South of the Mason-Dixon

By

Sam Kench

Sam Kench

A HellBound Books LLC Publication

Praise for South of the Mason-Dixon

"Sam Kench's SOUTH OF THE MASON-DIXON is a dark exploration of religious terror and cult brutality deep within the rural confines of the American South. It's a wicked journey full of twists and turns that build to a shocking climax you'll never see coming." - Chad Michael Ward (Writer/Director of Strange Blood, Black Kiss Stigmata)"

"Sam Kench hits a horror home run with his sophomore novel. This could easily sit among the Stephen King canon — except it goes one step further by offering a blood-curdling commentary on contemporary bigotry and the frightening current wave of Christian nationalism. It doesn't require a great leap of imagination to extrapolate the actions of some real-life lunatics and end up inside this uniquely American nightmare." — Jeff Jackson (Writer/director of Daemon_9, Frankenstein: The Musical)

"The finale made my jaw drop! The best horror novel I've read in years, it pulls no punches." — Preston "Phat Samurai Guy" Downey (Critic)

"An eerie look into society that feels uncomfortably relevant today. Sam Kench creates characters you fall in love with only to put them in peril and a world that is as terrifying as it is mesmerizing. South of the Mason-Dixon starts with a bang, and the momentum keeps going, you won't want to put it down. — Marissa Pistone (Star of Cruel Will, 4/20 Massacre)

South of the Mason-Dixon went well beyond what I could imagine at the outset, taking the reader on a journey that is both shockingly horrific and deeply affecting. I couldn't turn the pages fast enough. — Jennifer Grand (Writer of The Beast of Bedburg)

Reviews for The Fall of Polite:

(Five Stars) "Once I picked up The Fall of Polite I couldn't put it down until I had read the last page. The Fall of Polite is one book that will stay with me for many years to come." — The Avid Reader

(Five Stars) "Good strong characters and diverse settings make this book a must-read. Kench does not disappoint." — Novel News Network

(Five Stars) "Wonderfully written with great imagery and no skirting around topics. Sam Kench brings you a gritty tale that will keep you flipping pages." — The Indie Express

(Five Stars) "The author does not let his foot off of the gas at all over the course. It's an edge-of-your-seat kind of read that will have you engrossed." — Texas Book Nook

Contents:

Part I

Nulla

Trixie couldn't believe she had expected selling calendars to be fun. She posed her stuffed giraffe, Mr. Girafferie, atop a stack of novelty calendars that nobody in their right mind would be interested in purchasing. Her dad had written her name along the giraffe's oversized tag.

"How much longer?" she asked her big sister for the fourth time.

Lindsay sighed. "Come on now. This is for *your* field trip. You don't get to complain."

Lindsay wanted to leave too, though she pretended otherwise. She would have rather been at the beach working on her tan on this hot spring day but she kept up her cheery façade in hopes of attracting one of the handful of browsers milling about the parking lot.

Spread throughout the parking lot of a small-town Baptist church were a half-dozen folding tables manned by an equal number of children and retirees. In addition to the sisters' calendars, baked goods, candles, paperback books, picture frames, and stationery supplies were also on offer, though there were fewer shoppers than there were sellers. The tiny town of Gatlinburg, Tennessee rarely attracted a large crowd on even the biggest of holiday events, let alone on a random Saturday afternoon.

Across the parking lot, an old man with a crooked back raised an *Ocean Breeze* candle to his nose and pretended to take in the aroma. His eyes were locked on the eighteen-year-old with the long blonde hair and the eleven-year-old with the short pigtails and the stuffed giraffe.

Trixie couldn't sit still. She had progressed from fidgeting atop her folding chair to casting it aside and standing up behind the table. Even Mr. Girafferie was struggling to hold her attention.

"Go get a muffin," Lindsay said, handing her sister a dollar. "That'll keep ya busy awhile."

Mr. Girafferie joined Trixie on the journey to the baked-goods table.

A gruff man in a camouflage baseball cap wandered over to the calendar table and blocked Lindsay's view of her sister. Greying hair hung from the sides of his cap, and stubble had begun to collect on his fifty-five-year-old cheeks.

Lindsay switched to salesman-mode. "Hi. Lookin' for a calendar?" she asked, as chipper as could be.

"Maybe," the man said, looking over the offerings. "These for next year or the rest'a this year?"

"We have both, actually." She stood and spread out two tall stacks of calendars.

***

Trixie accepted a saran-wrapped chocolate-chip muffin from Mrs. Haverforth at the baked-goods table. She had taught Trixie in Sunday school a year earlier, and the two rarely got along. Trixie struggled to keep up with the lessons, and Mrs. Haverforth was not a woman of great patience.

On her way back to the calendar table, Trixie heard a quavering voice to her side.

"'Scuse me, li'l miss. Ya mind givin' an old man a hand with the good book?"

Trixie looked up at his smiling face. He reminded her of her grandfather, who was laid up in the hospital.

"It fell in a spot I can't quite reach," Sardus added.

***

Lindsay held a calendar aloft and flipped through the pages for her prospective customer. "The fire department made this one. That's them posin'." She feared she was losing the man's interest.

She failed to notice her little sister following the old man with the crooked back across the street.

***

Sardus moved along the hot sidewalk with shuffling steps. His eighty-three-year-old knees weren't as reliable as they once were.

Trixie glanced back toward the church as they moved farther and farther away from her sister. She felt like she should have told Lindsay before leaving to help this friendly old man, but it hadn't seemed necessary just a moment ago.

"Where's ya car?" she asked. "Ya said it was right nearby."

"It is," Sardus said, not looking back at her. "It's right around the corner."

"Ah dunno. Ah ain't s'pposed to go--"

"No, no. Look, it's right there. That's the bumper." He pointed to the front grill of a station wagon poking out from around the corner beneath the shade of a tall oak tree. The rest of the vehicle sat out of sight behind a thick row of hedges.

***

As her prospective customer flipped lazily through a muscle-car calendar, Lindsay took a glance toward the baked-goods table. Her chipper smile dipped.

"Trixie?" she called out, looking around the parking lot. She circumvented the table. "Trixie?!" Her little sister was nowhere to be seen.

"Whoa, whoa, calm down," her prospective customer said. "What's goin' on?"

"My sister—did you see a little girl wander off?" Her eyes scanned the small parking lot for a third time.

"With a li'l giraffe? Yeah, she went with her grandfather it looked like."

Lindsay shook her head, feeling frantic. She scolded herself for letting Trixie out of her sight. She was her responsibility. "Which way?"

"Uh," the man turned and pointed in the direction they had gone. "This way, I think."

Lindsay took off in a jog across the parking lot. She was surprised to see her prospective customer following along. His company helped ease her nerves the slightest bit.

***

The handle clicked in Sardus's grip. He swung the back hatch out to the side. The seats were folded down. The interior of the station wagon stretched long and flat up to the front seat.

Trixie hugged Mr. Grafferie to her chest as she looked in at the flat interior.

"There it is, right there," Sardus said, his pulse racing. He pointed to a bible at the far end of the wide trunk space. "My knees ain't what they used'a be."

Trixie stared at the black tome. She stood still and silent. Birds chirped and fluttered through the air. A gentle breeze swayed the branches overhead and changed the shape of the shadows that stretched across the old vehicle.

"Ah dunno. Ah don't think Ah wanna climb in--"

"Are you serious, young lady?"

Trixie felt a chill. The kind old man's tone had changed completely. He sounded like her dad when she misbehaved or her teachers when she failed her assignments.

"After ya made an old man walk all this way, ya ain't even gonna do what ya promised and help him get his bible back?"

"But Ah—"

"I just got done tellin' ya I got bad knees," Sardus said in the stern voice he used to scold his grandchildren before their parents cut off all contact with him. "I can't climb in there and I can't be walkin' all over tarnation neither."

"Ah'm sorry, Ah'm sorry. Ah didn't mean to--"

"If ya didn't mean it, then help me out like ya said ya would."

"Okay. Okay, sorry."

Trixie took a breath, then climbed up into the back of the station wagon.

The second her foot lifted off the pavement, Sardus unbuttoned the leather strap wrapped around his belt. He unfolded the lead-filled sap and gripped it in his wrinkled fist.

Trixie pulled Mr. Girafferie along as she crawled forward on her hands and knees. She reached a hand out for the bible.

Sardus leaned into the back. With a quick swing, the lead-filled leather sap thwacked across the back of the eleven-year-old's head. Her little body fell limp atop the stuffed giraffe.

The birds up above paid the act no mind and continued to twitter their afternoon tunes.

Sardus backed out of the station wagon just in time to see the sister and her prospective customer rounding the corner.

***

"Hey!" Lindsay shouted at the old man. She remembered seeing him in the parking lot now. "What are you—what'd you do with Trix--" She found her voice cut off and she grabbed at the arm wrapped around her throat by her prospective customer.

Joseph pulled with his other hand on the wrist of the arm he held the eighteen-year-old with. She struggled against his grip, so he pulled tighter.

"We're taking her, too?" Sardus asked, checking their surroundings. The suburban street was still unoccupied and still silent with the exception of the birds that chirped obliviously overhead.

"Hurry up, will ya?" Joseph said, flexing the arm with which he choked the teenager.

The girl's face was changing colors by the time Sardus shuffled up to them and brought the sap down on top of her head.

A thin line of blood trickled down her reddish-purple face as she continued to thrash in the gruff man's grip. It took a second swing to knock her out.

Joseph hauled her limp body to the station wagon and tossed her in the back, beside her sister.

"You might've told me we were taking two," Sardus judged.

"The opportunity presented itself," Joseph said as he swung the back hatch shut. "You know older's better anyway."

The fifty-five-year-old and the eighty-three-year-old made their way to the front of the station wagon and climbed inside. The engine awoke with a cantankerous grumble, and the vehicle puttered off through the quiet suburb.

Southern Hospitality

PENNSYLVANIA was etched into the north face of the small stone obelisk that poked up out of the weeds. Etched into its south side was *VIRGINIA*.

"This is it?" asked Andy, disappointed. He circled the obelisk with an accordion map of the U.S. in hand. The obelisk didn't even come up to his waist. He used his flip-flop to pin down a sprig of dandelion and reveal the lettering carved into the base spelling out *MASON AND DIXON LINE*.

"Yep," Harrison replied, crossing his muscular arms over his chest. He watched from behind his sunglasses as Andy circled the obelisk again. Sun glinted off of the big, silver belt buckle engraved with his initials: HW. He would have normally considered it a tacky accessory but he was committed to wearing it for the duration of their trip. Pa had given it to him as a going away gift when he left for college. "You thought it'd be bigger?"

Andy nodded and consulted the map, "I thought it would be lower too. The south starts farther north than I expected."

It was only Andy's second week in the United States. He had lived the rest of his twenty-six years in South Korea. He was a slender fellow; handsome and well-groomed. Adults had always called him theatrical growing up, even though he had never been involved in theater. This trip had been a long time coming, and everything felt fresh and exciting to him, sometimes too exciting.

The sight was nothing new to Harrison, who had passed by more than one of the obelisks spread across the Mason-Dixon line in his time and thought nothing of them. He was surprised when Andy had wanted to stop and check it out. A typical tourist destination it was not.

Harrison had turned thirty a few months earlier, which he called *reaching triple digits*. Most people considered him tall at six-foot, but he had always wanted to be taller. He would have liked to be tall to the point of noteworthiness; six-four, six-five. His beard got lighter in the summer and darker in the winter. His tan sat deep on his arms, face, and neck, and light everywhere else. Harry had a knack for never looking dirty but never looking too clean either. He always had the look of someone who had just finished working outside in the yard, even when he didn't leave the house for days on end. Andy enjoyed how rugged, yet well-groomed he was. A tricky balance to strike perfectly, and he sure did strike it perfectly.

"There's more to a state being part of the south than just geography," Harry said, stepping away from the Mason-Dixon line.

"Like what?" Andy asked, following behind Harrison toward the quiet, two-lane road beside the field.

"Well, slavery was the big one."

"Of course."

"But there are some good things too. Lifestyle things." Harry's accent still slipped out sometimes on certain words despite his best efforts. He feared his drawl would come back with a vengeance the second he was around his parents again. "People are friendlier down here. Sometimes anyway.

Southern hospitality. You ever hear'a that?"

Andy shook his head. He had heard of *southern comfort* but was pretty sure those were two different things.

"Things move slower down here," Harry continued. "A nice gentle pace."

"You miss it, huh?"

"Parts, yeah. The food, especially." Harry pulled open the driver's door of the dusty grey car parked off to the side of the dirt road. "But I wouldn't ever want to move back here for good."

The two climbed inside the car, and Harry hit the gas before Andy could buckle his seat belt. Streamers flapped from the bumper. Washable paint on the back window proudly proclaimed *JUST MARRIED!*

***

In a 1950s-themed diner with no name beyond the word *DINER* done up in neon, Harry and Andy sat on torn polyester bench seats the color of cherry limeade. Holes where springs poked through were covered over with red duct tape that almost matched the color of the polyester but not quite.

They still had another full day of traveling to reach their destination in Tennessee. Harry's car was the only one in the parking lot aside from those of the waitress and the cook who doubled as the diner's owner and tripled as the town mechanic who did repairs and oil changes around back, often without washing his hands when switching from motor oil to cooking oil. *A little grease never hurt nobody,* he would say if anyone ever called him out on his hygiene. So far, no one ever had.

The late-fifties waitress sauntered up to their table. Her nametag proclaimed, "*Maude.*" She wrote the specials down on a slip of paper and stuck it to the novelty mini jukebox bolted to the end of the table. Her accent was as thick as molasses. "You fellas pick out whatever tickles yer innards, and I'll be right back." She flashed a smile and twirled away with the energy of a bubble-gum-blowing school girl.

Andy leaned over the table and whispered, "Did you ever have an accent like that?"

Harry smiled. "I'm from farther south than this. My accent was twice as thick."

"What?!" Andy exclaimed, no longer making an effort to keep quiet. "No way!"

"I worked really hard to lose it." When Harry first moved to New York for college, his classmates would relentlessly ridicule him for his accent. They were classmates he would grow to consider friends. They didn't mean it to upset him, but it did hurt his feelings anytime one of them called him a hayseed or mocked his drawl. He spent countless hours working with his roommate and on his own to ditch his hometown dialect for something closer to the flat, unplaceable accent spoken by most TV news anchors.

"I guess I'm glad," Andy said of Harry's lost accent. "I probably wouldn't have been able to understand you when we met otherwise."

Harry tapped his napkin-bound silverware on the tabletop, poking a fork and knife up out of the rolled paper. "Could you understand her?" Harry pointed slyly toward the waitress with his fork.

"Barely. I caught, *I'll be right back.*" The newlyweds shared a chuckle.

"I guess you've probably only heard southern accents in movies, huh?"

"Uh, yeah. Cowboy movies," Andy said, grinning. "I need the subtitles on."

Maude returned, interrupting their giggles. "You fellas decide on sum'in?"

Andy wasn't one hundred percent sure of the actual words

she had spoken, but her return and the way she held her notepad and pen told him everything he needed to know. "I haven't even looked yet," Andy said, reaching for the menu.

Harry reached across the table and stopped him. "He'll have the chicken and biscuits. Extra sausage gravy. Same for me."

Maude pointed a finger-gun at Harry and made a clicking sound with her mouth. "Good call." She fired her finger-gun before heading back into the kitchen.

Harry leaned back in his seat and smiled at his new husband. "The first of many comfort and soul-food meals comin' your way."

Andy rubbed his hands together. "I'm actually very excited. You've hyped this comfort food up a lot." He rocked back and forth on his polyester cushion.

"It won't disappoint." Harry licked his lips in anticipation. When he realized he still had his strawberry Chapstick on, he wiped it all off on his napkin. He then encouraged Andy to do the same. *Comfort food must remain pure.* "When we get to Jonesborough, I'll take you to my old go-to spot. The best chicken and waffles in existence."

"I don't understand how that combination could possibly be good."

"Just you wait, Andy. You'll see."

Andy sat back and thought for a moment. His mind quickly drifted, as it often did. He straightened up and slapped the table. "Oh my God!"

"What?" Harry asked, not as alarmed as Andy's sudden, over-the-top reaction may have warranted had he not known him better.

"What if I can't understand your parents?"

Harry chuckled in response.

"They must have super thick accents, right?"

"I think you'll be fine," Harry said, still chuckling.

Andy rubbed a hand through his hair, exasperated. "But-

but what if—"

"I'll translate," Harry interjected to keep Andy from freaking out.

"How? Your Korean is awful."

Harry's Korean wasn't great but he had learned enough to get by in broad strokes ahead of his semester abroad. He tried to speak entirely in Korean on his first dinner date with Andy. His Korean-vocab reservoir was thoroughly depleted before the entrées had arrived. "I mean I'll translate from southern English to non-southern English."

"Oh, right." Andy groaned, his stress not alleviated in the slightest. "I just want them to like me."

"They will," Harry said with confidence.

"How can you be so sure?"

"Because you're an inherently likable person."

Andy cocked an eyebrow and cracked a mischievous grin. "My parents didn't like you," he said, teasing.

An embarrassed smile took hold of Harry's mouth. "Oh, man. I thought I was winnin' 'em over a bit by the end."

"My mom didn't mind you after a while."

"Didn't mind me?"

"But my dad still doesn't like you to this day… mostly just because you're not a woman who I can procreate with to carry on the family line."

"Yeah, well, neither are you." Harrison kicked his husband's shin under the table.

"Ow!" Andy kicked him back.

Soon enough, they were playing footsie underneath the diner table, flailing about rambunctiously, giggling the whole time.

They were still at it when Maude returned with their food. They didn't notice her arrival until she cleared her throat. Her bubbly energy had been sapped by their display of affection. Her eyes narrowed at them.

Harry blushed and sat up straight. "Sorry," he said out of

instinct.

"Enjoy, *fellas.*" The word held the barely masked intent of a different F-word as it left her mouth. She set their plates down with a clatter and leveled another judgmental glare at each of them before turning and striding away. *Won't be refilling their coffee, that's for damn sure.*

Harry rubbed at his neck, mad at himself for feeling as embarrassed as he did and doubly mad at himself for apologizing. What did he have to be sorry for? Maude wouldn't have batted an eye if they were a straight couple doing the same thing, Harry was sure of it. He shook off the feeling and found himself returning to high spirits as Andy picked up his silverware and took aim at the chicken and biscuits.

Andy looked over the plate with virgin eyes. The only time he had ever heard of chicken and biscuits was from Harry, and this was not what he had been expecting. It was the gravy that was really throwing him off. *Why didn't gravy make the title of the dish?* he wondered. *They really smother everything in the stuff,* he realized. His excitement was dwindling, but Harry's eager gaze conveyed clear expectations for his enjoyment.

Before digging in, Andy met Harry's gaze. "Are you going to stare at me while I eat?"

Harry considered the question. "… Yes."

Andy suppressed a sigh and readied himself a forkful of chicken and biscuit from the driest part of the plate. He brought the food toward his mouth.

"Wait, wait, wait!" Harry shouted, alarming his husband.

"What?!" Andy lowered his fork and scrutinized it, expecting a bug or hair to have made its way into the food or something of the sort.

"Ya gotta get gravy with it."

Andy's eyes dropped back down to the pool of excess sausage gravy on the plate.

"Swirl that bad-boy around," Harry said in earnest.

At length, Andy did as instructed. He hesitated just a moment before placing the sopping bite into his mouth and chewing. *Disgusting!* was Andy's immediate reaction. He tried to hide his distaste in the face of Harry's big, eager smile. Andy chewed laboriously before finally swallowing. He faked a smile.

"Did that just blow your mind?" Harry asked, miming a head explosion.

"I, uh, well--" He could see the disappointment begin to creep onto Harry's face. "Maybe I—um, let me try a bite without the gravy." Andy's fork shot for a dry corner of biscuit.

"No, no," Harry protested. "No way. The gravy is key. Don't do yourself a disservice. You need equal parts chicken, biscuit, and gravy in each bite." Harrison pointed wisely at the dish's ingredients as if giving a TED Talk.

Andy sighed. *The things we do for love.* "Okay." He prepared another soggy forkful.

Harry dug into his own meal with a smile. He was satisfied, calling 'comfort-food meal #1' a moderate success.

***

The car hydroplaned as Harrison took the exit off the highway. Andy hung onto the dashboard and overhead handle for dear life. Driving in even the best conditions already made him a little bit anxious, so the whole road trip had been an ordeal. But now that the road was masquerading as a shallow river, he was ready for the trip to come to a conclusion. He wanted to be off the rainy road ASAP.

Back in primary school, a teacher had told him and the rest of the class the yearly statistics on vehicular accidents and the mortality rates associated with them. She had meant it as a cautionary lesson in the importance of wearing a seatbelt, but Andy had taken it as a dark omen. From that point on, he had felt certain that if he were to ever die a premature death, it would be by way of a car crash. It was the reason why he had never learned to drive, why The Birthday Party's 'Dead Joe' was the most terrifying song he had ever heard, and why Harry's occasional speeding, or his lax, one-handed grip of the steering wheel made Andy clench every muscle in his body.

They had been caught in a sudden downpour after nightfall and would be losing at least a couple of hours' worth of travel time to the rain. Harry had been forced to cut his speed in half to make it safely to their lodging for the night. Andy wished he would slow down even further. Harrison would have taken the first exit following the emergence of the rain if not for a motel room further down the road having already been booked in advance of their trip. They were reaching the same destination, just a couple of hours later into the night, which meant sacrificing some sleep or getting back on the road later in the morning than planned. Sticking to so tight a schedule took away some of the spontaneity that Harry craved in life, but Andy preferred a roadmap of activities. This, then this, then this, in that order with no exceptions, if it could be helped. *For someone so easily excitable, he sure likes routine*, Harry thought. *At least it makes him easy to surprise.*

He was glad there weren't many other cars on the road at this hour. He could hardly make out the lanes ahead of him. The windshield wipers were not cutting it, even on their highest setting.

"Is that it?" Harry asked, gesturing through the wall of falling water toward a neon glow on the street corner. In the split-second after the windshield wiper arced by, he got a glimpse of a two-story motel on the corner beyond the sign.

Andy squinted at the sign out front. It was difficult to make out the lettering through the shimmering windshield.

The rushing water reflected the red glow of the stoplight above them. Andy checked his laminated itinerary of the trip, bathed in a wash of red light. "I think it's the right one," he finally said. His beloved laminator was one of the more painful items he was forced to leave behind in the move from S.K. to U.S. Not enough room in his luggage.

"Right, then." Harrison cranked the wheel and pulled into the parking lot without bothering to use his indicator, which always annoyed Andy. Harry wouldn't wear his seatbelt for anything he considered a "short drive" and he wouldn't bother with turn signals if they didn't feel necessary to him in the moment. He would go as far as to flat-out ignore stop signs and traffic lights if he was confident there was no one else on the road. *At least he's not one of those jackasses who texts and drives*, Andy thought. He was beholden to Harry's laissez-faire driving attitude. The times Andy had questioned him on his driving had resulted in only a chuckle or scoff from Harry. It was not a subject open for debate. Harry was confident in his driving abilities and wasn't about to take input from someone who never learned how to drive in the first place.

Eight-four-year-old Cora sat at the check-in desk before a wall of keys. With one hand, she flipped through an issue of Rolling Stone from 1974. Kris Kristofferson was on the cover to promote the release of *Alice Doesn't Live Here Anymore*. Cora used to think he was such a heartthrob. With her other hand, Cora stroked her calico cat, Mitsy. This time of night, she always listened to the rebroadcast of Reverend Danford's morning sermon on her Zenith MJ1035. Tonight, she had to crank the volume extra high to hear the good Reverend over the downpour outside the propped-open lobby doors. Thunder boomed not far off in the distance.

She lifted her eyes from an advert for a lotion brand that had been discontinued thirty years ago and watched the rain slap against the concrete outside the glass double-doors. A car pulled into view and took a parking spot in the quarter-full lot. Lightning flashed on the horizon.

With no umbrella to speak of, Harry and Andy sprinted across the parking lot and in through the double-doors. Harry let out a sigh of relief, dripping onto the rubber mats on the floor.

"Hi. I booked a room."

"Name?" Cora said, turning down the radio and flipping open a long, black ledger.

"Harrison Winters."

Cora scanned the ledger, sliding her pastel-pink fingernail down the ruled page. She looked up at them, then back down to the ledger. She sucked her teeth. "I see you here but there's been some sort of cattywampus I'm afraid."

The look on her face made Andy's stomach tighten up in knots. He looked back across the parking lot toward their car. The rain had turned their just-married declaration into a mess of colored streaks, and the thin streamers on the bumper had all but disintegrated.

Cora continued, "We've only got you down for a single."

"That's right—"

"Don't worry a pretty little hair on your head. I'll get you fellas switched over to a double in no time at all." She retrieved a bottle of whiteout from a desk drawer. Mitsy hopped off the desk and lapped from a saucer of milk by Cora's feet.

"A single is fine," Harry protested.

"Oh, nonsense. It's no trouble," Cora said, painting a white line over their single booking and blowing on it.

"But ya see, we're—"

"We got plenty'a two-bed rooms vacant."

"Well, we—"

"And!" Cora blurted. "Since it was clearly a mistake on my end, I'll only charge ya the single rate."

Harrison and Andy shared a look and a shrug.

"Ya want first floor or second floor?" Cora asked, reaching for keys on the wall behind her.

"… Second floor."

Harry led the way up the stone steps to the second level, rainwater gushing over their shoes. The narrow roof of the motel sent most of the rain cascading over the railing beside them and into the parking lot below. It felt like following a trail as it passed behind a waterfall.

They hurried to the room on the corner and Harry unlocked it as quick as he could. The door swung wide and two parallel beds with separate end-tables and lamps greeted them.

Wet clothes were piled up on the bathroom floor. The mirror was a blur of steam from the heat of the shower.

Harry had pushed aside the end-tables and shoved together the two twin beds of the double-room. While Andy showered off the rain, Harry lounged atop the makeshift double-wide bed in his boxer-briefs and watched TV to kill the time.

On screen was a news report, re-rolling a package from earlier in the day. A pair of teary-eyed parents spoke into a bouquet of microphones at a small press conference. A graphic was on screen beside them: an old photo of two sisters hugging and smiling for the camera.

"Today was Trixie's birthday," the mother said. "And we didn't get to wish her a…." She could not continue. She buried her face in her husband's sleeve as the tears came.

A lower-third graphic scrolled across the bottom of the screen: *Eighteen months since disappearance…*

"Please, if you're watching," the father took over. "We'll

pay whatever ransom, we won't go to the police, just give us our girls back." He refused to entertain the notion that Trixie and Lindsay may no longer be alive. His wife, however, couldn't stop imagining that dreadful possibility.

At the sound of the shower shutting off, Harry thumbed the power button on the remote and struck a seductive pose atop the blankets.

Andy strolled from the bathroom, a towel wrapped around his waist. "Ah, I like what you've done with the place, Mr. Winters."

"Get over here, Mr. Winters," Harry said with a lascivious grin. He reclined onto the pillows as Andy climbed atop the bed. Andy lingered above him, holding his breath. Harry reached up and stroked Andy's cheek with his fingertips. "Tell me you love me."

"I don't," Andy said, cocking his head.

"What?"

"I only married you for the green card."

Harry smiled, laughing without sound.

Andy leaned down and kissed him.

"You proud to be an American?" Harry asked in a played-up Southern accent, a stone's throw from a *yee-haw*.

"Ugh, shut up." Andy kissed him passionately.

Harry's hands slid smoothly down Andy's hairless torso until he reached the towel. He took hold of it and threw it across the room.

Without pulling away from their lip-lock, Andy stretched for the lamp on the cast-aside end table to plunge the room into darkness. The lights of the parking lot cast rapid shadows across the bed in the fall of the rain.

The Oldest Town in Tennessee

Tennessee Welcomes You, read the blue sign with the white outline beside the road. Devo blasted through the radio, the live version of "Auto Modown" off of *Hardcore*.

Andy read the sign aloud. "*The volunteer state.* Why's it called that?"

"Uh, I don't know," Harry said as they blew past the sign. He was glad to finally be back in his home state. *Not much farther to Jonesborough.*

"They didn't teach you in school?"

"No, they did. Something about the war of, uh, Eighteen-something." Harry paused to think. "1815? 1812? That's the one. War of 1812. I think."

"I don't think I've ever heard about that one."

"We don't talk about that one much. I don't know why. It was like the revolutionary war part-two… I think. That could be completely wrong."

Static began to overpower Devo. Harry fiddled with the radio knob but knew it was no use. Following an intermission of static, a man's voice came through over an acoustic guitar singing about pickup trucks and blue jeans.

"Aww," Harry lamented, turning the radio off. "And there it goes; the last good radio station for a hundred miles." He flipped open the center console and reached inside at a pile of CDs.

"Uh, I can do that for you," Andy said, wanting Harry to keep both hands on the wheel.

Harry glanced over before returning his hand to the wheel. "Sure. Just pick whatever looks interesting to you." The two didn't share very similar tastes in music, but Andy was rather passive when it came to what he listened to and would usually defer to Harry on all auditory decisions.

Andy lifted a tall stack of jewel cases and set it atop his knee. He looked through them. Half of the cases were broken. Some of them were empty.

"In Jonesborough, there's nothin' but country-western, gospel, and public access on the radio." It was a quiet little town with a population of just over five thousand.

Andy picked a disc at random and put it in the radio.

Harry continued. "And, around here, public access usually still means country-western, just played shittily by locals." The CD started, and Harry's face lit up with a smile. "Oh, hell yeah!" He turned up the volume on Dr. Dog's *Be the Void.*

Andy cleared his throat. "Hey, I've got kind of an awkward question."

Harry looked over, then back to the road.

"Are your parents—I don't know how to ask it…"

"What?"

"Are they open-minded about… the gay situation?"

"*The gay situation?* That sounds like a propaganda movie from the forties." Harry teased.

"The thing is—"

Harry put on a movie-announcer voice. "*Don't smoke the reefer or you'll turn homo and disappoint your parents—*"

Andy slapped him on the arm.

Harry stifled his laughter. "Sorry, sorry. Go ahead."

"I guess they must be open-minded about that but… but what I'm more worried about is, well, are they… they're not racist, are they?"

Harry busted out in raucous laughter. He slapped the side of the steering wheel.

Andy went beet-red. "It's just, I hear that kind of thing about the American south. I don't know how true it is."

With residual laughter still in his gullet, Harry shook his head. "It is certainly true of plenty of southern folks— plenty of Americans in general— but not of all of them, and certainly not of my parents."

Andy let out a sigh of relief. "Okay, good."

"They are still decidedly Republican otherwise though, so maybe avoid politics at the dinner table. Just don't try to take their guns away or have an abortion at the dinner table, and you should probably get along fine— Oh! Check it, check it, check it!" Harry pointed out through the corner of the windshield on Andy's side.

Andy laid eyes on a small, hand-painted *Welcome to Jonesborough* sign planted in the ground on the end of a fence post. *The oldest town in Tennessee* was scrawled in white at the bottom of the sign. Buckshot had perforated the lettering, but it remained legible.

Home Cooking

Ma Winters sat in her favorite of three rocking chairs braiding a rug by hand. In her early seventies, she had shrunken with age. She was now closer to four feet than five. Her floral jumper was big enough on her to serve as a dress. Her huge glasses stretched from an inch above her eyebrows to two inches down her cheeks, just in case the smooth parts of her face felt like viewing the world too.

With one foot, she rubbed Howie as he slobbered on a bone. She stopped braiding when the dog lifted his head and pointed his snout toward the front door.

"Hear sum'in, boy?"

The doorbell rang, bringing Howie to his feet and calling all of the other canines into the room; two sheep dogs and three border collies.

Ma Winters hopped to her feet with a wide smile. She was still sprightly for her age; Pa less so, but he did his best to keep up. She could hear his footsteps creaking down the stairs already.

She hurried over to the front door and threw it open.

"Hey, Ma!" Harry said, standing in the doorway with a bouquet of flowers. Andy, a couple of feet behind him.

"Harrison!" she squealed, throwing her arms up in the air. "Get inna ya mama's arms!"

Harry bent low at the waist to hug her. It was his first time seeing her in person since moving to Seoul a couple of years earlier.

The dogs hurried over to lick and jump at him fondly.

"How you boys doin'? Ya miss me?" Harry's accent had gotten thicker the second his mom opened the door. He grabbed onto the youngest dog and kissed its head. "Clive, you're huge! You were about ten inches long, last I saw!" He rubbed the dog all over. Clive's tail thumped against the floor as he rolled onto his back and presented his belly for scratches.

"Did I hear Harrison?" Pa Winters called from the hallway. He wobbled into the room on his Eighty-one-year-old knees wearing an old red-and-black flannel shirt and his marine-vet hat.

Harrison stood up from the swirl of fur. "Pa," he said with a respectful tilt of his head.

They shared a handshake. The old man still had a strong grip and kept calluses on his hands by playing around on his workbench in the garage. He noticed Harrison was wearing the monogrammed belt buckle he had given him all those years ago and he felt a swell of pride for his boy.

Harry turned around and waved Andy inside. He looked to his parents and put his arm around Andy's shoulder. "This is Andy Lew— Or, actually, it's Andy Winters now." He grinned from ear to ear.

Pa shook Andy's hand. "Pleasure to meet ya, Andy."

Before Andy could respond, Ma jumped in at the end of the handshake and hugged him. "We've heard a lot about you," she said with her neck craned to look up at him.

"It's great to finally meet the two of you," Andy said with

a nervous smile. The interior of the home smelled of dogs and cinnamon.

***

Later that day, Harrison and Andy strolled hand-in-hand through the Jonesborough farmers market.

This outdoor market was a permanent fixture of Jonesborough and ran all year long, only ceasing operation on Sundays or the rare snowy day in the coldest of winters. A number of residents made their full income through their market stalls.

Shoppers milled about, passing the newlyweds in both directions. Their eyes drifted down to Harry and Andy's interlocked fingers. Grimaces, sneers, and dirty looks were fired at them with alarming regularity. Andy could hear a few passers-by whispering to their hetero partners, but couldn't make out the words. He didn't really want to know what they were saying, but he did want them to stop.

Andy tried to let go of his husband's hand, but Harry held tight.

Harry turned and gave Andy a reassuring look. He was determined to not let their sneers bother him. He had promised himself before heading south that he would not give a shit about any of the judgment leveled on him while he was back. His apathy was forced, but it wasn't wearing him down yet, and he didn't want it to wear down Andy either.

After a brief exchange of silent looks, Andy retightened his grip on his husband's hand and tried to ignore the hateful gazes all around him.

But it was difficult. The stares were pervasive. He could swear the same glaring shoppers were coming back around for second sneers.

Eventually, they finished a loop of the farmers market and

rejoined the Winters' stall, where Ma worked a table selling her hand-braided rugs and wicker baskets. She had embraced retirement and her monthly farmers market proceeds were now her only source of income. Pa slept in a lawn chair behind her, a newspaper open across his chest like a tiny blanket.

***

Ma and Pa Winters led the newlyweds on a gentle hike through the woods. They followed a well-worn trail through the same lush, green vegetation that they had traversed hundreds if not thousands of times in their lives.

This was more pleasant for Andy than the market. Isolated in nature. No circumambient eyes to judge him. Much of the stress left his body and he felt somewhat comfortable for the first time since entering Jonesborough.

There were patches of dense forest scattered all over Jonesborough. More land was dedicated to the forests of the area than to residential and commercial zones combined.

Pa looked back at Andy over his shoulder. "How much ya know 'bout berries, Andy?"

Andy had to focus intensely whenever Harry's parents spoke directly to him. He could usually discern the gist, at least, if not their every word with enough attention paid. "About berries? Um, not much, I guess."

"Well, lem'me tell ya," Pa said, moving over to the side of the trail. "These right here are poisonous." He pointed to a stout shrub covered in bright red berries. "But right up here…" he picked up the pace and maneuvered down the winding trail. He stopped beside another bush: slightly taller, less dense, and covered in lumpy, purple, nearly black berries. "These berries—" He made a chef's kiss gesture and put a hand over his heart. "Delicious."

"And they're not poisonous?" Andy felt stupid

immediately after asking.

Pa blinked at him. "Correct," he said with a nod. He hunched over to pluck some berries off the bush.

Harry nudged Andy with his elbow. "Congratulations on becoming a berry expert, Andy," he said with a smile. "Your certificate's in the mail."

Ma helped Pa fill a little basket with berries from the shrub. It was one that she had made by hand and decided not to sell because the handle had turned out a little wonky. It was good enough for herself to use but no one else, she determined. When they were finished plucking, they continued down the trail. A gentle stream came into view past a few rows of trees.

"There's all kinds'a fine grub out here," Pa said, popping a berry into his mouth and squishing out the juice.

Andy missed that one entirely. He had not a clue what was just said. He held a neutral expression as Pa glanced back at him over his shoulder.

Pa continued. "You could live off this land, just foragin', if ya wanted to."

Andy's comfort was leaving him the longer this hike continued. He leaned in toward Harry's ear and said, "I need to pee."

Ma spun around to face him; great hearing for her age. "Go ahead, son. Just make sure ya don't wander too far off'a the path. There's hunters out here. Might-could mistake ya for a deer."

"Or a moose," Pa added.

With a red face, Andy pivoted from his new in-laws and hurried off the trail.

***

Andy stared down at the empty dinner plate set for him at

the long, glossy dining-room table. Harry sat across from him, and Pa sat at one head of the table. Ma's place was set but her chair was still pushed in as she finished up in the kitchen.

After comfort-food meal #1, Andy was doubtful that his further comfort-food experiences would improve moving forward and he was afraid of disliking Ma's food and offending her. *It does smell good though*, he thought, *certainly better than that diner food.*

Ma Winters made the first of many trips from the kitchen carrying serving plates and bowls. Andy had offered to help and been refused. Harry knew better than to offer. Cooking was a point of pride with Ma, and she wouldn't have anyone interfering with her process under any circumstances. And, for her, setting the table and clearing the dishes was all part of cooking, and it would remain a solo effort until the day she was unable to manage on her own.

Dishes of corn, green beans, mashed potatoes, and biscuits were spread across the table. A hand-painted ceramic gravy boat in the shape of a mallard was set in the center of the table. The foraged berries from their hike had been pureed into something resembling a chunky cranberry sauce.

"I know ya must'a been missin' my cookin', Harrison," Ma said in between journeys to the kitchen.

"Absolutely. Less than I missed the dogs, more than I missed Pa." He flashed Pa a cheeky grin.

"Hey!" Pa said, chuckling.

Ma disappeared through the swinging door into the kitchen again and quickly returned with the main course. "Hell, ya must be all kinds'a homesick after living in Ko-rea so long." She began serving everyone.

Andy found his plate filled with a heaping helping of chicken and biscuits with sausage gravy. It looked suspiciously similar to 'comfort food meal #1.' Andy gulped. *Did Harry plan this?* he wondered.

Harry sipped from a glass of milk. "Andy just had chicken and biscuits for the first time. He's a big fan now." He smiled at Andy, who forced a smile back.

Pa readied his silverware. "Smells delicious, Ma."

"Mm-hmm!" Harry affirmed. He rubbed his hands together and licked his lips like a cartoon wolf about to devour an entire turkey.

"It all looks great, Mrs. Winters," Andy said convincingly.

"Ya best get used'a callin' me 'Ma', son."

Andy smiled. "Will do, *Ma.*" It sounded weird coming out of his mouth. He cringed and wanted to fold in on himself, but no one else lingered on the awkwardness or even acknowledged it, they were too busy digging into their food now that Ma had finally taken her seat.

Sometimes Pa said grace but, usually, he didn't bother. They were what the church-folk called *casual Christians.* Once upon a time, Ma and Pa had been devout Catholics but, over the years, their participation in the religious infrastructure had waned. They both still believed in God and felt His love, but no longer cared for the worldly Christian mechanisms. They had begun to grow disillusioned with the Catholic church following the first news of the pedophile-priest scandals, and by the time Harrison was born, they were all but checked-out from official church worship. The meteoric rise of televangelists sealed the deal in their disinterest in the monetization of faith. Pa hated no one on earth more than the likes of Kenneth Copeland, Joel Osteen, and the rest of their ilk. *Scum of the earth!* he would say if he ever happened to catch a glimpse of one of them on television or was forced to listen to them speak over one of the public radios in the handful of diners and shops around town that were avid listeners.

Harry was grateful that his parents hadn't forced religion

upon him when growing up like had been the case with so many of his classmates; disallowed to think and decide for themselves. He couldn't imagine how different his life would have been if he had grown up in the typical Jonesborough echo chamber.

Wary of round-two with the chicken and biscuits, Andy started in on just the sides. He helped himself to a roll and some mashed potatoes, thankful that Ma hadn't doused them in gravy for him.

After two-and-a-half minutes of ravenous, uncommunicative eating, Pa wiped his mouth on a napkin and said, "Say, Andy, you got a uh, whatdoyacallit? An extra-Asian name?"

Harry snorted into his milk. "Jesus, Pa."

"What?" Pa said. "His name ain't actually *Andy*, right? That's just for us Americans?"

"My real name is difficult for non-natives to pronounce," Andy said. "Even Harry still struggles with it."

"Well, gimme a shot at it, son."

Andy took a sip of water. "My full name is Seung-jeong Oh."

Pa set his silverware down and focused as hard as he could. He slowly over-pronounced the name, "See Ong Jee, uh, Jee Jong Ooh?"

Harry had to cover his mouth to hide his snickering.

"Not bad," Andy said with a smile. "Not bad."

Pa smiled proudly.

Ma scooted her chair further in. "So, where does the name *Andy* come from?"

"Oh, have you ever heard of Andy Lau, the actor?"

Ma shook her head and took a forkful of mashed potatoes.

"He big in Ko-rea?" Pa asked.

"Hong Kong, actually. When I was little, I had a bootleg of his movie *Fulltime Killer*. I mean…" Andy leaned back in his seat and blew a puff of air. "That's when I knew I was gay."

Ma and Pa Winters each shifted in their seats, growing slightly uncomfortable as soon as the 'G' word left Andy's mouth. Pa more so than Ma.

They were okay with it as long as they were able to partially ignore it. They knew Harry had married Andy, of course, but it made it easier moment-to-moment if they could think of the two of them as just really close friends. Pa didn't like being confronted with the naked truth so directly.

Andy didn't notice their growing discomfort. He was lost in thoughts of Andy Lau's charismatic smile. "I used to watch that tape over and ov—"

Pa cleared his throat loudly, snapping Andy's attention back to the dinner table. "That's maybe a mite, um, *indelicate* for the dinner table, ain't it?"

Andy was mortified. He wanted to bury his face in the mashed potatoes. "Oh my God, I'm so sorry."

"It's all right. Quite all right," Pa said, fidgeting in his chair.

Harry found himself gritting his teeth. *All that talk of accepting me and he still can't hear the word 'gay' without crawling out of his skin.*

"I— Look, I'm fine with it," Pa grumbled, avoiding eye contact. "Just… maybe let's not talk about it so out in the open, hmm?"

Andy stared down at his plate. He twisted his fork through a mound of corn.

An awkward silence hung in the air.

Ma picked her head up and looked at each place setting around the table individually. She produced a forced-sounding exhalation and made a show out of scooping some more mashed potatoes onto her plate. "So," she finally said, breaking the silence, "… how was the road trip down here?"

"A lot of fun. Cape Cod was gorgeous right at the start," Harry quickly replied, eager to be out of the pregnant pause.

He looked to Andy for confirmation.

"Oh, yeah. Incredible," Andy said, forcing the smile back onto his face.

"Enjoy it while ya can," Pa said, pointing with his green-bean-tipped fork. "Before normal life comes rushing back at'cha. I tell ya, retirement could not come soon'nuff. Oh, the drudgery of working-life. Mind-numbin' stuff."

Andy turned toward his husband and spoke softly, "Uh, the *what* of working life?"

"Drudgery. It's like, um, boring, repetitive stuff."

Pa studied his new son-in-law. "What do you do, Andy?"

"Uh, for work? I'm an artist."

"Being an artist pays the bills?"

"Graphic design work does."

Harry leaned forward. "When we find a place and settle down in New York, I'm gonna help him get a spot in a gallery." He bit a chunk of chicken and biscuit off the end of his fork and spoke with his mouth full. "Ya 'member my first roommate? Gary?"

Ma and Pa nodded.

"He manages a gallery now." Harry reached over and gave Andy a squeeze. "Andy had shows in Seoul all the time."

"Soul?" Ma echoed, perplexed.

"It's the capital city where I'm from."

"Ooh, that's bougie!" Ma said.

Andy and Pa both pulled confused faces.

Ma clarified. "Uh, it means something like *fancy*."

"Oh, I see," Andy said.

"Right. Yeah, I knew that," Pa quickly added.

Later that night, Andy explored Harry's childhood bedroom. He had never seen so many David Bowie posters in his life. But the real showstopper was the twin bed in a frame modeled after a red number twenty-one racecar.

Dressed in pajamas, the newlyweds snuggled into bed. It was a tight fit.

"You never told me you had a race-car bed."

"Ugh, I know. Can you believe I hadn't outgrown it by high school? It's embarrassing."

"Are you kidding? You get a bonus cool-point for having a race-car bed."

Harry smiled. "How many cool points do I have in your book?"

"Hmm…" Andy made a show out of tabulating the results. "Like four."

"Four?!" Harry exclaimed, outraged. "Is that including the bonus point for the race-car bed?"

"Oh, yeah," Andy said, grinning. "Of course." He gave his husband a quick kiss, then ran his hand along the race-car frame. "You ever make love in this cruiser?"

Harry considered lying. "Yes, actually."

Andy was shocked. "Really?! Details."

Harry was blushing already. "I went to high school with her."

"Her?! Oh my God, one of the elusive *hers* of your past!" Andy pressed down on Harry's chest with a flat palm. "Tell me everything."

"Her name was Sherry Bright— uh, Bright *something*. Brightly or Albright or… Damn. I should remember this." He couldn't think of her name for the life of him. "The only other one was in college. We're still friends." Harry perked up with a realization. "You know her actually. We hung out on Facetime. Holly."

"You had sex with Holly?!" Andy shouted, mouth agape. "Wow. I thought you said she was like a sister to you?"

"She is. Now."

"Gross," Andy said bluntly with a grin.

Harry shoved him, not that there was any room for him to be pushed within the confines of the race-car frame.

Andy propped himself up above Harry and teased him in a soft, sing-song voice, *"Harry boned his sister."*

"Shut up," Harry said, chuckling. He gave Andy another shove.

"You never took a boy for a ride in your race car?"

Harry shook his head. It wasn't that he hadn't wanted to. Whenever he had felt a pang of attraction toward one of the boys in his school, he had thought there was something wrong with him and tried to block it out. It wasn't until he was immersed in a new environment in college that he felt comfortable enough in his own skin to fully accept his sexuality.

"How about we change that?" Andy said, cocking an eyebrow. He straddled his husband in the small bed.

"No, no, no," Harry said, shaking his head.

"Why not?" Andy asked, feeling rejected.

"My parents' room is right across the hall."

Andy glanced toward the door. Silence beyond it. "Come on, you've done it before."

"Not when they were home. It's too weird. They're already uncomfortable enough with us sharing a room."

"Oh," Andy said. He hadn't known that. "Okay." Andy settled back down beside him. He could see on Harry's face that he was about to apologize and make excuses for them, and Andy didn't want that. He lightened the mood. "This speed demon's too small anyway. I need something at least SUV-size to maneuver properly."

Harry gave him a deep kiss, then shut off the light.

***

Ma Winters poured batter into a mini-muffin tray. The batter was spotted with the rest of the fresh berries picked along their hike the day before.

Andy enjoyed a plate of buttery pancakes doused in

maple syrup. American breakfast food was more his style. That is, until the biscuits and sausage gravy made a cameo.

Harry bit into a strip of bacon. "Pork Whistle tonight, right Ma?"

"Already made the reservation."

"What's a pork whistle?" Andy asked, fearing the answer.

"Just the greatest chicken and waffle joint in this-here hemisphere," Harry said joyously.

Pa lowered his newspaper and looked over the top of his halfmoon reading glasses at Harry. "In this-here solar system, ya mean to say." He lifted the newspaper back up.

Andy tried to feign excitement but he lacked any confidence in his façade. "Oh. Yay." Both fried chicken and waffles were fine enough independently as far as his palette was concerned, but the combination made his stomach preemptively churn.

Pa crossed one leg over the other. He couldn't cross his legs the other way any longer. Not since his last knee surgery. He was grateful to still be able to walk without any pain.

Ma slid her muffin tray into the oven. "You boys have anything planned beforehand?"

"Yes, actually," Harry said. "We're going on a hike."

"We are?" This was news to Andy.

Ma smiled. "That'll be fun."

Harry winked at Andy.

***

Harry drove fast down the dirt road, kicking up dust.

People must not care about speed limits around here, it seemed to Andy. He held on tight to the polymer handle on the ceiling, trying not to appear anxious.

"I thought you might be craving a little alone time."

"Mmm. I like the sound of that." He was telling the truth,

but his top priority was getting wherever the hell they were going and climbing out of this speeding, metal box.

Luckily for Andy, it wasn't too much longer before Harry turned off of the dirt road. Unluckily for Andy, he made the turn by drifting ninety degrees and charging down a different road straight into the neighboring forest.

A yelp escaped Andy's mouth, and he found himself clutching the overhead handle with both hands and shutting his eyes.

Harry decreased speed once on the forest road. It was narrow and winding. He glanced over at Andy and chuckled at his fright.

A minute later, they were parked in a small dirt lot at the entrance to a massive state forest. A trio of walking paths branched off from the lot. They climbed out of the car.

Andy felt disappointment rising in him. "So, we actually are going hiking?"

"Yes and no." Harry gave his husband a coy smile and strode backwards down the central path.

Wounded Prey

The wooden hunting blind smelled of beer and homemade jerky. It was a welcome scent to the three hunters within.

Joseph was the oldest in the blind by more than two decades, so he called the shots on this excursion. His greying hair had lost the rest of its pigment in the months since abducting the sisters. The grey hair now reached down to his shoulders. His tan skin was leathery and mottled with small scabs. On this day, he wore a head-to-toe camouflage ensemble to match both his hat and the outfits of his compatriots. He sat on the floor of the blind with his back against the wall, finishing off the dregs of his fourth Jackalope beer. He crushed the can flat and tossed it into the graveyard of can corpses in the corner.

It was less than thirty seconds before Whitney placed another beer in Joseph's hand from the cooler. Whitney was still in his early twenties. He sported a dark goatee and an intense gaze. Whitney was only on beer number two, himself. He felt the need to catch up to Joseph, so he chugged the rest of his current beverage and quickly cracked into the next one.

Across the small blind from the imbibers, Judd knelt by the narrow viewport with a pair of binoculars to his eyes. Beside the leaning stock of his rifle, an open Jackalope can sat on the floor with not but a sip or two taken. He was the one on active watch for the time being.

Judd was thirty-two, six-foot-six, and built like a brick shithouse. He was the one the others knew they could count on when they needed to get shit done. It was a role he was proud of and happy to fill but also felt immense pressure from. He never wanted to let the others down and he often pushed himself too far or made concessions on his own priorities for the good of the group.

"Ya need a fresh'n, Judd?" Whitney asked between sips.

Judd shushed him. "Got eyes on one." He lowered the binoculars and got a grip on his rifle, raising it to his shoulder and taking aim through the horizontal window. He paused his chewing of the tobacco wad in his mouth and stuffed it behind his gums with his tongue.

"Think ya can make a heart shot?" Joseph asked. "Li'l Rhoda wants to learn how'ta mount a buck head."

"'Course I can make a heart shot."

Whitney got up off the floor and peered over Judd's shoulder at his prey off in the distance below.

Judd could feel the younger man's beer breath on the nape of his neck. He leaned into the stock of his rifle and switched the safety off. With his eye to the scope and his crosshairs over the creature's heart, Judd took a deep breath.

His finger moved into the guard and came to rest on the trigger. He squeezed gently.

The rifle barked a flash of fire.

Birds shot up into the sky from nearby trees.

Whitney hooted and clapped a hand down on Judd's back, breaking into obnoxious laughter.

Joseph sucked his yellow teeth and bit off a hunk of jerky.

The prey ran deeper into the forest in a zigzag.

Judd lowered the rifle. He shook his head; mad at himself. He grit his teeth and slung the rifle over his shoulder on its leather strap.

"How'd ya miss that sumbitch?" Whitney asked, teasing.

"I didn't miss him."

"Ya missed his heart."

Judd rose from his kneeling position, keeping ducked under the low roof of the blind. "Just takes a while to bleed out is all." He hoped that was true. He was only fifty/fifty on whether or not he actually hit the damn thing.

"You hit none but meat. Missed all them organs," Whitney continued. He laughed loudly.

Judd lifted the hatch in the floor and lowered his foot down onto the top rung of the ladder.

"Hold up a second, boy," Joseph said.

"I'll track'im, Joseph, don't you worry."

"I ain't worried 'bout that." He slid a walkie-talkie along the floor of the blind to Judd. "Tell us if and where ya drop him, and we'll meet ya there."

Judd gave an affirmative grunt and continued down the ladder with the walkie-talkie clipped to his belt. He hadn't bagged any meat on his last hunt. He couldn't go back empty-handed again and face that shame.

He neared the spot where the deer had stood when he fired. He looked back over his shoulder as he stepped forward. Whitney was watching him through the horizontal window, but Joseph must still have been seated on the floor, not visible at this angle.

Blood on the leaves. *Good,* he thought, *I didn't miss altogether.*

He was a good tracker. Not as good as Joseph, but pretty good.

Judd followed a trickle of blood along the ground for fifty yards before rounding a bend. He stepped quietly, his eyes flitting between the ground and the path ahead.

A narrow river came into view up ahead.

"Shit," Judd said aloud. The trail led straight across the river. He considered turning back and accepting failure. He stood for a moment, motionless aside from the movement of his jaw masticating the tobacco in his mouth. "Fuck it."

With his rifle balanced over his shoulder, Judd waded through the waist-high water.

He spent a couple of minutes milling around the muddy shore on the other side of the river, failing to find any trace of blood.

A noise coming from somewhere not too far away enticed Judd's gaze from the ground. He looked in the general direction of the disruption into the dense forest. *What was that?* he asked himself, unable to provide an answer. It certainly hadn't come from a deer.

He paused to listen, standing still and holding his breath, but he didn't hear it again, whatever *it* was.

Judd was about to give up and head back across the river when he finally spotted a hoofprint sunken into the mud. A quick scan of the area revealed a second print followed by a third and a fourth.

He had picked the trail back up. Clutching his rifle with both hands and stepping lightly, Judd followed the hoofprints.

Soon, the tracks became speckled with droplets of blood once again.

Judd passed through some broken branches and froze at the sound of the odd noise repeating. It was louder this time, closer. He whipped toward a row of tall bushes at his side.

The sound was of human origin, he was sure of it. Breathy, male.

Judd crept toward the bushes, unable to see through to the other side.

It sounded like someone moaning.

Judd looked for a gap in the bushes.

Another voice spoke over the moaning. "Ya like that?" Another male.

The moaning paused briefly. "Mmm, yeah." Then, back to moaning.

"Tell me how much you like it."

Judd's throat filled with bile. He felt disgust and outrage rising in equal measure within him. He pushed his way past the bushes.

The sight made him feel sick to his stomach.

Faith for Violence

Harry was on top of Andy, making gentle love atop a bed of freshly fallen leaves in a spotlight of warm sunshine through a gap in the canopy above. It was a flat, picturesque clearing with a view of the river sparkling brilliantly in the afternoon sun. The spot was just as perfect as he remembered it all those years ago.

For a brief period of time, this clearing had become the go-to hangout spot for Harry and two of his high school buddies. They would camp out on the weekends or just hang out after school around the fire pit they had constructed one afternoon. He had his first alcoholic beverage as a freshman in this very spot, though Pa thought his first taste of ale didn't come until his birthday two years later.

Harry had feared the spot would be overgrown, but luck was on his side, or so he had thought.

Their heaving breaths were a duet. Ecstasy in the friction between them. Every stitch of clothing cast carelessly aside on a smooth boulder.

"I love it," Andy said for the satisfaction of Harry's ego.

"What the fuck is goin' on here?!" Judd shouted, pointing

his rifle at the center of Harry's back.

Andy let out a shriek.

"Jesus!" Harry exclaimed. He fell onto his side, scrambling, desperate to cover himself up.

"What in the name of Second Christ is goin' on here?!"

Harry got to his feet, covering his crotch with both hands. "Look, man, we—"

Judd jabbed forward with his rifle from eight feet away. "Stay down in the dirt, ya filthy degenerate!"

Andy shrieked, still down on the leaf-covered ground. He curled up, shutting his eyes tight.

Harry lowered back down to the ground.

Judd stepped toward them. He pulled the walkie-talkie off his belt, brought it to his mouth, and thumbed the talk button. "You better hurry over here! I just caught a couple of queers fornicating in *our* woods!"

Joseph's voice quickly responded, tinny through the handset. "If this is a joke, it ain't funny, Judd."

"North-west, cross the stream, in a clearing. Hustle up." He clipped the walkie-talkie back onto his belt and returned his hand to the rifle to steady it.

Fuck, fuck, fuck! was all Harry's mind could string together. He swallowed hard and managed the first words that came to mind. "We didn't think anyone was out here—"

"We don't want any trouble!" Andy added in a panicked shout, peeking up at Judd.

"You are trouble!" Judd spat chaw juice onto the ground. "Filthy fuckin' faggots!" He took another step towards them, thrusting the rifle forward.

Andy curled back up into as close to a shell as he could get. *Faggot* was the first word Andy had ever heard in English outside of the movies. The juvenile son of a tourist couple had barked it at him in the Dongdaemun Market. Andy didn't know what it meant at the time, but the kid's sneering face gave him some idea. He tried to look it up in the Korean-English dictionary at school, but the word was absent. It wasn't until he visited an internet café, and figured out the correct spelling, that he confirmed the meaning.

He reached a trembling arm out toward Harry, and the two embraced in a shared fear.

"Stop touchin' each other!" Judd roared.

Andy yelped and let go.

"Put some air 'tween ya."

Harry slid away from Andy. Leaves clung to his sweaty, nude body.

Andy's whole being trembled uncontrollably.

Harry was doing everything he could to hold it together. He knew he couldn't afford to panic. His breath came out shaky but his senses remained sharp. His brain searched for a solution whether it be a means to escape, to attack, or to diffuse.

Judd began to shake his head as if trying to dislodge something. He paced back and forth in a short line, muttering under his breath. "Make me fuckin' sick." He spat again into the leaves, coating the green in brownish-yellow. *"On Second Christ's haven?"* he said more to himself than the others. "In *our* fuckin' forest?"

Harry found Judd looking at him as if he were expecting a legitimate answer to his last query. "We're sorry if we upset you," he said, attempting to be diplomatic.

"So sorry. We're so sorry," Andy added with a whimper.

Harry got up on his knees. "We'll just get dressed and leave." He began rising to his feet. If he could just get to his cellphone… *then what?* he asked himself. *One step at a time.* "You'll never see us in here ag—"

"Oh, no you don't!" Judd yelled. He brought the rifle to his shoulder and aimed it straight at Harry's head.

Harry dropped back down to the ground.

Andy instinctively reached for his husband but found

Judd's aim pivoting towards him.

"I said stop touchin' each other, queers!"

As the words left Judd's lips, Joseph and Whitney arrived at the clearing in a rush. They both had their rifles at the ready and were both taken aback upon sight of the nude men on the ground at the end of Judd's gun barrel.

Whitney let out a hoot of laughter. He pulled off his hat and slapped his knee with it, grinning broadly.

Joseph couldn't share in Whitney's delight. His chest heaved with anger. There was fire in his eyes.

"Look'ee what we got here!" Whitney whooped. "Coupl'a nudie-boys!" He laughed like a schoolyard bully.

Judd looked over at Joseph, keeping his aim on Harry. "They were… *fornicatin'* when I come upon 'em." He hoped Joseph would have the answer. "What should we do with 'em?"

Whitney assumed a quick execution. "Let me shoot one of 'em! I want the slant-eyed faggot. You can do the other'n." Whitney brought the stock of his rifle to his shoulder and his eye to the iron-sights.

Andy shrieked and curled up into a ball.

"No! No!" Harry shouted, putting himself between Andy and the rifle.

"Now, wait a second, Whitney," Judd said. "Ain't it our Christian duty to try 'n save their souls?" He looked from Whitney to the elder hunter for confirmation. Judd didn't want to be the one to make this decision one way or the other.

"Ain't no savin' their kind," Whitney spat.

Judd looked at Joseph: silent, contemplating. "Gotta try convertin' 'em first, don't we?" Judd asked. "Isn't that what Conrad always says? Faith 'fore violence?"

Whitney scoffed. "He wasn't talkin' 'bout these fucked-up blasphemers."

Finally, Joseph spoke. No words at first, just a grunt, but it brought pause to the two younger hunters. They looked to him. The words were difficult to say. He wanted to have it Whitney's way but knew Conrad would disapprove. "Judd's right, Whitney."

Whitney lowered his gun. He spun on his heels toward Joseph, outraged. "He's what?!"

Joseph took a moment to shake his head and glare at the fornicators before speaking. "Gotta bring 'em back to Conrad. It's for him to decide."

With a bastard sigh/groan, Whitney gave up on arguing. He stewed in the anger and disappointment for a moment, then he nodded. "All right. Fine. But either of these fags steps an inch outta line, and I'mma blast 'em in two."

"That'll be on them," Joseph condoned.

Whitney hoped they would step out of line. He willed them to try and run.

With his gun aimed from the waist, Joseph stepped toward the newlyweds and gave his meanest glare. "On…" he said commandingly, "Your…" he said, dripping venom, "Feet," he said with finality.

With his hands over his crotch, Harry rose to his feet.

Andy followed Harry's lead, missing about fifty percent of what the hunters were saying. He at least understood Joseph's piece-meal command.

"Look, we're really not any trouble," Harry said. "We'll just leave and never come back." Harry's eyes flashed to his crumpled clothes. The corner of his cellphone protruded slightly from the pocket. He averted his eyes and regretted looking. He hoped the hunters hadn't tracked his eyeline.

Whitney actively avoided looking in their direction. He gestured blindly toward Harry's crotch. "Make'im put his fuckin' pants on at least." Now that there was no plan to kill them, the whole thing felt obscene to Whitney.

Judd waved towards the crumpled clothing atop the boulder with the end of his rifle. He gave Harry a *go on* look with his eyes.

Holding his breath, Harry advanced towards the clothes. Willing his pocket-encumbered cellphone to glide towards him.

"Wait!" Joseph commanded.

Harry froze. *Shit!*

"Check down them pockets first." Joseph kept his eyes glued to Harry.

Whitney went over to the clothes and emptied the pockets. He stuffed Harry's wallet and keys into his own pocket then pulled out the cellphone. He smashed the screen to pieces against the boulder.

Harry felt his heart sink. That was the point of no return if they hadn't crossed it already. He shut his eyes and took a deep breath, feeling his slim composure failing him. He fought to maintain control, his chest heaving.

Whitney did the same with the contents of Andy's pockets, then he threw their clothes at them.

The newlyweds slowly dressed at the ends of rifle barrels.

Tears streamed down Andy's face. He could not help it. His best efforts to stop the crying only made him feel more helpless and hopeless and made his cries heavier.

"Pathetic," Whitney muttered aloud in response to the tears. *Real men don't cry.*

Harry tried to come up with some kind of solution, anything at all, but he was having trouble thinking straight. His amygdala burned with red-hot panic.

Once they were fully dressed, Judd motioned down a trail with his rifle.

Harry looked toward the direction Judd had gestured to. It stretched long into nowhere. It was not the direction he and Andy had come from. He could hear Andy whimpering behind him and wanted so badly to spin around and hug him. He had seen Andy cry before, at movies and after fights with his father, but never like this. Never out of fear or desperation.

He looked at the hunters. Three gun barrels looked back at him. "Please don't—" It felt pointless trying to communicate with them but he couldn't think of anything else to try. "… Just— Just let us leave."

"You are leaving," Whitney said. "With us."

Whitney strode toward the trail and turned one hundred and eighty degrees once he passed the newlyweds. He walked backwards down the trail, keeping his gun trained on Harry's center of mass.

"Move," Joseph commanded with authority.

Andy hoped and begged and wished that Harry had a plan. He felt useless but had faith in his husband.

Harry cursed himself for his inability to think of a viable course of action. *There must be a way out of this*, he told himself, but he could think of nothing other than to comply to buy them some more time. Maybe an opportunity would present itself if they could play along for long enough. It was as close to a plan as he could devise under the immense pressure.

With shaky steps, Harry followed Whitney down the trail.

Andy stuck right behind his husband, barely able to see through the tears in his eyes. He wanted to grab onto Harry's sleeve as a guide, but the hunters' admonishing words had finally sunken in.

Judd and Joseph walked side-by-side behind the newlyweds with their rifles aimed from hip-height. Fingers rested on triggers all too ready to be pulled.

Smiling Upon Us

The staggered group trudged on. How long had they been following the trail?

Harry guessed forty minutes.

Andy guessed over an hour.

Judd knew it had been less than ten minutes since they left the clearing. Time limped like a condemned man to the gallows.

Andy's tears had subsided. His chest was tight and his eyes stung. He felt like he hadn't slept in two days.

Whitney was still moving in reverse, only occasionally twisting to look where he was going. As he walked, he whistled *I Wish I was in Dixie*.

Harry's attention was glued to Whitney's gun and his finger resting right on the trigger.

The heel of Whitney's boot caught on a tree root and made him stumble. He accidentally squeezed the trigger, just halfway, but enough to make every muscle in Harry's body tense up.

Harry shut his eyes tight and stopped his forward march.

Andy stopped too, but quickly felt the stock of Judd's rifle shoving him forward. He staggered forward and bumped into Harry.

Harry caught his balance. His eyes opened and landed on Whitney who had resumed both his backwards movement and his whistling, his finger still on the trigger.

Andy whispered, his voice small, "Harry…"

Harry fought the urge to ignore him and keep trudging on indefinitely. He looked back over his shoulder at Andy and silently mouthed, *it's okay,* twice.

Joseph suddenly perked up. "Eh, well lookee here."

The deer Judd shot had finally bled out and collapsed right atop the very trail they now walked.

Judd smiled at his bounty. "All worked out, huh Joseph?"

"The lord is smilin' upon us today, yes siree."

Whitney halted his backward progression, prompting the newlyweds to stop as well.

Andy watched as Judd slung his rifle onto his shoulder on its leather strap and approached the deer. He listened as Joseph and Whitney, still aiming their rifles, each murmured something; the same something. He couldn't make out any of the words. They were speaking quickly and mumbling under their breath.

Harry missed most of the words too but he surmised they were saying some sort of prayer.

Judd lifted the buck by its antlers and got a grip on its underside. He returned upright with the deer slung across his shoulders.

Fuck… was all Harry's internal monologue could muster at the display of strength. The thing must have weighed close to two hundred pounds, and the hunter carried it as if it weighed no more than a jug of water.

With the deer balanced on his shoulders, Judd even managed to keep ahold of his rifle with one hand.

Before they had walked too much farther, the trail came

to an end. It terminated at a muddy parking lot which hosted a single vehicle: a dark-blue pickup truck with badly scratched up sides revealing the silvery, metallic color underneath.

Three pairs of boots and two pairs of sneakers squelched in the mud.

Beyond the lot was a sunny country road. The sunlight—unaffected by the shadowy gloom of the overhead leaves—had a magnetic draw to Harry.

Andy felt the same draw, watching the wide-open road over Harry's shoulder. Beyond the canopy of green leaves, the sun shone golden against the two-lane road and the wheat field that lay beyond it, swaying gently in a breeze that couldn't be felt in the forest.

A car drove lazily past the forest entrance about a hundred feet away. Andy lit up at the sight. His mouth opened and he nearly blurted out a cry for help but he stopped himself just in time. He knew it wouldn't be heard from this distance, even if the windows had been rolled down, and the attempt might have been enough to get him shot. He tightened back up and stayed in line as the hunters led him and Harry over to the pickup truck.

As if taking off a backpack, Judd tossed the deer into the bed of the truck. The pickup bounced on its shocks under the weight.

"Keep 'em peeled, Whit," Joseph ordered as he climbed into the driver's seat. Judd got into the passenger seat after taking a moment to stretch out his shoulders.

Whitney didn't like Joseph playing leader all the time. He respected Joseph for his seniority—as he would respect any elder—but Joseph didn't have legitimate rank over him. He sure acted like it, though. Okay, he had been with Conrad since almost the beginning, but that shouldn't matter so much at this point, Whitney thought, or rather wished.

Harry stood in place at the end of Whitney's gun barrel.

Whitney jerked his head toward the truck bed. He clicked in the side of his mouth as one would when giving a dog a command.

At length, Harry and Andy climbed into the back of the truck. Harry wondered if he was making a mistake even as he sat down with his back to the gate. What chance did he have of just making a run for it? Less than five percent he guessed, closer to zero percent of both him and Andy bolting and making it away scot-free.

Whitney climbed in after them, stepping into the wheel well and lifting himself up on the tire, being sure to never take his finger off the trigger or his aim off his prey. He sat down with his back to the cab, the deer carcass between him and the captives. He liked the smell of the deer in front him. It made him hungry. He thought of the jerky and beer they had left behind in the hunting blind, forgotten in all the commotion. *Damn it.*

Andy couldn't take his eyes off of the dead animal. The bullet hole in its chest stared back at him. He had never seen a wound like that up close. He wondered if he would feel it or just die instantly if it happened to him.

The window into the cab slid open beside Whitney. "Keep your finger out the guard 'less they try somethin'," Judd cautioned. "Lots'a potholes on the way."

Whitney gave a half-hearted grunt in response that just barely passed as affirmation rather than a scoff. If he didn't like taking orders from Joseph, then he *really* didn't like taking orders from Judd. His finger stayed right where it was.

The engine turned over and the truck pulled out of the muddy lot, making a right turn onto the road.

Harry recognized the road. They were moving away from the lot where his car was parked. Away from his home.

Andy drew up his knees as blood from the deer sloshed towards him down the ridged truck bed like rainwater down a gutter.

Joseph followed the straight road running parallel to the forest. The old asphalt was cracked and run through with grooves of dirt and sand from the neighboring farmland environs which stretched as far as the eye could see. The truck bounced and rocked from side to side as it forded potholes.

The Wages of Fear popped into Andy's mind. He shook off the distraction, confused as to how his mind could wander at a time like this. His brain wished to transport him anywhere else. *Stay focused*, he urged himself, *think*.

Harry couldn't stand looking into Whitney's hateful glare. It made his skin crawl. He could see in the young man's eyes that he would follow through on his promise to shoot them and not feel one bit bad about it. Harry could see just how easy it would be for him. Like checking a box on a form.

He lowered his gaze from Whitney's piercing eyes to his finger, resting against the trigger of his rifle.

The truck hit a nasty pothole and jostled everyone in the back. Whitney squeezed the trigger halfway before releasing.

Harry worked up the nerve to speak. "He- he said to keep your finger off the trigger." He could feel the words trembling on their way out of his mouth.

Whitney couldn't believe his gall. "What'd you juss' say to me?" He leaned forward aggressively. His leg stretched out and his boot came to rest against the belly of the deer carcass.

Harry put his hands up innocently and leaned back over the gate of the truck bed. "Ju- in- so you don't accidentally—"

"You shut your cock-suckin' mouth, boy!"

Whitney postured up tall in the back of the truck, kneeling on the grooved bed. He braced the stock of the rifle against his shoulder, aiming with his teeth bared.

Harry tried to cower away but had nowhere to flee. His face was mere inches from the end of Whitney's rifle barrel.

Andy curled up into a ball in the corner, hating the cowardice that stopped him from leaping in front of Harry. He wished he could say he would take a bullet for his husband but that would be a lie.

The truck hit another pothole.

Harry braced himself. His eyes clenched tight like vices.

Whitney lost his balance. He pulled the trigger.

A flash of bright light was scored by a loud bang with a long decay.

"Harry!" Andy shouted as a gust of smoke from the rifle blew back into his eyes.

The truck swerved.

Harry screamed. His trembling hands clawed at his bloody torso.

Cracked Asphalt

arry's hands searched for the wound to plug the bleeding but couldn't find it. He felt Andy's hands join in the frantic search. Harry felt no pain. He figured shock must be overpowering physical sensation.

Whitney righted himself and yanked back the bolt of his rifle. The expended shell spun from the side of his gun and clinked down into the truck bed, slotting into one of the grooves. "Get away from him!" He shouted at Andy, gesturing with the rifle, his finger already back on the trigger.

Harry's search for the bullet stopped when he felt a gush of warm liquid against his thigh. He thought he had pissed himself and took that to be his final, pathetic act as a mortal man. But he was wrong.

It wasn't his urine, but rather the blood of the deer flowing from a newly formed bullet hole near its heart. Whitney's bullet had blown through the deer and bit into the metal gate at the back of the pickup truck.

"I'm all right," Harry blurted. He turned to Andy and repeated, "I'm all right."

"What the fuck you doin' back there? They givin' ya trouble?" Joseph asked. He had twisted around in his seat to look through the little window out of the cab.

Whitney tried to save face. "Just showin' 'em who's boss!"

The truck's speed picked back up. Judd was glad there were no other cars on the road. Out in the forest, Judd didn't care *too* strongly whether Whitney killed the fornicators or not but, out in the open, he didn't want to risk witnesses. He considered driving around in circles for a while instead of going straight to Conrad's holler but he felt confident that they were alone and at no risk of being followed. This road didn't see too much traffic, and the neighboring farmland was hardly ever tended. He didn't want to risk transporting their captives any longer than necessary.

Without looking back, Judd asked, "We need'a switch places, Whit?"

"I got it handled!" Whitney spat off the side of the truck. He hated feeling belittled. It was all because of his age, he thought. They never took him seriously. If he were older, he'd get a little more respect. He had thought, foolishly, that growing out his facial hair might have led to more respect as a man. All it led to was a bit of teasing from the others when his goatee was growing through its patchy phase.

Judd tilted the rearview mirror to get a clearer look at the mess in the truck bed. He spotted the new bullet hole in the deer. "Don't seem like ya got it handled. Why you perforatin' a dead buck?"

Whitney twisted toward the cab. "Ugh, ya know what, Judd?" He stuck his head in through the little window. "You ain't above me, so stop actin' like y'are!"

The second Whitney looked away, Harry leaned over to his husband and whispered, *"We need to jump, Andy!"*

"What?! We can't!"

"I ain't acting like I'm anything," Judd said. "Just

commentin' on—"

"You're always treatin' me like I'm some fuck-up," Whitney said spitefully.

Harry got into a squat. He looked down over the back of the truck. The cracked asphalt rushed by in a hot blaze.

"No, they'll shoot us!" Andy said, fearing his husband would jump anyway. *"They'll kill us, Harry!"* He could see it playing out: Harry leaping from the back of the truck, his leg breaking on impact, the big hunter slamming on the brakes, a bullet going through the back of Harry's head as he tried to crawl away…

Harry was frustrated with Andy for his cowardice. He wanted to grab hold of Andy and dive off the back of the truck with him.

"Calm down, Whitney," Joseph said from the passenger seat.

"Y'ain't the boss'a me either, Joseph! I answer to Conrad, not you. I ain't your inferior."

Harry guided Andy's view toward the back of the truck.

Andy looked down and felt his stomach drop at the sight of the blur of blacktop flying by under the tires. *"No, I can't! Please, Harry, don't!"*

Harry grit his teeth, knowing he needed to do something now, anything. He glanced toward the hunters: still preoccupied. He scrambled to remove his belt buckle.

"Okay, Whit, okay," Joseph said in a calming voice. "Settle down. We'll talk about this later."

Harry released his monogrammed belt buckle off the side of the truck. He watched it bounce off of the white line painted on the edge of the asphalt and land somewhere in the brush off to the side of the road. His parents would recognize it instantly. *But how would they ever find it?*

He retook his passive sitting position just in time for Whitney to turn back around. *That was useless*, he scolded himself. He needed to navigate this situation more carefully.

Dropping the belt buckle was too big of a risk, and for nothing. Mistakes like that could get us killed.

"Damn right, we'll talk about this later. Ah, sheesh." Whitney sat down and fixed his pissed off glare on Andy. The foreigner engendered the most hatred in Whitney. He was confident that Conrad would approve the death of the homosexuals. It would be a mercy; on them and on the world.

The truck slowed, seemingly at random. Then, Harry noticed the narrow trail into the forest; overgrown and hard to spot from a stand-still let alone while in motion.

At a gentle pace, the truck made its first turn since exiting the forest, right back into a different part of the same forest, a few miles down the road.

The trail had faint tire tracks set in the not-quite-dead grass which the truck now traced into the forest.

Judd always had to flip on the headlights for this leg of the journey. The overhead foliage was so dense and all-consuming that this stretch of forest seemed out of place and time. A natural canopy smothered the sky. Nighttime seemed ever-present beneath these sacred limbs.

Sharp tree branches and thorny bushes alike reached out towards the sides of the truck to scratch away its outermost surface. The newlyweds inched closer together to avoid being poked and prodded by the piercing nature.

The truck rocked side to side as its tires forded dips, rises, rocks, and roots like a boat on rough water. Andy thought of *Heart of Darkness,* of *Apocalypse Now.* He feared the Colonel Kurtz at the end of this journey. Again, his mind wandered. *Why? Damnit,* he cursed himself. Andy had learned English from movies. Sure, he had English classes at school to supplement, but the majority of his linguistic education came from foreign films on VHS tapes rented from his local video shop. It wasn't *just* foreign language and culture the films exposed him to but also an escape. An escape from the bullies at school. An escape from his dad when he went too hard on the soju. And now, an escape was what he wanted more than anything. His wandering mind sought escapism where there was none to be had.

It was slow-going down the trail. The truck puttered below a walking man's pace. Judd made careful, micro-adjustments to the steering wheel with only the slightest pressure applied to the gas.

Eventually, the headlights shined against the rusted metal of a chain-link fence overgrown with roots and vines at the end of the trail. Beyond the fence lay a wall of foliage. A metal sign was bolted to the chain link. The letters *H-A-Z* were legible before a patch of moss and rust obscured the text. From the other end of the obfuscation stuck out the letters *I-C-A-L-S*.

The pickup truck slowed to a stationery idle.

Harry looked back the way they had come. The forest seemed to stretch on into infinity. The open road they traveled seemed a distant memory in this place of darkness. He flinched at the sound of the driver's side door opening.

Judd climbed out of the truck. He strode to the fence and grabbed ahold of the chain link with his two big hands. With minimal exertion, Judd peeled the fence aside. Each link on one side of the fence that blocked the trail had been snipped with bolt cutters. It was imperceptible from a distance of more than a few inches.

With the fencing peeled aside, Judd began dismantling the wall of carefully-arranged foliage that precluded the rest of the trail as a form of camouflage.

Harry mustered up the courage to speak, knowing it was unlikely he would receive an answer. "Where are you taking us?"

"Shut your cock-hole," Whitney menaced in a low tone.

"I ain't gon' tell ya again."

Joseph slid over into the driver's seat. When Judd had cleared the path head, Joseph gassed the truck the few feet forward past the fence and foliage. He shifted back into the passenger seat as Judd dragged the fencing back into position and reassembled the camouflaged roadblock.

A sense of entombment rushed through Andy despite being out in the open air, but where or what he was walled inside of, he had no clue.

The truck navigated deeper into the dense woods, making wide turns through tight foliage.

Eventually, the trail widened, and an exit appeared to the darkness. Golden sunlight shined brilliantly ahead: at first, a pinprick in the dark, then the light at the end of the tunnel.

As the light slowly grew to greet them, Harry laid eyes on their destination and couldn't keep from muttering under his breath, "*what the fuck?*"

Part II

The Holler

The large clearing was walled on all sides by the dense forest. The sun, directly overhead, cast the rustic settlement in a wash of amber; a veritable village of modest construction.

The truck rocked over the greenery. There was no road, though one was slowly being formed from travel in and out of the holler over time.

Harry's brain struggled to process what he was looking at. The pieces dotting the landscape ahead of him came from two different jigsaw puzzles. A dozen wooden, two-story homes were arranged in the shape of a horseshoe opening up toward the slowly advancing truck. A pointed church stood proudly in gleaming white at the apex of the curve. In the center of the horseshoe was a raised platform—halfway between stage and gallows—in front of an audience of outdoor pews. Cornucopias full of fruits and vegetables lined the front of the platform, and a tall, wooden cross emblazoned with intricate carvings stood erect in the stage's center. Behind the pews was a large, cuboid monstrosity of wood and metal that the newlyweds could not make heads nor tails of.

A new chill ran through both Harry and Andy's bodies without either of them knowing precisely why. The implication seemed too abstract to possibly be correct. Their minds settled somewhere short of comprehension.

Two dozen yards behind the church was a large, man-made lake: stagnant and swarming with insects and algae. A rusted, out-of-use drainage pipe burst out of the ground on the shore and hung above the surface of the water.

Alongside the twelve homes was a covered workshop filled with tools and lumber but lacking walls or a floor, a long mess hall with a welcoming facade, and a large, round building the color of the sky with a metal door painted red. The round building lacked windows or any signage. Further away from the homes, was a stone well with a hanging bucket and a row of modest gardens where fruits and vegetables grew. One garden and a neighboring workstation was dedicated solely to the cultivation of hemp.

Less than half of the structures were painted, but a few others were works in progress. A pair of men with brushes worked by hand on the side of the mess hall, painting it white to match the finished structures.

The pickup truck parked atop a patch of dead grass alongside the station wagon used for "recruitment." A third vehicle sat tireless and up on blocks. Another had its hood open with jumper cables clipped to the battery and frame.

Andy noticed a pair of women crossing the greenery from the village center over to the parked vehicles: one in her twenties, the other in her thirties. They were both wearing homemade, ankle-length dresses. The drab material was coarse and scratchy; rough burlap. Their dresses weren't a perfect match, but it was clear an attempt at uniformity had been made if not quite succeeded.

The women walked with rigid movements, bending unnaturally at the joints like playthings with each step. Their movements looked painful to Andy, like strained limps in both legs and odd rigidity in each arm as it hung straight against their hips rather than swinging with their gait. The faces of the women betrayed no discomfort. Subtle smiles hung on their mouths, but their faces were adorned with something… Andy couldn't tell what from the distance.

A man dressed in casual blue jeans, work boots, and a red flannel shirt with the sleeves rolled up stepped out of one of the unpainted homes and headed toward the parking area. He jogged to get there before the burlap clad women.

Judd and Joseph climbed out of the truck. Judd was glad to be back in the comfort of the holler. He knew the stress of dealing with the degenerates was far from over but he felt infinitely calmer now that he was in such close proximity to the church. It felt like he was away from home for far longer than he actually had been. He was glad to see Abigail heading towards him. She was a good one. So was Joseph's Damaris. Whitney's spouse was a whole other story.

"We eatin' venison tonight, boys?" the man asked as he closed the distance between them.

Judd gave Clayton a welcome confirmation.

The women were close enough for Andy to see clearly now. The marks on their faces made him avert his eyes. A deep scar curled across most of Damaris's cheek, over her jawbone, and down into her neck. Abigail's left eye was badly mangled and stitched shut with black thread. The wounds didn't exactly look fresh but they didn't look fully healed either. The contented smiles accompanying the injuries made Andy shudder.

"Who're they?" Clayton asked upon seeing the newlyweds in the back of the truck. "What's goin' on here?" He cocked his head at Joseph.

Joseph didn't want to explain the situation twice. He had no say in the matter. "Need a word with Conrad. He available?"

Clayton shook his head. "Been in his writing room since first light." That was always great to see. Conrad spending the day working on his tome filled Clayton with excitement and wonder.

Abigail arrived in front of Judd. Without hesitation, she dropped to her knees and kissed his muddy boots with a string of eager pecks.

Damaris knelt before Joseph. She felt his fist tighten in her hair and force her down to his boots. She was going there anyway, but he enjoyed the show of force.

The women returned upright with muddy faces. Judd gently wiped the mud from Abigail's nose and mouth. Joseph left Damaris dirtied.

Judd cupped Abigail's chin in his hand. "Fetch me a pair'a ropes, will ya?"

Abigail nodded, the smile unmoving upon her face as if etched in stone. She turned back towards the village center and strode home. On her way, she passed by Trixie, who was now twelve years old after a year and a half away from home. She had been renamed Shiloh and grown used to the sound of it. *Late, as usual*, Abigail thought, judging. *She doesn't appreciate how good she has it.*

About fuckin' time, Whitney thought as he watched Shiloh's lazy approach. The sight of her swinging her arms, the sound of her noisy humming, it made him furious. He despised her. *Why'd I get stuck with the runt of the litter?* That question often kept Whitney up at night.

She wore a similar burlap dress as the other women but didn't share in their same strained movements. Her arms swung lackadaisically by her sides, and her stride was even.

"Gimme a hand with the carcass, Clayton?" Judd said, circling to the truck bed.

Clayton nodded and joined him at the side of the truck. He looked skeptically at the strangers at the end of Whitney's gun.

Judd stared Harry in the eye. He could tell Harry was the one he had to worry about more than the other one. He spoke in a neutral tone. "Be smart. Be civil. Be respectful."

As Judd and Clayton reached for the deer, Harry inched away.

Whitney stood up in the truck bed and looked down at Shiloh as she finally arrived.

"Welcome home, Whitney," Shiloh said with a curtsey.

Ugh, her fucking mongoloid voice. Whitney hated hearing her. He hated looking at her just as much. He at least had the carnal satisfaction to look forward to in the not-too-distant future.

"Ya need some giddyap, Shiloh. Y'aint be gettin' away with this disrespect much longer."

"Disrespeck? Ah were fixin' a snag in mah dress." She held up a ruffle of her coarse dress. An off-white patch was stitched onto it with black thread.

Whitney scoffed at her. He looked to Clayton, who strained to lift the deer from the back of the truck—Judd was doing most of the lifting. "Was Judith this bad before her bleedin'?"

"Oh, yeah. Worse even," Clayton said, thinking back on the beginning of his matrimonial union. "She knows how'ta act now."

Whitney found some comfort in that. "Don't know which I'm lookin' forward to more, the copulation or the silence." He let out a single loud laugh, then turned pointedly toward the twelve-year-old. "A little early peace and quiet wouldn't kill ya, would it?"

"You juss mad ya c'aint hit me yet."

Oh, the nerve. The fucking belligerence. Hot breath pumped from Whitney's nose, his mouth clenched tight.

Abigail returned with two lengths of black, hempen rope. She bowed deeply as she proffered the strands to Judd. He lowered the deer to the ground to take hold of the ropes.

Whitney climbed from the truck to make way for Judd, who took his place.

Judd stood tall in the truck bed, his six-foot-six frame towering over Harry and Andy on their knees.

Harry tried and failed to mask his terror. Andy left his fear out in the open like a puppy left outside in a thunderstorm.

"Don't make this harder on ya-self. Flat on ya belly, now."

Andy shared a scared look with Harry. He didn't know what was being asked of him, the accent and vernacular too thick for him to parse. In the blink of an eye, he felt Judd's big hands on him. He let out a shriek as Judd forced him flat, his face pressed hard into the ridged truck bed.

Judd pinned Andy's arms behind his back and knelt to hold them in place while he tied his wrists together.

Andy called out in pain. "Stop! Stop, please!" The weight on him was immense, the pressure was crushing.

"Don't hurt him!" Harry shouted, momentarily overcoming his fear for the sake of worry. He grabbed onto Judd and tried to pull him away from his husband.

Judd easily rebuffed him. The reaction wasn't unexpected.

Whitney and Clayton grabbed hold of Harry's arms from beside the truck. They bent him backwards over the lip of the bed and had him at their mercy.

Andy tried to wriggle free from beneath Judd. The pain in his arms was unbearable as Judd pressed down with his full bodyweight. He felt himself being pressed to a breaking point.

In response to the wriggling and the cries of pain, Judd let his full bodyweight press down on Andy. He heard and felt the crack of bone beneath his knee.

Bound & Broken

"Stop! Get off him!" Harry yelled but could scarcely be heard over Andy's wails of pain.

Judd finished tying Andy's hands together with a French-bowline knot. He stood up off of the crying man and looked down at the discolored bulge in his forearm. It looked as though a golf ball had been surgically implanted under Andy's skin where his cracked ulna diverged from its natural path. Judd was unfazed by the injury.

Whitney, on the other hand, was delighted. *About time these faggots suffered a little*, he thought. They had worse coming to them, of that he was sure.

"Andy, you're gonna be okay! It'll all be okay! I promise!" Harry had no idea how he could fulfil that promise. He hoped to sound confident, and that his confidence might quell his lover's overwhelming fear.

Now free from Judd's weight, Andy lay flat on his chest, crying. His fractured arm trembled behind his back as his tears collected in the ridges of the truck bed. He had thought he was out of tears but was proven wrong.

Judd left the scrawny one where he was and climbed out

of the truck bed. He grabbed hold of Harry. "That doesn't have'ta happen to you too," Judd told him plainly. "Make this easy."

Harry wanted to spit in his face. He wanted to make it as difficult as possible for the hillbilly bastard who hurt the love of his life… but he retained just enough presence of mind to know that would only make matters worse. He needed to be smart and play his cards right. He would need to avoid debilitating injury to have any hope of escaping or fighting back when the time was right. It was a heart-breaking waiting game. He didn't want to play along but knew he had to or else seal their fates.

With Clayton and Whitney's help, Judd forced Harry to the ground, face-down. Judd was not met with any resistance as he tied Harry's hands behind his back. *Good*, Judd thought, *stay docile.*

Andy had never broken a bone before; never fractured, never sprained. He had expected it to feel awful, but the reality was even more painful than his imaginings. The crooked angle of his arms tied behind his back made the pain even worse. The bindings were far too tight to attempt a more natural position.

When times were tough, it usually helped Andy to remind himself that things could always be worse. Now, he was in such a dreadful situation that he struggled to think of an unfavorable alternative. The search gave him the slightest of distractions from the searing pain. *Better an arm than a leg*, he rationalized. It would be harder to escape with a broken leg than with a broken arm. There it was, the elusive silver lining, always there no matter how dark the cloud. When circumstances kept getting worse and worse, the light seemed further away, but Andy knew it was still there, just needing to be uncovered.

Harry was brought back to his feet by Judd. *Funny*, Harry thought morosely. He didn't feel much more trapped or endangered with his hands bound behind his back than he did when in the hunters' presence unencumbered. The forest was a knot tightening around them.

Pork Whistle

Ma Winters was getting worried now, and Pa could tell, though he didn't feel the same level of concern.

They had been sitting outside at one of the Pork Whistle's three patio tables for quite a while at this point. The waiter came by to check on them for the fourth time but was again dismissed.

Pa had skipped lunch to be extra hungry for the Pork Whistle, and his stomach was rumbling something fierce. Watching the dinner patrons at the next table over dig into their aromatic food sent him licking his lips absently.

Ma had her cellphone out, the one with the frustrating touch screen that she barely knew how to use. She regretted letting the young lady at the shop downtown talk her into upgrading to a 'smart' phone. She called Harrison for the third time since arriving at the restaurant, whose very building looked to be saturated in grease.

Again, the call went to voicemail. She returned her phone to her purse with a sigh.

Pa looked over the menu again, though he had no reason

to. He knew exactly what he would order before he arrived at the restaurant. He had known what he would order the next time he was at the Pork Whistle since the last time he was at the Pork Whistle. He had no plans to deviate from his usual order until his dying day.

He glanced up at Ma, fidgeting in her seat and scanning the sedentary parking lot again. "No use gettin' all worked up, Ma," he said. "I'm sure they just lost track'a time."

"What if they got lost hiking? Oh…" Ma found herself reaching for her phone again immediately.

"Harrison? Get lost hiking?" Pa said incredulously. "Prolly hooked up with his old buddies. He still got friends in town, don't he?"

Ma wasn't sure. She guessed, probably. Harrison didn't speak much of any old friends but maybe that was just because his new life overseas dominated their conversations.

Harry had a small pocket of friends that he had been close with in high school who were still located in the Jonesborough area. They kept up with occasional light correspondence—happy birthdays and merry Christmases— but they had largely fallen out of touch otherwise. Harry had taken college as a chance for a fresh start and left behind a lot in favor of self-discovery. It was the best decision he ever made.

Ma and Pa had wanted him to go to college closer to home, but a complete change of scenery was important to Harry. The open-minded, liberal, cultured land that was New York City sounded like a fantasyland the way his Jonesborough neighbors described it with disdain. He made sure to temper his expectations with alternative viewpoints of the city that painted it in a less delectable light. Even still, he was practically crawling out of his skin with excitement on the whole drive north. It hadn't delivered on everything he hoped for but it delivered enough.

Ma returned her cellphone to her bag. It was Harrison's

first full day back home. She knew Pa was right not to worry. After all, she never found herself worrying about his safety when he was all the way over in South Korea and would go for a few days at a time without replying to her messages. His being in close proximity had reignited a long-dormant maternal protectiveness in her that she was sure was now getting the better of her and making her paranoid.

She shrugged off her worries, understanding that Harrison had surely just been swept up in visiting the old haunts or some such harmless time-wasting as Pa suggested. Harrison deserved a little fun, and Andy certainly deserved a tour of Jonesborough, did he not?

"Ya know something else I'm sure of?" Pa asked. "That they won't mind if we go ahead and order."

Ma felt her stomach grumble. "Oh, go on."

Pa's hand shot up into the air and waved the waiter over with an eager flourish.

The Two Churches

The sun began to dip behind the tall trees encircling the holler.

Andy sniffled. He wanted to wipe his nose and dry his eyes but could do neither with his arms bound behind his back. He was no longer crying but his eyelashes were host to residual tears, as were his wet cheeks. The pain in his arm had not lessened in the slightest. The bulging bone of his forearm had bumped against the back of the pew when he took his seat, and the tears had almost started flowing all over again. It was taking a significant amount of willpower to keep his pained vocalizations bottled up inside. He feared what his captors would do to him if he kept blubbering. He could tell it was getting on their nerves, and that their nerves were not the sort you wanted to get on.

The newlyweds were seated in the back row of the outdoor church's two columns of weather-worn pews. Judd sat in between the two, and Joseph stood right behind Harry, looming over him.

The traditionally constructed church stood just beyond the stage in front of them, not a stone's throw away. Two churches in a row, one for warm weather, the other cold. The white coat of paint on the traditional church looked brand new or otherwise kept meticulous care of. Bird droppings, dust, dirt, and rain could all easily tarnish the bright paint job, but the structure gleamed immaculate. The stained-glass designs set in the church windows never failed to strike awe into virgin eyes, and the newlyweds were no exception. Conrad had the windows specially made and trucked into the holler when the settlement was still in its infancy. It was the largest startup cost by far, but there was not a soul amongst his followers who considered the investment to be made in vain.

Harry's eyes drifted along the arc of homes now that he was seeing them up close. The houses were simple: two stories, bare-bones construction, windows with wooden shutters, no outward signs of electricity. They resembled the sort of modern cabins that vacationers might rent for a modest sum. Each home was identical, aside from some having been painted and others not, save for the one beside the church, which was much larger than the rest. Above the entrance of the first home, hung a wooden oval with beveled edges. The names, *Bo — Rhoda,* were painted onto the oval. Above the next home's doorway, *Clayton — Judith* was painted on a similar sign. Each and every home had a matching sign about the entrance.

The larger home beside the church was not taller but longer and wider. Grander. Above this home's embellished doorway hung an ornate plaque with *Father Conrad — Mother Mabel* carved in cursive lettering. This was the only home to have a porch, which was supported by intricately designed columns and balustrades. The second floor of the home even had brilliant stained-glass windows to match those of the neighboring church. Though the home was already a sight to behold, it still appeared to be a work in progress with certain aspects of it lacking the embellishments of others.

A loud ticking brought Harry's attention back to the strange wood and metal creation situated just behind the pews. Up close, Harry thought the boxy device resembled an organ. It was fitted with pipes and bellows and a row of horns but no visible pedals or keys by which to operate it. Exposed gears ticked loudly within the instrument at an irregular rhythm. He had never seen anything like it. He could imagine encountering it an ancient-history museum just as easily as a modern-art museum.

Judd spoke to Andy while looking down at the dirt under his feet. The grass was worn away around the pews from all of the sitting and shuffling of feet the ground undertook during their outdoor masses. "If Conrad decides you're worth saving, we'll get that arm of yours patched up. Hailey's good with the first aid. Heck, if your conversion's successful, Second Christ may even take away your pain altogether. I seen him do it. One touch was all it took."

The big man waited for Andy's response— his gratitude —but it never came.

Judd swiveled his body atop the pew, knocking knees with the injured outsider. He looked down at Andy, who shrunk away in response. "Ya know? Here in America, it's considered respectful to—"

The tall doors of the church swung open.

Judd shut his mouth and rose to his feet as if for the national anthem.

Joseph snatched the hat off his head and held it against his heart. He smoothed out his hair to make himself a mite more presentable for the Father.

Father Conrad strode from the church with a big smile on his face. He was fifty-six years old, six-foot-three, and over the cusp of three hundred pounds. He was beaten in height within the holler by Judd alone. But even then, Conrad had many pounds on him. He wore long, handmade robes and a blue, silk stoll embroidered with crosses, doves, and various plants and flowers found in the garden of Eden.

Joseph hurried over to Conrad, engaging him in the limited space of flat grass between the indoor and outdoor churches.

From their seats on the pew, Harry and Andy watched Joseph and Conrad converse inaudibly for a time. Joseph pointed back towards them.

Conrad stared over Joseph's shoulder at the newlyweds for a long, hard moment, deep in thought. The cheery smile was gone from his face. His stare made both of the newlyweds deeply uncomfortable. The longer it went on, the closer it felt like he was to the newlyweds despite neither party advancing toward the other, as if the empty space between them was somehow contracting.

At length, Conrad's stare relented. The smile returned to his face, albeit in a more menacing form. He placed a gentle hand on Joseph's shoulder and spoke words that Harry desperately wished he could hear.

Andy tried to read Conrad's lips, forgetting in the moment that he could only manifest that talent if the speaker was conversing in Korean.

Joseph gave Conrad a confident nod, then accompanied him on the short walk around the stage and between the two rows of pews.

The approach made Harry so tense he felt as though he might snap like dry spaghetti under the slightest pressure.

Judd moved out of the way so Conrad could form a direct connection with the captives, and Joseph remained at a respectful distance in the outdoor church's central aisle.

Fear bubbled in Harry's chest as he looked up at the massive man before him, his torso blotting out the setting sun. The face looking down at him was wide-eyed and slack jawed. Andy set his eyes to the grass and tried to keep his quivering down to a minimum.

Conrad stood still above them. A moment of silence passed as he lingered in their discomfort. Then, he spoke. His deep timbre and thick drawl gave the sensation of leather on catgut. "Joseph tells me you're a pair'a homosexuals." He paused to gauge their reactions. "Does he speak truth?"

The newlyweds remained silent. Harry knew the truth would not be welcomed but also knew that attempting to lie would be futile and likely bring about severe punishment. He feared the punishment for the truth would be damningly severe enough already.

Conrad put on a friendly face. "Oh, don't worry none. I don't condemn anyone, 'less they're beyond savin'." His friendly face dropped just as quickly as it had appeared. "Are you beyond saving?" he asked in a lower register.

Harry shook his head under the weighty glare. "No," he said, trying to keep the fear out of his voice. "We- We can be saved." He shot Andy a telling look. "We can be saved," he repeated for Andy's sake.

Andy wasn't entirely sure what the massive man was asking but he caught on to Harry's nudge. "Uh, yes. We can be saved," he said, chancing a glance up at Conrad.

"We want to be saved," Harry added.

The smile returned to Conrad's face. "I don't believe any man is truly evil at his core but rather corrupted by outside forces."

Andy peeked over at Harry. He was hardly able to catch a clear word of Conrad's speech. His drawl was too damn thick.

Conrad raised his arms and settled a hand on each of their shoulders.

Andy's eyes slammed shut and he inadvertently held his breath in his attempt to remain still.

"Search your souls and know this corruption is true," Conrad said, swiveling his gaze between the two newcomers. "Do you understand homosexuality is sinful?"

"Yes," Harry said without hesitation.

"Yes," Andy added right afterward.

"Under Second Christ's watchful eye, do you swear to renounce the vile ways you've fallen into or else suffer God's wrath?"

"Yes," Harry said through gritted teeth. He couldn't seem to make his jaw unclench.

"Yes!" Andy squealed, louder than he intended. He was quivering, *damn it*, despite his best efforts. *Fucking pathetic*, he cursed himself. *Stop trembling!* But that only made it worse.

"Why do you tremble, my lamb?" Conrad asked in a soothing voice.

Andy found Conrad's full attention leveled upon him. The hand came off Harry's shoulder and came to rest tenderly against Andy's cheek. He hated how soft the touch felt, how smooth his hands were. Andy would have rather been smacked across the face than feel a touch so gentle from this man.

"Is your corruption too great to renounce?" Conrad asked in a soft voice. The softness drained from Conrad's voice in an instant as he spat, "Do you feign repentance out of fear alone?"

The large hands gripped tight onto Andy's shoulders. He gasped and choked on his saliva. Andy hoped to God a breath so pathetic wouldn't be his last.

"Do you sit before me and lie?!"

"No!" Harry shouted. "He's repentant! He'll change! Convert! We both—"

"A man speaks for himself!" His words hung in the air.

Judd and Joseph shared a look, both ready to intervene but not wanting to interrupt Conrad's process.

"No. No. I- I'm sorry," Andy said. "I'm- I'm not lying. I promise. I'll change. I'll- I'll—"

"Good." Conrad released his grip on Andy's shoulders.

"Second Christ will aid in your transfiguration where he is able, but you must meet him halfway."

Harry made no attempt to parse the strange information coming out of the man's mouth. He would agree to anything to decrease their proximity.

"Your intentions and your repentance must be true. As long as you are willin' to do what must be done, you shall not be harmed under Second Christ's loving gaze." His tone of voice was that of a seasoned teacher ingratiating himself to new students on the first day of class. "I do not ask much of you, my lost lambs." He gave each newlywed a gentle pat on the shoulder. "Now, let's get you boys unbloodied, huh? Joseph, you can track 'em down some clean clothing in their sizes, can't ya?"

"Of course, Father Conrad," Joseph replied, bowing his head.

Conrad grinned broadly at the newcomers. "Second Christ told me something earth-shaking was on the horizon. Perhaps your conversion and the growth of our flock is what he intimated."

He took a deep, ponderous breath in through his nose. At length, he let the breath escape his mouth and nodded to himself.

"I see the potential in you, my lost lambs. You are not bound as slaves to your sin. It can be overcome..." He looked upon them with warmth. "Our humble congregation will continue to grow and expand outward until all that is other has been subsumed. It will be a long and trying road, surely outlasting my own lifetime, but as word of my son spreads, so too will belief in our new gospel."

"Amen," Judd and Joseph said in perfect unison.

Conrad nodded contentedly with his eyes closed. "If you faithfully commit to the necessary change, then, in time, I will send you into the world for recruitment and the distribution of our message to the unknowin' masses."

He'll let us go! That was Harry's takeaway. That if they could just play along for enough time and convince this deranged man of their *conversion or transfiguration or whatever the hell*, then he would let them go. *But how long could that take?* He was not ready to settle on that as plan-A quite yet. A means of escape, a means of retaliation, a means of rescue — all still paths he sought.

Conrad's eyes drilled into Andy. "If you prove to me your spiritual mettle, I will bestow upon you the honor of translatin' our holy book and proselytizing to those lucky few Orientals deemed worthy of God's love."

Andy returned a blank look. He struggled to hold eye contact with the man and broke to look at the ground.

Conrad took it as a show of respect, a sort of bowing of his head. He reached out to Harry and held the newcomer's cheek in his meaty palm. "I am Father Conrad. What is your name?"

Harry wondered if he should lie. How might it help him? Would they be able to tell? *One of them took my wallet,* Harry remembered. Whitney had his ID in his pocket. "Harrison Winters," he said after a bout of hesitation.

"No *Winters,*" the huge man said. "Not anymore. We renounce our surnames here, for we are all one family." He gestured lovingly toward Judd and Joseph. "We are the kin of Second Christ and belong to no other."

There it was again, 'Second Christ'. They kept saying it, and Harry kept fighting a sense of intrigue over the moniker. He didn't care to learn the details of their fucked-up rhetoric. There was no curiosity nor intrigue. Religious extremists? Cultists? The specifics didn't matter to him. The danger they were in was real. Getting out of harm's way was what mattered.

Now, Conrad took Andy's cheek in his palm. "And your name, lamb?"

Fuck, that was a question; Andy could tell from the

inflection. What he couldn't tell, were the words. Conrad was looking at him expectantly. He had just heard Harry say his name, so he took the risk of it being the same question now posed at him. "Andy," he said, lacking confidence in his own anglicized name for the first time since he had chosen it so many years ago.

Three loud horn blasts of increasing pitch made the newlyweds jump and brought smiles to the faces of Judd and Joseph. The sounds came from the mass of wood and metal behind the pews. Harry understood now, it was a type of music-box. The horns were preceded by a loud grinding of the intricately arranged gears.

A broad grin came to inhabit Conrad's mouth as if by stop-motion. He clapped his hands together a single time and strode away from the newcomers as a dozen doors swung open, and the rest of the congregation flooded out of their homes.

Three Horns

"Ah! Three horns! Glorious!" Conrad proclaimed to his entire flock as they gathered in the village center.

Clayton returned from the mess hall. He had just finished dragging the buck carcass to the back door and found himself drained of energy. It would usually have been a task for Judd. Clayton took up a position at the periphery of the outdoor church and was joined by his fourteen-year-old wife Judith. The wounds covering her body were finally beginning to scar over.

Bo, a soft-looking twenty-two-year-old, escorted Li'l Rhoda from their home by her five-year-old hand. Hearing the Grand Decider always made Li'l Rhoda giddy with excitement, though she did not yet understand the details of its proclamations.

Hoyt and Earl set down their paintbrushes and made their way toward the pews. Their wives, Cilicia and Bethany, hurried over to their sides with rigid strides. One of Cilicia's eyes had been plucked from her head. The socket had healed over as much as it ever would. At thirty-five years old, she was the oldest woman of the group aside from Mother Mabel. Bethany had just recently turned twenty-one, though she had still never tasted alcohol and likely never would, unless Earl had a change of heart and was feeling generous. The jagged X-shaped scar was a permanent feature over her entire face. The crisscross of the X converged right on the bridge of her nose. It had been cut deep, and she still struggled to smell even the strongest of scents. She was thankful that Earl hadn't gone straight across her eyes with his blade.

Walt sauntered out of the workshop with a toothed saw still in hand. Wood shavings clung to his overalls. He looked around for his woman and found her circling the others to take her post at his side. Marabella was fifteen. She wasn't as badly scarred or permanently disfigured as some of the other women, not yet anyway, but her face was marred by fresh bruises and welts. Her lips were swollen and blue and bloodied on the inside from where her teeth dug into them.

Fifty-five-year-old Cappie stepped out of his home right alongside Hailey, the holler healer. She was a couple of years younger than Cilicia but still older than most of the other wives. She had tried to run away more than once to no avail. Her knowledge of medicine at least kept her from being punished as badly as she would have been otherwise. The men were afraid to damage her hands or eyes, lest they diminish her healing capabilities.

Duke and Myra returned from the gardens and joined the others around the outdoor church. There were twenty years between them in age, and two feet between them in height. A black eye—swollen completely shut—graced Myra's smiling face. Her visage looked like a boxer's following a tough defeat.

The oldest of the entire congregation was Sardus with his crooked back. He was now halfway through his eighties, and his shuffling gait had slowed down even further since his last excursion from the holler. He still had plenty of bite when he needed it. He knew to conserve energy for the important things. He was the last of the men to answer the Grand Decider's call. He let Eve walk ahead of him with a dishrag held to her bleeding head and a smile forced upon her face. *Bleeding head*, that reminded him. He shook the clump of blonde hair out of his fist and let it fall to the ground underfoot. He felt blessed to be paired with such a beauty as Eve, who hadn't heard her real name uttered aloud in eighteen months. Nineteen years old she was. Such a young, pliable body to receive his cruelty. When he and Joseph had plucked her from Gatlinburg, he hadn't imagined the pleasure of her matrimony would be bestowed upon himself.

So many new faces surrounded the outsiders. Half of them threatening, half of them disconcerting and pitiable. All of the women were bone-thin and all but Shiloh and Li'l Rhoda shared similar rigid movements, like second-hand dolls with simple ball-in-socket joints. Harry was disturbed by the injuries surrounding him and perplexed by the smiles accompanying them. Andy felt his skin crawl. Before today, he had not thought such cruelty possible.

"Whose turn is it?" Conrad asked of Joseph once the entire congregation had gathered.

Damaris waited patiently as Joseph left her side to go check the list pinned beside the red door of the round building.

"It's Sardus's turn," Joseph proclaimed.

"Take up your station, Sardus!" Conrad declared, joyously.

A smile crinkled across Sardus's wrinkled face. He enclosed Eve's hand in his fist and set about shuffling over to the windowless building.

Harry could see Eve's cheery façade falter. He watched her smile crack, and distress fill her eyes. Her feet were dragging even more than the old man's as he shuffled ahead of her. This view into her true disposition lasted only a moment. The content expression was plastered back onto her face in the blink of an eye, but now there was no doubt in Harry's mind that it was false.

He studied the smiles of the other women surrounding him. He could see how phony they were, but a couple smiles looked genuine to him. Maybe some were better pretenders than others.

"Need fluids, Sardus?" Hoyt asked.

Sardus grunted a *no*. "I'm good to go."

Conrad produced an iron key from within his robes that seemed better suited to unlocking a treasure chest than a doorway. He opened the door to the round building and locked it again once Sardus and Eve were inside.

Harry tried to get a look into the windowless building while the door was open, but his angle of the doorway occluded any clear view. There was some intrigue after all, it seemed, despite his best efforts to the contrary.

Conrad spoke to Judd and Joseph without looking toward their directions. He knew they would receive his call directly. "Turn the newcomers away. They do not have permission to lay their sinful eyes upon Second Christ. Not yet." With his order given, he turned and headed toward the church

Judd and Joseph grabbed hold of Andy and Harry and turned them to face away from the round building.

Andy allowed Joseph to maneuver him like a plaything. He was putty in the congregant's hands.

Harry wanted to know more now, wanted to see what they didn't want him seeing, wanted to see just how far their shared delusion went; a dangerous cocktail of curiosity and spite. In the corner of his eye, he watched Conrad disappear into the church.

A moment of stillness followed. The holler lingered in total silence save for the gentle breeze that ruffled leaves on trees surrounding the settlement and the low ticking of gears in the music-box behemoth they called The Grand Decider.

An awful shriek pierced the silence. Then, another followed, both emanating from the round building.

Andy flinched at the sound and cowered lower on the pew.

Harry twisted toward the round building.

Judd refocused Harry's view in the other direction and tightened his grip.

No one else in the congregation bat an eye at the awful sound as it split the air for a third time. It didn't sound like any scream Harry had ever heard before. He couldn't place his finger on how, but it was different in some way. The vocalization had a flat warble to it. It was a sickening fusion of fear and pain intertwined, each emotion constantly escalating to outdo the other.

The other congregants lowered down to their knees in an arc several feet from the edge of the round building. They began to pray for the souls inside the building.

The prayers were spoken aloud as a flood of overlapping utterances but were unintelligible to the newlyweds.

Judd felt strange about not joining the prayers. It felt bad that he wasn't doing his part in this matter, contributing to the shared effort, but he had to hold the newcomer in place. He knew it didn't carry the same weight, but he prayed anyway, silently inside his head.

Mother Mabel stepped out of the church alongside Conrad on his return. Though she was in her late forties—the oldest of the women in the village—she looked younger than some of the others. The copious scars added a great many years in appearance to the younger women. Mabel's skin was fair and unblemished. She was an exception to the scarification, it seemed, Conrad's pious wife. Her skin bore none of the cuts, bruises, scars, or disfigurements that graced the rest of the congregation's females but she did amble with the same rigid movements that were becoming a familiar sight to the newcomers.

She held in her arms the tiny body of Second Christ.

The baby looked to be but a bundle shrouded in gilded cloth. Harry only caught a quick glimpse in the corner of his eye as she exited the church before her and the faceless form in her arms were out of his peripheral vision. He saw no child. *A bundle of rags? Is that what they're worshipping?*

Harry tried to turn his head for another look but found Judd's grip on him holding firm.

"Ya can't rush this, Harrison," Judd said. "You'll witness Second Christ's miracles as we have when you are deemed worthy of his love."

"Sorry. Yes. I understand."

Mother Mabel and Father Conrad stood between the line of prayer givers and the round building from which pained noises continued to escape at irregular intervals.

Conrad gently took Second Christ in his own arms. He adopted a wide stance in the doorway to the windowless building, pressing the sides of his feet against each end of the wooden frame and laying his forehead against the red metal that looked out of place in the otherwise blue, wooden building.

He cradled Second Christ with one arm against his heart. With his other hand, he clutched onto the wooden frame overhead. His grip was tight enough for his fingertips to go white from the pressure.

"Lord, I ask alongside Second Christ that you grace our pious Sardus and Eve with the gift of fertility in their blessed union."

A scream of agony emerged from the round building but was cut off before its natural conclusion. The air went quiet once again.

Mother Mabel placed a hand on her husband's back. She stood slightly behind him with her head bowed in reverence.

Conrad continued, "Lord, please bless the church of Second Christ with a new member for our flock so we may continue to grow our congregation; so that we may uncover and understand your word in truth… as so many before us have misinterpreted and misrepresented."

Each and every male congregant replied in perfect unison, "Amen!"

Li'l Rhoda added an excited, "Amen!" of her own. Bo smiled at her and tickled her sides.

Shiloh quickly followed suit. "Amen!" Whitney shot her a dirty look for lagging behind the others as usual.

Another shriek flew from the round building before ending in a choked gurgle.

Harry looked over at Andy, who was hyperventilating. He whispered to his beloved, *"We'll be okay. We'll get out of this."*

Andy mustered a tiny, trembling nod. He believed Harry. Or at least, he wanted to. Harry was his hope. He had no other.

Gone Nowhere

Ma Winters paced the length of the living room with her cellphone to her ear. The dogs swirled around her, picking up on her nervous energy. They were well-trained and never barked, but they were whining and whimpering something fierce. They knew not what, but that *something* was wrong

The call went to voicemail. She hung up before her son's recorded voice could utter a single word. She had already left multiple messages. She tossed her phone onto the couch and hurried into the kitchen where she lifted the landline off of the hook. As if a change of hardware would make some difference, Ma tried to call Harry again.

While it connected, she stretched the cord over to the kitchen doorway and popped her head back into the living room. "Anything?"

"Nothin'," Pa said, standing by the window with the curtain pulled aside. It was dark out now. He had his face right up against the glass to see past his own reflection in the light. The gravel driveway looked like the surface of the moon in the white illumination of the exterior light mounted above the garage door. Mere feet into the distance, the outside world plunged into total darkness where the driveway met the dirt road. Jonesborough didn't have many street lights, and their road had precisely none.

Again, the call went to voicemail. Ma slammed the phone back onto its cradle. "God dang it!" She returned to the living room, rubbing a hand through her tangle of gray hair. "Should I call the police?" she asked Pa.

He rotated away from the window, leaving the curtain drawn. "Now, hang on. Don't get carried away, Ma." He shuffled across the room and brought her to a seat beside him on the floral loveseat. "Let the boys have their fun. I'm tellin' ya, Harrison just lost track'a time or sum'in."

Ma was getting frustrated with that response. She was struggling to understand why her husband wasn't sharing in her worry to anywhere near the same degree. "Why wouldn't he answer his phone?"

"Left it on silent? Battery died? Forgot it in the car? You don't gotta always jump to worst-case scenarios, Ma."

She sighed. He had a point, of course, she thought. It had been so long since she had Harrison nearby to worry about. Maybe she was subconsciously making up for lost time? Their boy had been unresponsive like this in the past. Surely, she was stressing out over nothing, she rationalized. She felt some of the tension leave her body but not all of it. "I can't help but worry."

"I know, I know." Pa put his arm around her and gave her shoulder a comforting squeeze. It wasn't entirely unlike Harrison to bail on plans without notice. As a teenager he had a habit of disappearing at odd hours with no explanation. He routinely missed dinner at least once a week throughout high school, and his time remained unaccounted for even in the face of punishment, groundings be damned.

Sometimes, Harry had snuck off to hang out with friends, drink alcohol, and dabble in drugs. Other times, he truly had no answer to the question, *where were you?* Sometimes, he would go *nowhere*. On certain tormented nights, his senses of loneliness, self-loathing, and alienation would compound to the point where he found it difficult to breathe. On nights like those, he would slip out of the house, pick a direction, and walk through the dark for hours on end with no destination in mind. The fresh air of a Jonesborough night was unlike any he had breathed anywhere else in the world. The air in this small town seemed to confer a sense of liberation, even when so many who lived within the town sought the opposite for Harry.

He would walk and walk until either the crushing sensation in his chest went away or he began to worry about making it home soundly. Those walks freed his mind up for introspection in a way he could never achieve at home. He had so many questions about himself with no way to ask them. Ma and Pa were older than most of the other kids' parents, but Harry doubted their age made much difference in the matter. They might have been there for him more if only he could have opened up to them, he often thought. His inability to express his thoughts and feelings, even to those closest to him, was an additional source of self-loathing.

"Tell ya what," Pa said. "They don't show up overnight, we'll head on in to the police station first thing in the mornin'. How's that sound?"

"Deal." Ma made him shake on it.

Tiki Torches

Harry hadn't been to church since he was a child. His parents had brought him to the local catholic church until his first communion, at which point they left the decision entirely up to him whether or not he wanted to continue attending.

He was a miracle child to them, arriving after a decade of trying and failing to start a family. A string of miscarriages had plunged the growth of their family-unit into uncertainty. It wasn't until they had given up on the idea of natural childbirth and begun looking into adoption that Harrison was finally conceived. A little miracle out of the blue. His sexual orientation was not what they had expected and certainly not what they would have preferred if the choice were up to them, but they loved their miracle son too damn much to let it come between them. They refused to risk letting anybody or anything push him away.

Harry hadn't hated religion when he stopped attending church. As a child, he had mostly just found it mind-numbingly boring. It wasn't until later on in life when he began to take umbrage with much of what the church stood for. Sure, the church offered some worthwhile teachings—good morals and such—but it also offered up a lot of excuses. Confession to excuse sins. The acceptance of Jesus Christ as your savior to excuse all manner of wrongdoing and wipe the slate clean. The church itself not only excused the actions of pedophilic priests but kept them safe from outside persecution, allowing them to remain within the same framework of authority and trust they so readily exploited.

The religious excuse that most directly and so often plagued Harrison was tied to homophobia. *It's not bigotry, it's religion. The bible says so.* While he faced it the most in his hometown, this excuse was one not limited to the South nor in fact to the country. Even while living with Andy in South Korea, Harry had been accosted by bigots who used their Christianity as an excuse and as a justification for their homophobia.

Though he had grown to somewhat despise the Christian faith he grew up with in particular, Harry paid no ill will nor in fact any mind at all to the various other religions of the world. He hesitated to call himself an atheist, opting instead for the less-committal "agnostic" label. If he was being truthful with himself, he knew he was a full-blown atheist in actuality but he detested the way that stance made so many people look at him differently.

At least Andy had given no strong reaction when they first spoke deeply of their religious views with one another. Andy had grown up in a predominantly non-religious community but he remained more open to the various ideas and teachings of different religions than Harry. His education as a child had been spent alongside an equal number of atheist and agnostic students as Protestant and Buddhist students. The dominant religion in South Korea was constantly in flux throughout Andy's lifetime, and the majority of the population typically held no religious affiliation of any kind. Andy and his parents counted themselves amongst that majority.

Now, for the first time in nearly two decades, Harry found himself sitting in the midst of what was without a doubt *a church service.*

The entire congregation filled the pews of the outdoor church facing the raised platform and, beyond it, the indoor church. Rows of tiki torches were planted in the ground alongside the pews to light the brisk night with dozens of orange flames. The overpowering scent of citronella soured the Jonesborough air Harry loved so much from his past. The smiling faces of the congregants distorted in the flicker of the firelight.

Sardus had rejoined the congregation after exiting the round building. It had taken Eve a little longer to make her exit but she now sat beside Sardus with fresh bruises on her face and a thin line of blood running out from one nostril. She did all she could to maintain the anguished smile upon her face.

Judd and Joseph sat bordering Harry and Andy, like bodyguards on duty if bodyguards did the opposite of protect. They in turn were flanked by their wives whose hands they held as they eagerly watched the door of the community's largest home.

Andy's fractured arm had mostly gone numb. A dull throb lingered. He was afraid of how or even if it would heal, but that fear was far down the list of things that presently terrified him. Andy wanted desperately to go to sleep or, better yet, to wake up and find this all to have been a comfort-food induced nightmare.

Harry felt as though he had been transported into another world; one out of place and time. He had been transferred from a homophobic society to a homophobic *society*. He found himself in a subculture built entirely upon hate rather than one which simply reinforced and prospered upon prejudices at every turn. Conrad's holler was an echo of familiar sentiments magnified to an extreme, a reflection displayed on disturbed water; a jittered rendering of the real world, like watching a 3D-movie without the 3D-glasses.

Finally, the door of the grand home swung wide, and Conrad strode out, waving like the Queen of England.

Voracious clapping consumed the audience upon the pews in the wake of the Father's stately emergence. Cheers and a pair of whistles were thrown into the mix.

"Lean forward," Judd said to Harry.

Harry hesitated, just for a moment. He knew he had no recourse, no alternative. If Judd wanted him to lean forward, it was going to happen one way or another. Harry went along with the command. To his surprise, Judd untied his hands.

"Thank you," Harry said.

"Clap for Father Conrad." In the midst of the entire congregation, Judd no longer felt concerned over the captive's actions. *He wouldn't dare try to escape now*, Judd thought.

Harry performed something close to a mime instead of a genuine clap. The sound of his personal applause would be lost in the cacophony of pounding appendages at any rate. It was the only miniscule act of defiance he dared to attempt.

Judd didn't bother to untie Andy or tell him to clap. He knew it wouldn't be possible with his injured arm and that it would be cruel to make him try. Judd did not consider himself a cruel man. He knew what they were doing could be viewed as harsh, brutal even, but it was in no way cruel as it was for their own sake. He knew they wouldn't see it this way, but bringing them here was an act of generosity. Judd took less pleasure inflicting pain upon Abigail than the other followers of Second Christ seemed to take from the suffering of their wives, and he figured that must be worth something.

It took Conrad a while and a not-insignificant amount of effort to haul his bulky frame up the steps to the top of the tall stage. The wood creaked under his weight. Dust lazily drifted down to the dark grass below. Conrad took his stance at the head of the stage. Behind him, in the center of the stage, was a small, square-shaped hole with dried blood encircling it. The tall cross was no longer slotted into the opening. The new cross, assembled in the workshop, was almost ready.

Judd spoke to the newcomers at his side. "Listen closely. You'll learn a lot."

The clapping continued for a seemingly interminable time. Harry watched Conrad bask in the adulation, loving it, demanding it. *Pathetic*, Harry thought, *deranged cult-leader psycho fucking prick asshole….* It wasn't just fear he felt any longer. Now, there was anger alongside it.

Conrad lifted a hand into the air. His congregation ceased their applause on a dime. He listened to one, final pat from the tiny hands of Li'l Rhoda before she too stopped.

"Today was a glorious day." He projected his voice to the back row of pews with ease. "Much progress has been made on the divine text." He smiled fondly. "I tell ya, Second Christ was positively talkin' my ear off this mornin'."

As Conrad chuckled to himself, laughter and smiles filtered through the crowd.

Bo, with Li'l Rhoda seated on his lap, found Conrad's eyes meeting his directly. *What an honor.*

"You wanna know something he told me, Bo?"

Bo nodded eagerly.

"He said, Li'l Rhoda's gon' grow up to be a picture-perfect mother."

Bo grinned widely, as did Li'l Rhoda herself.

Li'l Rhoda stood up atop Bo's knees. "He did?!" She shook her little fists giddily, not yet knowing all that this proclamation entailed.

"That's right, Li'l Rhoda. You and Bo are gonna add a whole mess'a littl'uns to our flock one day."

"Yay!" Li'l Rhoda exclaimed, doing the start to a little jig atop Bo's knees before falling back into his lap.

Bo felt warm and fuzzy inside at this news. Knowing such grand results awaited him in the long run was comforting. "Bless you, Father," Bo said, swelling with pride for his five-year-old bride.

Conrad shifted on the balls of his feet atop the stage. He set his eyes on Harry and Andy with laser focus. An open-handed gesture was made toward the newcomers as he spoke of them, "I'm sure you've all noticed we have a pair of outsiders in our midst."

Heads swiveled toward the newcomers like a pack of wolves ready to pounce.

"Treat them as such until they've proven themselves," Conrad told his followers. "Forgive me as I inundate the rest of y'all with prevenient knowledge for the sake of these lost lambs." He knew his congregation was unlikely to be familiar with the word "prevenient," nor perhaps even the word "inundate." Conrad found not just enjoyment in flexing his vocabulary over his followers but control as well. His superior education was a part of what elevated the Father and made his status unassailable.

His steady gaze remained locked on Harry and Andy as he transitioned into a sermon aimed directly at the lost lambs. He spoke in a rehearsed, theatrical manner. It nearly sounded as though he were singing with how much his tone rose and fell and with how rhythmically he delivered his carefully chosen words.

"They said Mabel was too old. They said I was sterile. But what these so-called doctors failed to comprehend was…"

He slowly knelt at the edge of the stage and put a hand over his heart.

"… Divinity surpasses the limitations of mortal flesh." He mimed the holding of a baby in his arms. He rocked the invisible child to and fro as he continued, "Seventeen weeks premature, he was. And smaller than my fist."

A clenched fist rose before his face as he returned to his feet.

"And again, these so-called *experts in their field* underestimated the glory of God. They said my boy would not live beyond mere hours, but yet he lives on. Three years goin', stronger and stronger day after day… stronger than all who came before him."

"Amen!" cheered those of the congregation who retained the capacity for speech.

"He is *my* son but he is also *God's*," Conrad continued. "And just as before, so too will my son be a carpenter by trade. Once he is able to hold hammer and nail, he will devise his own version of our Grand Decider."

He gestured to the ticking music-box at the back of the church.

"I can only approximate so closely from God's word secondhand."

His eyes tracking the lambs, Conrad began to stride back and forth across the stage like a prowling animal plotting escape from the zoo.

"It was my son who first told me a new bible need be written. *A new bible for a new age*, he whispered in mah ear. God's word has changed, and it is spoken through my son's mouth. And when my illuminated transcription is complete, us followers of Second Christ shall spread that word en masse and reap the bounty of His everlastin' love and gratitude."

"Amen!" the men erupted.

Insomnolence

The darkened room was abuzz with the motorboat snoring of Pa tucked into their queen-sized bed. One of the dogs, Clive, was asleep atop Pa's feet. They kept each other warm.

Ma had no such luck in the soporific department. She tossed and turned; tired but unable to turn her mind away from her outlandish worries.

Do they drive on the wrong side of the road in South Korea? She wondered. What if Harry slipped into that old habit and got himself into a wreck? What if he was pinned under twisted metal while she and Pa slept soundly in their bed? It was no use trying to ignore the pervasive thoughts any longer.

Ma got out of bed, quietly so as to not wake Pa or Clive. She slid into her slippers and crept from the room.

She creaked open the door to the other bedroom anyway, knowing it would be empty. She peered inside at the empty race-car bed. Her heart felt heavy. *Maybe they got themselves a motel room for a little privacy*, she considered. They didn't call it the *honeymoon phase* for nothing, she thought. It was possible that the boys were just trying to be considerate and avoid disturbing her and Pa's homeostasis. It didn't feel right though.

Ma maneuvered down the hall and stood at the top of the stairs. She looked down at the dark living room and landing below. Her own shadow was cast crooked across the stairs by the hall light to her back.

Oh, I'm being foolish, she thought. But the worries didn't dissipate.

She brought a hand to her forehead and massaged her temples with her thumb and middle finger. Pa would be grumpy if she woke him up, and they *had* made a deal to stave off panic until the morning.

With a weary sigh and a shake of her head, she turned around and returned to bed.

Closeted

Harry stood against the exterior wall of the home that had *Whitney — Shiloh* painted above the doorway. They hadn't rebound his hands after the church service had concluded, and Andy's hands were untied now too. He and Andy were being brought into their fucked up little society proper. They had scrubbed the blood off of themselves with the aid of a barrel of water and a pair of washcloths, and they had each been given a change of clothes: simple, flannel shirts and slightly baggy trousers.

There had yet to be a single moment free from the armed watch of at least two men. It had become clear that if they played along, they would make it through the night. But that meant sleeping in these caustic environs and waking up just as trapped come the morning.

And, come the morning, then what? The prospect of extended time spent within this community was dreadful to say the least. The intensity of their guard had lessened over time as they lingered in the holler, so it followed logically that their guard may continue to lessen further.

While scrubbing themselves clean, Harry had managed to

pass an undetected whisper to Andy. He told his husband that they needed to play along—no matter how twisted things got— until the right opportunity presented itself. Harry knew not what this opportunity would look like nor if it would ever come, but he couldn't risk Andy making an escape attempt before the time was right. For now, it was a waiting game; a test of how long they could hold out. "Promise me you'll go along with what they say," Harry had whispered to him. "I'll get us out of here as soon as I can. Trust me."

Andy had passed back a whispered, "I promise."

Harry would ensure whatever opportunity they were awaiting would arrive sooner rather than later, even if that meant creating the opportunity himself. Playing along for enough time to convince Conrad and the others of their veracity in commitment was as comprehensive a plan as Harry could devise. If he could get them to believe he was truly one of them, or at least *becoming* one of them, then he believed their guard would eventually be reduced to a lax-enough state to escape, or they might even be allowed to leave willingly with the understanding that they would return just as willingly.

But that would take a whole lot of trust. Harry didn't know if he and his husband had it in them to play the long game. Building that kind of trust seemed like it could take months, if it was even possible at all, and every minute spent in this isolated community was a nightmare. A more immediate escape option remained elusive for the time being, but maybe come the night, when everyone went to sleep...

Andy sat on a short, wooden stool beside the front door, his hair still wet from the scrubbing. His broken arm rested in the gentle grip of Hailey, the holler healer, who knelt before him. She tended to his wound, just like Judd had promised.

Whitney stood out of earshot, chatting with Cappie who was there to watch over his wife while she worked. Whitney balanced the stock of his rifle in the crook of his arm, pointing it up toward the night sky. Cappie held a shotgun lazily by the stock, pointing the barrel down at the dirt by his feet.

It was quiet and peaceful in the holler this time of night. Most of the congregation had returned to their homes and retired for the evening.

Across the way, Duke and Earl shared a drink outside of Earl's home. They occupied wooden chairs, made by hand in the workshop over yonder. Orange firelight danced in the sconces affixed to either side of the front door.

Earl balanced his tin cup on the arm of the chair and picked up his guitar. It still needed to be varnished, and he would have to take the strings off to do a little more sanding on the fretboard, but he had finally got the sound the way he wanted it. The perfect amount of twang in his acoustic beauty.

He plucked away absently, being interrupted only ever-so-briefly by the shout of pain that came from the lost lamb across the way as Hailey set his bone in place.

Tears welled in Andy's eyes. He had cried more in the past twelve hours than in the past five years of his life combined. He stamped his foot on the ground and bit down on the collar of the flannel shirt to keep from screaming. The flannel tasted of stale tobacco. Whoever the shirt belonged to was a smoker.

Harry grabbed his lover's shoulder and wished to take some of his pain upon himself.

Hailey attached a splint alongside the break in Andy's arm and secured it in place with tightly wound bandages.

"Thank you," Andy said through the pain.

Hailey kept her eyes on her work.

Andy sniffled and dried his eyes with a wipe of his

uninjured arm. "What's your name?" he asked.

She ignored him.

Harry glanced over at Whitney and Cappie: still distracted. "Are you here by choice?" he asked of the holler healer.

She looked up at Harry. Her face was completely devoid of expression. She looked deep into Harry's eyes but gave nothing away. After a moment, she returned her eyes to Andy's arm, her face remaining blank, neutral, guarded.

"Can you speak?" Andy asked, wondering just as much if she had the ability as the inclination. "We won't tell on you. I promise." He felt like he was back in school, gossiping with classmates and afraid of the teachers.

Hailey stopped binding his arm. She went motionless. Without meeting his gaze, without even lifting her head, she took the risk and gave a tiny, near-imperceptible shake of her head.

Instantly, she regretted doing even that much. Hailey hastened to finish with the bandages and rose to her feet. She didn't dare look either of the newcomers in the eye. Without delay, she turned one hundred and eighty degrees and walked, rigid at the joints, away from them and over to Cappie.

Andy watched her leave. He watched as she bowed her head to Cappie, and the two made their way across the village through the dark. Then, he watched Whitney coming towards him.

"All better?" Whitney asked in a mocking tone.

Andy nodded.

"That's too bad." He grabbed Andy by his hurt arm and yanked him off the stool.

Andy shrieked and jumped to his feet, moving with Whitney's motion to mitigate the force on his arm.

Harry couldn't help himself. He grabbed onto Whitney's lapels and shoved him away from Andy. Caught up in the rush of it, his hand balled into a fist, but he stopped short of throwing a punch when Whitney's gun barrel rose to aim between his eyes.

Harry froze. The only movement he dared to make was the unclenching of his fist.

Duke gestured toward the commotion, and Earl set down his guitar and took up his firearm. They made their way over.

"Need a hand, Whitney?" Earl asked.

"As a matter of fact…" Whitney took a step back from Harry, keeping his gun pointed at the degenerate's eyes. "You fellas mind keepin' watch outside tonight?"

"'Course not," Earl answered readily.

"Wouldn't trust 'em in my home neither, Whit," Duke added. "Mighty noble of ya to offer up your abode."

"Just doin' my part." Whitney lowered his gun from Harry's face to Harry's chest and peered over the top of it.

"Hold up!" a voice called from off to the side.

Whitney turned to find Hoyt approaching him at a brisk pace.

"Conrad wants them two apart." Hoyt took hold of Andy's non-injured arm and tugged him away from Harry. "Come on, gook. You're stayin' at mine."

Andy felt a fresh rush of panic. He looked back at Harry with overwhelming worry. He couldn't bear to be separated. He wouldn't have survived this long without Harry as his rock.

Much to Andy's surprise, Harry said, "Great idea. Separation is just what we need as we overcome our corruption." He nodded with purpose.

Andy caught on to the ruse after a second's delay. He nodded back. "Right. Exactly." He tried to sound self-assured but doubted his ability to convince.

"Good fuckin' call," Whitney said. "One queer under my roof's bad enough." In truth, Whitney had been looking forward to housing and tormenting them both.

"I hear ya, brother," Hoyt said with a sympathetic raise of his eyebrows.

Whitney watched Hoyt escort Andy across the village center, nearly disappearing into the inky black outside of the various fire-light glows. He turned toward Harry and jabbed his rifle at his chest. "Inside. Bedtime." He nodded to the front door.

"I'll take first watch, Duke. You get some rest," Earl said, plopping down onto the short stool that Andy had just occupied. He wondered for a moment if he should have wiped it off first.

Harry pushed open the wooden door and stepped inside the dim home. This felt like entering yet another mouth of madness. He feared the muscular Judd and the imposing Father Conrad more as men, but feared what Whitney *might do* even more.

Whitney stepped inside behind him, then shut and locked the door.

The interior of the home was sparse, just a mere notch above subsistence. A wooden table with two wooden chairs, a fireplace that hadn't been lit since the past winter, a small kitchen nook with a wood-burning stove, and, most eye-catching of all, a large, hand-painted portrait of Father Conrad and Mother Mabel. Their smiling faces looked down in wonder toward Mabel's pregnant stomach. All four of their oil-painted hands held gently onto her rounded midsection. It was not a particularly well-rendered portrait, but the likeness was unmistakable. The simple, two-letter signature of "Bo" hugged the bottom corner in gold-colored paint. A similar though unique portrait hung in each and every home within the holler.

"Upstairs," Whitney said flatly, motioning for his captive to take the lead.

Harry ascended the rickety staircase of the narrow home. A half-built railing clung to the side of the unfinished steps.

It looked as if it might collapse before supporting anyone's weight, but the staircase proved more resilient than its appearance would suggest.

The second floor creaked loudly under Harry's feet. A light layer of sawdust covered the floor. Harry turned to his left and looked through an open doorway into the bedroom: two parallel beds with their own end tables. One each for the husband and his young wife. Harry heard rain, he smelled the subtle scent of wet brick, and he felt a rush a thick humidity to his back. He flashed to the motel two nights earlier when he swung open the door of the room on the corner and was greeted by the same sight. *What does it matter, the similarity?* He asked his subconscious but received no response.

Shiloh, seated atop one of the beds, waved at Harry with a smile.

"Not that way," Whitney said from halfway up the stairs.

Harry stopped in his tracks. He turned one hundred and eighty degrees and moved down the other end of the hall.

The only other door on the second floor was closed and stuck out like a sore thumb from the rest of the home's rustic decor. The door was made of riveted metal while everything else was constructed of plain wood. Up at eye-level was a small window, cut out of the metal and divided into fourths by a detailed crucifix mounted in the center.

With great hesitancy, Harry reached for the door handle and pulled it open. The inside looked like a storage closet: blankets, towels, knick-knacks, pickled vegetables, and a crate of what appeared to be stuffed animals and children's toys. The name *Trixie* had been written on the oversized tag of a stuffed giraffe, then scribbled over with a black marker.

"Shiloh," Whitney called into the bedroom, "clean this shit outta here. And show me some giddyap for once."

Giddyap was shown as Shiloh cleared most but not all of the junk out of the room.

As the tight space was cleaned, Harry noticed what was previously obscured: two metal bars mounted horizontally on the back wall of the closet. One was up high, and the other, down low. Black, hemp ropes lay draped over the bars.

Harry stepped into the confined space and turned to face Whitney, who filled the doorframe. His features were hidden in the dark.

"Back to the wall. Wrists against the bar," Whitney said with his gun aimed at Harry's gut.

Harry's hesitation was brief. He knew he had no choice. He was ground down. He raised his wrists up to the bar, level with his shoulders. The metal was cold against his skin.

Whitney cautiously set the stock of his rifle on the floor of the hallway outside the closet and leaned the barrel against the wall. He maintained laser-focus on Harry as he spoke to Shiloh, "His wrists comes off that metal, you holler for Earl downstairs."

He stepped into the closet. If his captive were to attempt an escape, Whitney mused, now would be the time to do it.

"I'd say *don't try nothin'*… but the truth is, I'd be happy for the excuse."

Harry averted his eyes from Whitney's glare. *Is this the moment?* he wondered. *Is this the opportunity I was waiting for?* Harry didn't have long to consider his options. A moment longer, and he might have acted differently.

He stood, motionless, with his wrists to the metal.

Whitney bound each of Harry's wrists individually to the bar. He was quick about it; one of the best knot-tyers in a community full of knot-tyers. He used constrictor knots, a specialty of his. Others—Judd and Joseph included—had asked him to teach them, but he didn't want to give away all his secrets for free.

"Spread ya legs," he said before he knelt down and bound each of Harry's ankles to the lower bar.

When the tying was done, Whitney backed up out of the

closet. He lifted his gun from the floor. "In case you're wonderin'… I'm a real light sleeper." He wasn't, but he was confident his bluff would be believed.

He shut the door and locked it with a sliding steel latch that scraped along the metal door like nails on a chalkboard. He leaned in close and stared at Harry through one quadrant of the crucifix divided window.

He stared long and hard through the opening, but Harry kept his eyes averted and his body still. He stood uncomfortably upright in his bindings. Whitney ambled down the hall and got into bed, leaving the bedroom door open.

As soon as Harry could no longer see Whitney through the crucifix bearing window, he began to yank aggressively at his bindings.

His wrists and ankles thrashed forward, his hands and feet strained, but he made no progress. He had no slack with which to maneuver, and the knots were tight enough to dig into his wrists and draw blood the more he wrenched around.

For ten minutes straight, Harry tried with all his might to force or otherwise wriggle out of his bindings. When he stopped to catch his breath, the bonds felt no looser. In fact, they felt tighter if anything.

He slouched forward, hanging limply from his wrists. He gritted his teeth and strained again. A vein in his neck bulged, and his face went red with exertion, but it was all for naught.

Now or Never

Hours passed as they always do. The argent moon hung in the night sky directly above the holler, as if to spotlight the strife of the bigoted microcosm. Duke and Earl had swapped shifts on the stool outside Whitney's front door. It was a pleasant night with warm air and a gentle backing track of chirping crickets and the occasional hoot of a distant saw-whet owl. Neither man minded the guard duty. Nightfall in the land of Second Christ brought with it a comforting sensation of peace and security that Duke and Earl savored as they sat in turns upon the short stool.

Back in the closet, Harry's eyes were red and his lids were drooping. He did all he could to power through the fatigue. He cared not about wearing himself out; he had adopted a *now or never* mentality.

He had given up on thrashing after the first full hour with zero progress. It had become clear that brute force couldn't free him from his bonds. He had then spent several minutes attempting to chew through his bonds, but the ropes had a waxy finish that hurt his teeth and prevented them from finding purchase or digging in.

Now, he was trying to pick apart the knot. When he contorted his hand in the right way, he was just barely able to reach the knot against his wrist with the very tips of his middle and ring fingers. He struggled to get a grip of any kind and, even if he did, he had no idea how to undo this particular type of knot. There was no clear spot to tug that seemed as if it would lead to an unraveling.

Still, he kept trying. *If I can just get one hand free...* That was all he needed, he kept telling himself, *just one hand free.*

"Psst! Mistah!"

Harry's heart leaped into his throat. He quickly relaxed his hand and looked innocently over to the window set in the door. Shiloh peered in at him.

She glanced over her shoulder through the open bedroom door. Whitney lay asleep in bed, snoring loudly. Shiloh pressed her face up against the window, standing on her tiptoes to do so. "What's ya name, Mistah?"

"... Harry. What's your name?"

"Shiloh. Mah name used'a be Trixie... but Mistah Conrad din' like that. Said it sounded too, uh, Ah forget the word he used. He changed up me and mah sistah's names to the bible kind."

"Could you open the door, Trixie?" Harry hoped using her real name might ingratiate himself to her, but it backfired.

She shifted uncomfortably. "Nah, nah. Shiloh, please. Ya gots'a call me Shiloh."

"Okay, Shiloh, okay," Harry said in a calming voice. He felt like she could be trusted if he played his cards right, or at least be of use to him and Andy. "Can you please open the door? And maybe undo this knot? I think your, uh..." he didn't know what to call Whitney in relation to her. The couples of the holler seemed to be paired as husbands and wives but the decades-long age difference between most of them made the matrimonial terms feel perverse. "Um, *Whitney* might've tied it too tight. It hurts." He hoped he sounded as weak and pathetic as he felt rather than coming across as manipulative.

"Sorry, Harry. Ah wou' get in heaps'a trouble if Ah do that. Whitney cain't hit me yet but he gots other ways'a punishin' me."

Harry understood her apprehension. If he were in her situation, he would have liked to think he would take the risk to help someone but he couldn't be sure what he would actually do without truly being forced to decide in the moment.

"He tie *me* up like that sometimes," Shiloh said softly. "He say he have this closet made special on account'a mah misbehavin'… but Ah'm not sure Ah b'lieve him." She wasn't usually allowed into the other homes within the holler but she was pretty sure at least a couple of the other men had 'misbehaving rooms' like this one.

"Would you get in trouble for talking to me?" Harry asked.

"Ah ain't had mah bleedin' yet, so Ah still 'llowed'a talk…." She stopped. A thought wormed its way into her mind that made her regret ever coming down the hall. "Not this way witchu, though." Her face pulled away from the window.

"I won't tell, don't worry," Harry said urgently. "Are they keeping you here against your will, Shiloh?"

"How ya mean?"

He chose his words carefully. "Could you leave this place if you wanted to?"

"Umm… they stopped Judith when she tried'a run off after her bleedin'. Ah wooden wanna leave wit'out mah sistah, though."

"Who's your sister?"

"Her name Eve now, but it still feel weird callin' her that.

The Grand Decider paired her wit' Sardus, non-fortunately. He a mean one, Ah tells ya." Shiloh felt so bad for her sister. She was afraid she would forget what her sister's voice sounded like now that it was gone.

"Andy and I could help you and Eve get out of here if you want."

Shiloh perked up. "You *cuh*?" Leaving had seemed impossible until the idea came from someone else.

Harry nodded, putting on a friendly, confident smile. *Now or never*, Harry told himself. This was the opportunity he had been awaiting, he felt certain. "Could do it tonight, if you help me out of this closet."

Shiloh felt excitement bubbling up inside of her. She nodded rapidly as she reached for the door's bolt. Then, she went stiff and cold. "Wait… nah, Ah cain't. Ah get punished hor'ble if Ah do."

"No, no. They won't punish you. They won't be able to, we'll be gone."

"Uh-uh, they will. They always do." She paced back and forth across the narrow hall, two steps at a time. "They punish me big time for some'tin like this, with the starvin' and the tyin', and they give mah beatin's to Eve. Ah cain't." She turned her back on him and stood still when he spoke.

"Wait. Wait. Don't you wanna get Eve outta here? Keep her safe?"

"Sorry, mistah." She started down the hall. She really was sorry.

Harry whisper-shouted, *"Shiloh, wait! You wanna get outta here before your bleedin', right? Shiloh?!"* He couldn't see her through the window any longer. She was gone. "God damn it," he said to himself. With this added burst of frustration, he returned to yanking furiously at his bindings. He didn't dare entertain the *now or never* thoughts any longer. *Now* had passed him by.

Gerald

It was sweltering in the police station. The AC was broken, and the handyman who worked on it with a screwdriver and wrench had no idea what he was doing. Crystal, the officer manning the lobby desk this morning, shook her head and tsk-tsked at the handyman down on his knees, pretending to know how to fix the problem. *He should just stop playing like he knows and give up already.* The sooner he admitted he couldn't fix it, the sooner they could shit-can him and bring in someone who actually knew what the hell they were doing.

Ma Winters felt like shouting at the lady behind the desk who clearly wasn't paying attention. Instead, she restrained herself to a simple but agitated clearing of her throat.

Crystal looked over, returning her pen to the half-filled out form. She raised her eyebrows in a *go on* expression.

"Brown hair, five-eleven or thereabouts," Ma said. "The fella he was with was Ko-rean. Dark hair. He's smaller. Maybe five-eight." She looked to Pa, who stood at her side, finally at the level of worry she considered appropriate. "Five-eight, Pa?"

"Maybe five-nine. They were drivin' a grey '13 Taurus. Oh, what am I doing?" Ma asked herself. "Hang on." She fished out her cellphone, figured out which icon brought up *the program with the pictures* on the third try, and muttered a drawn out "H-a-r-r-i-s-o-n" as she typed her son's name into the search field. When Harry's Instagram profile had loaded, Ma navigated to a photo of her boy and her new son-in-law on their wedding day. She showed the screen to the officer. "This is the both of them right here."

"Oh," Crystal uttered, squinting at the screen. She hadn't picked up on the two missing persons being anything more than friends before then. Crystal wasn't too concerned with concealing her surprise.

Once or twice, when Harrison had disappeared as a teenager, Ma had contemplated going to the police, but he always showed back up before she pulled the trigger on a search party. His longest withdrawals—different from his hours-long walks to nowhere—lasted from a day-and-a-half to two days, always situated on a weekend so he wouldn't miss school. It was a pattern Ma and Pa learned to recognize. Harrison never had a good explanation for where he had been or why he had slipped out without informing them.

Ma's best guess was that Harrison liked the attention; wanted to know he was missed and worried over in his absence, but everything about Harrison's demeanor upon return always suggested the opposite; annoyance over their concern, acting as though they were smothering him, always insisting that he was fine and they didn't need to worry, claims of premature adulthood and self-sufficiency. That behavior had all but stopped by his senior year of high school, though Ma and Pa were never informed of the real reason for his longest absences or why they suddenly stopped one day after becoming a routine.

Harry could never explain the truth of his missing

weekends to his parents. They wouldn't understand, and he barely understood it himself. Those fleeting weekends, once every month or two, had been spent in the company of an older man by the name of Gerald whom Harrison had met at the ring toss of the county fair in his sophomore year. Gerald— never Jerry— was two-dozen years Harry's senior. Their friendship was unlike any Harry had experienced before or since. The relationship never became sexual but the possibility that it someday could was never off the table in Harry's mind, though it was in Gerald's. There was a certain romantic longing between them that Harry had never before felt at that stage in his life.

Gerald lived in North Carolina, and whenever Harry couldn't stave off whatever nebulous force drove him to Gerald, he would make the trip by public transport. It took up to a half-day's travel depending on how many stops each bus made on that particular day. Harry and Gerald never communicated except in person, but Harry's sudden, unprompted arrivals never threw Gerald. He was always welcomed warmly no matter the time or company Gerald kept. The man's small, cluttered home felt like a safe haven where Harry could truly be himself, even as he figured out what that meant.

Years earlier, Gerald had been ostracized from his family and friends, but he was out and he was living a pleasant life without fear of others discovering what he used to keep hidden. He was both a sounding board and a fountain of wisdom to Harry, who had no one else he felt he could open up to. Gerald had been through it all and helped Harry to feel less alone in the world. He was always understanding and as gentle as could be. Whenever the two got together, they would sit cross-legged on Gerald's living room rug, drink Masala Chai from porcelain tea cups, and talk the night away in the warmth of the fireplace or the breeze of a box fan depending on the time of year.

One day, when Harry went for a visit after two months apart, it was a new face that answered the door instead of Gerald. Harry blinked at the middle-aged woman in the doorway. The furnishings behind her weren't Gerald's. The sounds of children playing in the next room put a knot in Harry's stomach that he couldn't unravel.

He took it as a personal affront. What had he done wrong? He ran through his last visit with Gerald in his mind looking for missteps, but there were none. There was nothing out of the ordinary to cause such a rift. Harry grew to look at the situation differently in time; less personally. Gerald had always spoken fondly of New York and mentioned his wish to move there someday. Harry couldn't be sure whether or not that's where he went but he liked to think it was true.

He still thought of Gerald from time to time; wondering where he went and what happened to him. It was years later when Harry began to wonder if some neglected part of his subconscious had chosen New York City as his college destination in the foolish hopes of one day bumping into Gerald again in the big city. Of course, it never happened.

Ma steadied herself on the tall police-station counter. The more they spoke to the police about finding her son, the worse she felt. It was counterintuitive to what she had expected when driving over in the morning, but as Crystal assured her they would send two officers in search of Harrison, Ma felt like she was saying goodbye to him.

"Do you have an article of your son's clothing with you?" Crystal asked.

"Uh, no," Ma said, confused. "But we can go get one from the house."

"What for?" Pa asked.

"In case we need to use the sniffer dog."

King-Sized

Birds sang up above the holler. It was a sunny day with a bright blue sky and puffy white clouds. Conrad's flock knew Second Christ was smiling upon them with such a gorgeous day.

Bo and Duke stood at the side of one of the half-painted homes, working with hand brushes to complete the white façade. It would take a few more days work before the home was painted in full.

Cappie and Walt were constructing wooden furniture in the workshop. The open-air building had only one wall, from which tools hung and a row of cabinets was situated. No other enclosure surrounded the large workshop, only support beams to hold up the slanted roof.

A pleasant breeze drifted through the workshop. Cappie nailed two boards together while Walt slid slats into a partially constructed bedframe. The frame would be quite large by the time it was finished; California-King large. It was to be Father Conrad and Mother Mabel's new bed. Walt had never worked much with tools before joining the congregation but now he felt like an old hand at woodworking. Conrad had proven to be an excellent teacher and he had decades' worth of experience as a carpenter to pull from. Walt could even take pride in his work from time to time. His skill had grown immeasurably in his time under Conrad's tutelage.

The community did not yet have the skills nor the resources necessary to fabricate their own mattresses, so the mattress for Conrad and Mabel's new bed would have to be brought in from elsewhere. Outside resources were brought in strictly on an as-needed basis, but the congregants did everything they could to allay that need. Eventually, Second Christ's holler would be an entirely self-sufficient sanctuary. Conrad promised that day wasn't too far off in the future. Growth had been slow and steady so far but would hasten exponentially in time as the congregation grew and Second Christ aged.

Clayton and Earl stopped by the workshop to grab a pair of wicker baskets. They strode toward the tree line, gabbing about Clint Eastwood movies. They were on gathering duty, which was usually uneventful and even a little boring compared to some of the other jobs. Clayton always looked forward to hunting duty, as much for the thrill of the hunt as for beer that came with it. Earl would have rather been tending the gardens but he was hesitant to admit this predilection as he didn't want to seem taken with a womanly interest. As the years had gone on, he had found increasing peace and joy in the act of kneeling down in the warm soil and cultivating plant life.

He had first taken an interest in gardening during the last year of his five-year stretch in prison. There was a ten by ten square of soil out in the courtyard that the inmates were allowed to tend under supervision, and it had become his one enjoyable pastime in the months leading up to his release. He continued the pursuit with his own home garden, learning more techniques and facts from books he checked out of the library. He had to put the kibosh on all that when joining

Conrad's ranks. Gardening was a task for the women only. *Oh well*, he thought. The benefits far outweighed this one minor drawback; it was no competition. He had the grand scheme of things to keep in mind.

Harry hung limp in his bindings in the closet, asleep. His knees were buckled, and the weight on his wrists would leave lasting joint damage. If he were less exhausted, sleep would have been impossible in this upright position.

His body managed a little over an hour's rest before the metal-on-metal shriek of the moving door latch shocked him awake like a bucket of cold water. In this narrow time between animation and soporism, Harry momentarily forget he was tied up and tried to flee from the sound

The sight of the captive sleepily flailing against the ropes brought a smile to Whitney's face as he swung the metal door and stepped inside. He was feeling fresh and rested. "Sleep well?" he asked in a mocking tone. He took two strides across the closet interior and grabbed onto one of Harrison's wrist.

Harry felt his pulse rise as Whitney eyed the bruised and bloodied skin beneath the rope. It was obvious he had been trying to escape. He feared the punishment that would follow.

But Whitney was not the least bit surprised. "Ah, I guess not. You kept busy, huh?"

"I- no, I—"

"That's why I prefer a good constrictor knot over the simpler clove hitch." When Judd and Joseph asked for instruction on how to tie the constrictor knot, he had taught them the clove hitch knot instead. They were in the same knot family, and the others couldn't tell the difference without examining one of their knots and one of Whitney's knots against each other side-by-side. It gave the illusion of him having a magic touch the others couldn't replicate.

"With a constrictor, the more ya struggle, the tighter it gets."

Whitney hoped he would get the chance to demonstrate his knot tying knowhow to Conrad up close some day. He wished dearly to impress Conrad— a fellow knot expert himself— and demonstrate his usefulness. He was jealous of Bo, who had breezed right into the holler and was able to curry favor with Conrad right off the bat by demonstrating his painting prowess. Whitney wanted the same treatment. He wished to be viewed as above the others in Conrad's eyes even if in just one category. The proper opportunity to demonstrate his skill had yet to arise. He prayed nightly that Conrad wouldn't think him a joke as Judd and Joseph liked to make him out to be.

Harry held his breath while Whitney untied him, starting with his ankles. Once both wrists were free, Harry found himself unable to keep from dropping to his knees, his strength depleted.

Whitney laughed again at him and retreated from the closet. He scooped his rifle up off the floor.

Harry willed the strength back into his legs to stand up. He was unsteady but he could stand without leaning against the wall. His wrists—discolored black and purple—felt like they were being pulled off the ends of his arms even still.

"Conrad says we have'ta get ya fed." Whitney waited, expectantly. "Well? Don't you think a thanks is in order? A thanks to me for untyin' ya and a thanks to Conrad for the sustenance?"

There was a lump in his throat as Harry swallowed his pride. "Thank you," he said flatly.

"Y'ain't hardly welcome," Whitney said, turning around and heading down the rickety stairs.

The husband and wife followers of Second Christ typically ate dinner in their own homes but most often they enjoyed breakfast as a community in the village's mess hall each morning. It wasn't a hard-and-fast rule— breakfast under one's own roof was always an option— but most chose each other's company to start the day.

The mess hall was a long, rectangular building with a high, arched ceiling and picnic-table style seating arranged in one long line. The cookware had been brought in from the outside world, but the rest of the mess hall and its contents had been built by hand by those who used it. It brought a sense of fulfillment or sometimes even pride to the simple act of sitting down with their fellow neighbors to share in a plate of eggs and bacon.

Today, there were no eggs and there was no bacon. In fact, there hadn't been for some time. The beginnings of a farm had been attempted in the holler in the not-too-distant past. They began small with just a few chickens and pigs, but the endeavor did not last long enough to begin incorporating larger livestock.

An illness befell the swine, and a separate strain of life-ending sickness decimated their poultry population. The congregants considered it a miracle that none of the holler's human inhabitants fell ill; a miracle they attributed to Second Christ and all his merciful protection. The inception of the illness, of course, could not be Second Christ's doing; the suggestion of it would be ludicrous.

Whitney shepherded Harry to a seat, then forced him down into it with a hand on his shoulder. "Any luck, we'll part ways after this," Whitney said, though he was actually enjoying tormenting the newcomer and wished to continue doing it. It made him feel powerful. It made him feel like a man.

Harry set his hands flat atop the wooden table on either side of the empty bowl set before him. It was surprisingly comforting to simply have a seat. He cautiously lifted his gaze from the splintery surface to the man sitting across from him. He stopped short of looking into the man's eyes, but saw enough of his face to recognize him as the one Conrad had called Bo; the one married to the five-year-old. If Harry didn't know any better, he would have thought Bo smiled at him.

Bethany stood in the kitchen stirring a tall pot filled with oatmeal. She gave it a sniff, then dropped in a clump of brown sugar and continued stirring.

There were six other congregants seated at the table. Harry pivoted his head to look down the table. That's when Harry saw him. Andy was seated at the far end, looking toward him apprehensively. Harry felt like a bastard for not noticing him right away. His eyes had been glued to the floor on his approach to the table. It was as though he were wearing blinders like a skittish horse.

Andy's eyes darted toward Hoyt across the table from him, then he looked down into his empty bowl. As Andy turned his head, Harry caught sight of the dark bruise on his cheek and his busted lower lip, both of which were new since last night.

Last night, Harry thought, *fucking hell.* It felt like it had been days since he last saw Andy—like it had been a week since they first encountered the hunters out in the woods— But it had been less than twenty-four hours.

Harry flinched as Bethany reached over his shoulder with a ladle and filled his bowl with oatmeal.

Whitney laughed at him. "Frightful li'l faggot, ain't ya?" He looked to Bo who shared in his laughter.

Bethany made her way around the table, balancing the pot against her hip and filling each congregant's bowl.

Hoping Whitney wouldn't notice, Harry risked a glance over at Andy. Their eyes met, and that meeting brought the tiniest sense of solace along with it before they both looked away again.

Harry's sore wrist worked his spoon through the oatmeal. The strained sensation lingered in his joints, like he was dragging an anchor around with every movement. He wondered if they would have given him a fork and knife if the meal were different. What he wouldn't give for a nice, sharp knife….

After such strenuous hours, his first spoonful tasted better than oatmeal should ever taste. As they ate, Harry and Andy periodically stole glances at each other, fearful of lingering too long. Sometimes their eyes met, other times they missed each other.

The bottom of the bowl was never reached. Two loud horn blasts thundered outside and disturbed the quiet atmosphere of the mess hall.

The congregation around them rose to their feet, so Andy and Harry rose too.

Outside, everyone put a stop to their respective tasks as the horn blasts decayed in the warm air. Tools were hung back on pegs. Brushes were laid flat on the rims of paint buckets. The gatherers made their way back from the forest edge. The door of each occupied home swung open, and the remaining congregants stepped outside to join the others awaiting Conrad's emergence.

In a manner he hoped was subtle, Harry drew closer to Andy outside the mess hall entrance. He didn't look at him, but he spoke in a hushed voice meant only for his husband.

"Are you okay, Andy?" Harry felt sick seeing the bruises on Andy's face. He feared further injuries hidden under Andy's borrowed clothes. "What happened to you?"

Andy looked over at his love. "I'm trying to do-" He caught on to Harry's off-base gaze and looked away himself. "I'm trying to do what they want but I keep making them angry. I can barely understand anything anyone's saying." In his time apart from Harry, he had been repeatedly beaten for what he thought was following orders. He was struggling with the thick accents, especially Hoyt's, whose overwatch he was remanded to. How frightened he felt at all times certainly didn't help his attempts to parse these foreign tongues. "I don't know what's going on. I'm so scared, Harry." He fought the urge to spin around and hug onto his husband. "I'm so scared," he repeated in a small, child-like tone of voice.

"I know, Andy. It'll be okay. I'm going to get us out of here."

"How?"

"I-" Harry hoped a convincing sounding plan would spring to mind in that instant despite failing to conjure one up since they first encountered who he thought were regular if bigoted hunters. "I don't know. But I will. I promise. We'll get out of this. I love you and I'm going to keep you safe." The *I love you* carried the inflection of an *I'm sorry*.

"I love you so much, Harry."

Harry noticed Hoyt and Earl looking their way. His pulse quickened. *Distance. Now.* "Just keep playing along. I'll figure this out, I swear to you." He casually stepped away from Andy without awaiting a reply.

He pretended to study one of the stained-glass windows of the church with great interest. In his periphery, he saw Hoyt and Earl look away.

Then, the doors of the final home swung open and Conrad stepped out. His stride was long, his girth rippling with each step down the incline from his home. He appeared as a magnificent beast to those who loved and respected him and as a contemptible horror to the duo who feared and despised him.

Mabel emerged from the home as well, though she was but a speck in her husband's eclipse of a shadow. Like every other female in the holler, she wore a smile upon her face at nearly all times, though hers was the only one to be genuine.

Conrad strode toward the center of the horseshoe-shaped village, projecting his voice to each and every attentive ear as he moved. "Job rotation! Hunters are now carpenters are now gatherers are now painters are now watchmen!"

This was good news for some, disappointing for others.

Conrad beckoned Harry and Andy with a swing of his arm. The baggy sleeve of his robe hung below his arm and rippled in the air; an inverted sail to navigate his sweeping wave.

No one left for their jobs yet. All stood with eyes on the newcomers, rapt.

Andy looked to Harry. Harry fought the urge to do the same. He looked Conrad square in the eye and held resolute on the journey to him across the field of trodden grass.

As they drew near, Conrad spoke. "I am still discussing the nature of your conversion with my son. There will be a proving and there will be a transfiguration, but there are some… particulars to work out." The most straightforward path was clear but not preferable, and far from fair to the men of the holler. "For now, it's time you join the fold, newcomers."

Harry jumped at the chance to present the front Conrad wanted to see, "Yes. We'll do whatever you need." He gave Andy a cold nod.

"Yes, absolutely," Andy added, following Harry's lead. He seemed to have a plan.

Conrad smiled a toothy smile. His chest puffed as if he were chuckling but no sound was produced. "I like the enthusiasm, lambs." He gestured to Harry with an open palm. "You shall join the gatherers today."

Fuck, he's separating us again. Andy thought of asking to remain together but knew the result would be a judgmental *no* at best and a severe physical punishment at worst.

Conrad motioned to Andy, then pointed a long-nailed finger toward the wet brush perched on the rim of the paint can across the village. "You shall take up brush and flush the barren white."

Andy had not a clue what was being asked of him. He

tracked Conrad's finger to the paintbrush and got the idea. He nodded.

Conrad knew his choice of words would baffle the foreigner but he couldn't help himself. He did so enjoy his grandiloquence. He continued, "You will grow competent in all the essential skills throughout your time here. Now go."

With his piece spoken, Conrad turned his back on the newcomers. He took Mabel's hand in his and returned to his home. With much hesitation and with congregant eyes still upon him, Andy made his way over to the half-painted building. He looked back over his shoulder at Harry, who gave a reassuring look.

The followers of Second Christ took to their newly assigned jobs.

Harry didn't know the protocol for serving as a 'gatherer' in the village, but it wasn't long before Cappie sidled up to him.

"Harrison?" Cappie said. "Follow me and Walt."

Harry gave a firm nod. It was the easiest gesture to display his willingness. He followed his two new guardians toward the edge of the village. He wondered if this meant he was no longer under Whitney's watch. He would welcome the change. He chanced a glance over his shoulder at Andy, who was taking up the white-dipped paintbrush.

Clayton and Earl, no longer on gathering duty, handed their baskets over to Cappie and Walt on their way over toward Andy to join him in painting. Clayton felt sure he would need to do-over everything the foreigner attempted on the side of the house. *No way he'll do it right.*

"I'll grab another basket," Cappie said to Walt. "Wait out here with him." Cappie sauntered into the open-air workshop where the spare baskets were kept. Mabel knew how to weave baskets and she had taught the craft to a handful of others within the holler so they were in no short supply.

Joseph and Whitney were both saddened to be off of the

hunting rotation but found workshop duty almost as fulfilling. Judd actually preferred it, though he would deny this fact if questioned directly. Hunting was the most masculine of all trades, and he *was* the most masculine of all men in the holler after all. He had to fit the model image the others had of him and that he had of himself.

Whitney sat atop a low stool and made dagger eyes at Harry as he dragged a bow saw back and forth across a thick plank of wood. Joseph pulled tools from hooks and settled into his station for the day's work. Judd noticed Harry watching and gave him a polite nod as he lifted a ten-foot wooden cross onto a work table. He began sanding it smooth. When the cross was finished, it would replace the one that previously stood in the center of the outdoor church's stage.

Harry returned the greeting while cursing up a storm inside his head. His eyes drifted to the row of tools hanging on the workshop's one wall; their sharp metal teeth glinting in the sunlight. The chisels and files and saw blades called to him. He could almost feel the weight of the keyhole saw in the palm of his hand.

If he could just get his hands on one… then what? How many of them could he take out before being taken down himself? One? Two? Would his last stand be over before it began? Could he bring himself to kill if it meant saving himself and the love of his life? *Yes*, he told himself. That was one question he could answer with confidence. He would kill to save Andy if it came down to it.

"Hey, um, what's the order of the job rotation?" Harry asked Walt while they waited for Cappie to retrieve an extra basket.

"Not always the same," Walt replied. "Up to Conrad."

"Ah, I see." Harry wanted to know how long until he would be assigned a carpentry job. He wanted to know how long until those sharp tools would be within reach. It might not get him very far, but he would feel a whole lot better with a weapon hidden upon his person. "And, uh, how often does the rotation happen?"

"Whenever the Grand Decider deems it so," Walt answered, feeling obligated.

Harry forced a friendly expression. He understood the 'Grand Decider' was what they called the strange music-box at the back of the outdoor church. He wondered how it worked. He hadn't seen anyone tend to it in his entire time within the holler, but at the same time, it did not seem complicated enough machinery to run autonomously. As near as Harry could figure, the timing of the horn blasts seemed randomly determined by the ticking gears. Although, he deduced, the deranged inhabitants of the village probably saw the ticking music-box as an extension of their prophet's will.

"Right," Harry said. "Hey, what do the different horn blasts mean?" He suddenly feared asking so many questions might arouse suspicion as to his true intentions. He added, "Just trying to get my bearings here and be a, uh, productive member of the flock."

Walt seemed to think nothing of the questions beyond their surface levels. "One horn means Second Christ has word to share through Conrad. You know what two horns means now. Three signals the act of procreation. Four means devils at the gates, *metaphortically* speakin'. And above that, well, you better pray you never hear five horns or more as long as you live."

Harry had more questions, but Cappie returned from within the workshop and handed him a wicker basket. Walt was clearly tired of waiting. He led the way into the forest. Harry savored the sight of the sharp tools hanging on the workshop wall and the minuscule amount of comfort the mere thought of attaining one brought. He refocused his gaze before the others had a chance to grow suspicious. He followed behind them into the forest.

Peoples is Peoples

Officer Faulkner had turned forty-six as of half an hour ago. For the first time since they met, his wife, Janey, had forgotten his birthday. They had been drifting apart for a while but even last year on the big forty-five, when things were at their worst, she still swept the animosity under the rug and made the occasion into a special day.

It was weighing heavy on his mind as he and his partner drove to the last known location of Harrison Winters and his husband, whose name Faulkner had not bothered to commit to memory. He wondered if Janey would ever walk out their front door for good. It was seeming a less distant possibility than ever before. They no longer had a child there to tether her to the home.

His partner, Lean, hadn't wished him a happy birthday either, but that wasn't his fault. Faulkner had never told him when it was. Lean was nine years younger than him, as of half an hour ago. Sometimes he seemed even younger to Faulkner, given how much pep he still had in his step. None of his enthusiasm for the job had drained yet. It would happen eventually, Faulkner was confident.

He wasn't jealous of his partner's zeal but he *was* jealous of his facial hair. *Good God, that walrus 'stache is magnificent,* Faulkner often found himself thinking upon seeing Lean at the start of their shift. His own face was follically challenged, but he was saved from feeling too inferior thanks to his full head of wavy red hair, whereas Lean had to shave his head or else live with the toilet-seat ring of hair around his ever-expanding bald spot.

Behind his mirrored sunglasses, Faulkner glanced at the rearview mirror. Bison was panting in the backseat, the sole JPD German Shepherd sniffer dog. He looked so cute in his little black vest, but Faulkner knew Bison's bite was far worse than his bark, he had seen it first-hand. Bison had sniffed out a baggy of weed on a local teenager and sunk his teeth into the burnout's knee. Nearly took the kid's leg clean off. Faulkner got a good laugh out of it.

The cop car slowed and turned down the short path onto the gravel lot. Harry's car was the only one parked outside this particular entrance to the state forest. Since his parents only knew they went hiking and not precisely where, the officers had checked three other forest entrances before arriving at this one.

The officers stepped out of the cruiser and made their way over to the empty vehicle at a leisurely pace. Lean slid a document out from his pocket and unfolded it. He compared the license plate printed on the paper to the one on the car. "It's a match."

"Okey-doke," Faulkner said, devoid of enthusiasm.

He sauntered back to the car and let Bison out. He wrapped the leash twice around his hand and knelt down to bring one of Harrison's T-shirts to Bison's snout. He wondered what Bison thought of the scent. Faulkner had sniffed it himself when Lean wasn't looking. He was curious how different a gay man's clothes smelled from his own. It wasn't as drastic a difference as he expected. In fact, he wasn't sure he detected any distinction whatsoever but he figured there *must* be a subtle difference. Bison could surely tell them apart, he thought.

"It feel different to you, Lean?" Falkner asked. "Workin' to find a couple homosexuals versus tryin' to save a pair'a normal folks?" He walked Bison toward Harrison's car.

"Don't see why that should matter none," Lean said.

Always one to take the high road. It was Lean's most annoying characteristic in Faulkner's eyes. "I don't know," he said. "It just ain't sittin' right with me somehow." He gave it some more thought, trying to figure out what was causing the pit in his stomach. "Like, maybe our time would be better spent elsewhere, ya know? More important crimes goin' on we could be workin'."

The leash went taut as Bison picked up the scent.

"Their bein' gay don't got no impact on your life, Faulkner," Lean said, disappointed that it needed explaining. "And it don't make them any less missin'. It's like they say in the greatest motion-picture ever made, 'peoples is peoples.'"

"What the fuck movie is that?"

"Muppets Take Manhattan, man."

Faulkner chuckled. The officers followed Bison down the trail into the state forest.

Bullydom

ndy dripped sweat. He was ten feet off the ground, balancing on a paint-splattered wooden ladder leaned against the side of the house. He had to stretch to reach the spot he was meant to be painting. He had hoped that painting, a task that utilized his real-world skillset, albeit in an abstract way, would finally offer an opportunity for him to prove himself worthy of the slightest degree of respect. But, his hopes had been dashed.

The ladder needed to be moved, but Clayton did not seem willing to let him come back down the ladder.

Earl was painting on the other side of the house and largely minding his own business, but Clayton had insisted on doing Andy the courtesy of holding the ladder steady for him.

He had a funny definition of 'holding steady'. Andy had nearly lost his balance a half-dozen times already. Clayton was gleefully awaiting the best moments to shake the ladder when Andy was the most stretched out from his center of gravity. It was bringing him immense delight. "Don't mind that. It was just the wind," he would say, snickering, after jostling the base of the ladder and watching the newcomer yelp and cling to the rungs like a cat fearing a bath. It made Clayton feel young again.

For as much as Clayton claimed to hate having the homosexuals in their midst, it was proving incredibly entertaining watching over the foreign one. He wanted to believe that Conrad and Second Christ could truly save their souls, and if that happened, he would apologize for the way he behaved. And they, having by then been fully transfigured, would surely understand his disgust toward them in their "gay state" and would not hold grudges.

If one of them could be saved, it was the one called Harrison, Clayton thought. He almost seemed normal to Clayton, but the other one? Everything he did had that unmistakable air of homosexuality about it that made Clayton's fists clench without him telling them to. *Not a chance in hell this chink's soul is salvageable,* he thought the very first time the idea of converting them had been floated. It's not like Second Christ would turn him white, he didn't think.

Work duty alongside him was bringing back a rush of good memories. *May as well enjoy it while it lasts*, Clayton thought to himself as he shook the ladder again. He heard the homosexual above him exclaim something in his native tongue, so Clayton shook the ladder harder. *Serves him right, speaking anything other than English in America.*

It reminded him of his middle and high school days when he used to torment the smaller and weirder kids. He had relished his bullydom. He was but one of a dozen bullies back when he still lived in Nashville. By his sophomore year, his family had moved to Jonesborough where the school was a mere fraction of the size. He was upgraded from 'one of the bullies' to '*the* school bully'.

It was a label he welcomed with open arms but it came with some drawbacks as well. It became harder to get away with his cruel acts when each and every authority figure in the small school knew where to point the finger. It meant more detention and even the occasional suspension but it also made him more imposing to those he tormented. He quickly learned he didn't necessarily need to use his fists to ruin someone's day. A simple gesture or intimidating look that conveyed his intentions of ill will could be enough to put the fear into someone and put them on edge for the rest of the school day. Passing them in the hall between classes and seeing the fear in their eyes was a sensation he learned to savor.

His bullying occasionally veered outside of school hours but something about it as an extra-curricular activity just wasn't quite as fulfilling. The danger of being caught and punished by the teachers was part of the spice that made it appealing to him. That he had to get away with it made their displeasure all the sweeter. Making someone shriek held more weight if the threat of detention loomed overhead.

"I can't reach from here," Andy finally said, gripping the sides of the ladder tightly.

"Are you saying you want to come down?" Clayton asked. Without waiting for an answer, he continued. "You know what the quickest way down is, right?"

"N- No--"

Clayton ripped the bottom of the ladder away from the wall.

Andy shrieked as he plummeted the ten feet to the ground. His legs buckled and half of his body slammed against the wall of the house. The wet paint he had applied on the wall before climbing the ladder was stamped onto his face and shirt. He instinctively tried to brace himself with his wounded arm, which proved a terrible idea.

Earl popped around the corner at the sound. For a split second, he appeared concerned, then he joined in Clayton's ridiculing laughter to a lesser degree.

For the first time, a new emotion joined fear and sadness in the constant tug of war over Andy's disposition: anger. He felt an unactionable rage toward the men before him and the entire situation he found himself in. Maybe a final straw had just been pulled, or maybe his fear tank had dipped into reserves and his anger tank had just been tapped into. He pouted, he fumed, the hand of his uninjured arm balled up into a fist.

"Oh, oh, oh, look'a'that! He wants to hit me! Ya see that, Earl? The faggot wants to hit me. Well, go on then." Clayton folded his hands behind his back and presented his jaw like a gloating boxer.

Andy had to look down at the grass. If he kept his eyes on Clayton's smug face, he just might have taken a swing, and he knew there was no chance that would end well.

"All right, cut it out," Earl said. "We've got a job to do."

"Look at you," Clayton said, gesturing with disgust at Andy and motioning over his paint-covered person. He was getting into it now. He was grooving. "You're a mess. Don't you know it's racist to wear white-face?" He reached out and smacked at Andy's paint-splattered cheek.

Andy flailed and backed up into the wall.

"Let me help you get that off," Clayton jeered as he took another swing at Andy's face.

"Stop it!" Andy shouted. The words left his mouth before he could stop himself.

"Stop what?" Clayton asked innocently as he laid another open palm on Andy's cheek.

Andy raised his fist halfway. He only just barely managed to hold himself back from throwing the punch. He could tell his restraint wouldn't hold out much longer and that a lack of restraint would very likely spell disaster.

"Clayton," Earl said in a cautionary tone. "What would Conrad say?"

Clayton whipped toward Earl. "About what?! I'm just

helping the little bitch clean himself up."

"We all know that's not what's happenin' here, Clayton. Get a hold of yourself. Remember Conrad's teachin's. Faith 'fore violence."

Clayton paused. He remembered his age. He remembered Conrad's gospel and Second Christ's miracles.

"Conrad said he ain't beyond hope of salvation. You keep fuckin' with him, you're spittin' on Conrad's intentions."

"I would never--"

"Then don't," Earl said. "You don't gotta be nice to him but you don't gotta be so mean neither."

"… You're right," Clayton said.

Andy unclenched his fist. He looked in Earl's general direction without lifting his gaze all the way from the grass. "Thank you," he said quietly.

"Don't misconstrue it for a favor," Earl said with his eyes locked tight on Andy. "I'm lookin' out for Conrad's will, not you. Conrad says you've failed—says you ain't worth savin' no longer—then I'll take my knife to ya quicker'n anyone else." And with that, Earl returned around the corner and resumed painting.

Fertile Ground

They had traveled a little over a mile away from the village. The patch of forest they were to forage was lush with varied vegetation. Cappie, Walt, and Harry milled about the area adding berries, mushrooms, and other edible and/or medicinal plants and herbs to their baskets. Walt had given Harry a brief overview of the specific plants they were to look for, describing their appearances, textures, and purposes.

Once they had been at it for forty-five minutes, Cappie and Walt stopped keeping as close an eye on Harry as they had been at the start of their foraging session, but Harry never took his eyes off of them for long.

Harry might have been able to slip away and hide until they gave up the search, but that thought never crossed his mind. He wouldn't be leaving without Andy. Instead, he thought of ways he might attempt to get hold of one of the firearms each man kept strapped to his back.

While the congregants had their eyes to the ground, brushing through low foliage, Harry wandered a little farther into the forest. He pushed past some shrubs and froze in his tracks. He felt goosebumps rise on his arms despite the heat. Before him was a bush covered in red berries; the very same berries Andy had recently learned were poisonous under Pa's tutelage.

Harry glanced back over his shoulder. Cappie and Walt were both doubled over, shuffling with hunched backs from one bit of foliage to the next. Harry creeped closer to the bush. He was outside their sight lines now, and they, out of his when he glanced over his shoulder again.

With his heart beating fast and his breath coming out heavy, Harry began plucking as many berries from the bush as he could as fast as he could. He shoved handfuls into his pockets and went back for more. His fingers trembled as he reached back for more of the poisonous berries, fearing with a dreadful certainty that he was about to be caught.

"Hey, Harrison?!" Cappie's voice shouted from beyond a tangle of foliage. "Where y'at?!"

Harry dropped the last couple of berries held between his fingertips. His muscles were tight as he turned toward the source of the voice. Plant life stood between the men, preventing each from seeing the other. "Uh, sorry! I'm here!" Harry rushed back over, unsure whether he should emerge with his hands held over his head or not. It was a gamble, appearing subservient could mean appearing guilty, and maybe he wasn't *that* to these men just yet. "I'm right here," he said as he stepped back into view, both hands crushing the handle of his basket.

"S'all right," Cappie said, stepping toward Harry. "Just don't wander off too far..." He took another slow step toward Harry. "These woods is dangerous if you stray too far from Second Christ's watchful eye."

Again, he stepped closer to Harry, infiltrating his personal space. Harry fought the urge to retreat. It felt like a test of intentions and of resolve.

After a brief pause, Cappie extended his right appendage

for a handshake. "I'm Cappie, by the way. Don't think we had ourselves a proper introduction."

A gentle wave of relief lapped against the shores of Harry's nerves.

Walt scowled. "Ugh, ya really gon' shake his fuckin' fag-hand? Talkin's one thing, but touchin'?"

"Ain't a fag-hand no more," Cappie said with confidence. "Conrad and Second Christ are cleansin' his soul. They fixin' him right up proper. He's one o' us now."

"We'll see," Walt muttered, returning his attention to the ground and resuming his foraging efforts.

Cappie left his appendage extended, so Harry completed the handshake.

"I was glad to hear Conrad's word got through to you. Always happy to see our flock grow. How *is* your recovery goin'?" Cappie cocked his head and leaned forward like a genial morning show host. "Any ill thoughts still creepin' in since Conrad's word?"

"No," Harry said, perhaps too eagerly. "No, Conrad straightened me right out. I've, um, seen the error of my ways and I'm-" he searched for the right word, "… repentant."

"Well, I won't hold nothin' but your present against ya. I *know* Conrad can save ya. I seen him do it. Firsthand." Cappie took yet another step closer to Harry, close enough to embrace him. He spoke softly and with great candor. "I once was addicted to the crack rock, if ya can believe it." He sucked his teeth and shook his head. "It surely would have meant mine end, sooner rather than later. Conrad and Second Christ got me clean, got me focused, and got me back on God's path. To Conrad, and to Second Christ and his divine teachin's, I owe my life."

Harry nodded firmly; that simple gesture seemed to be working so far. He thought of the berries in his pockets and wished an opportunity to poison these sons of bitches would present itself in the not-too-distant future. "Amen," he said with feigned reverence.

Snuffling

Bison's snout was low to the ground as he prowled forward, leading the officers at a comfortable walking pace.

"I'm just sayin' it would be a heck of a lot easier if I had *something* in common with him," Lean said, feeling like a bad father.

"Ya just need a bondin' activity," Faulkner said reassuringly. "What's Todd like doin'?"

"Ugh, he just sits in front of his computer all day, playin' that thing with the forts or whatever. I can't get through to the kid. Hardly says a word outside'a dinner time. Even then, he's scarfin' his way through his mom's cookin', tryin'a get it over with ASAP."

Lean used to take Todd fishing and hunting all over the county and even took him hiking in this very state forest. Then, Todd grew out of quality time with his dad. Lean tried to remind himself it was just a part of growing up, but it was hard to take comfort in that sentiment when he knew the worst of it was still to come in a year or two's time when the teenage angst really took root and sprouted limbs.

"Play the fort thing with him then," Faulkner said as if the solution were the most obvious thing in the world.

"Ah, I can't do any of that nonsense." Lean had tried out video games a handful of times at his son's behest. Each and every time left him feeling embarrassed and old. The controls just didn't compute with him. He couldn't wrap his head around moving the camera and moving the character at the same time, which spelled instant doom for his foray as a gamer-dad.

"Well," Faulkner said, stepping over a dead possum in the middle of the trail. "Don't let *him* play it neither then."

"And have him outright hate me? No thanks. I'll stick to the indifference I'm gettin'."

"Todd won't hate ya for takin' away his video games. He might think he does for a little while but he won't really. He'll get over it. Lay down the law. Y'are a cop, ain't ya?"

They emerged from the forest into a parking lot. Bison sniffed his way over to where the hunters' pickup truck previously sat. His nose told him it was the end of the line. He barked and turned in a tight circle between the tire-track depressions in the mud. The ground had dried but the marks were preserved with remarkable clarity. Nobody had driven in or out of the lot since the hunters departed.

"Must'a got into another vehicle," Faulkner said. He pulled a treat from his breast pocket and flipped it to Bison as one would a coin. Bison snatched it out of the air, hoping for more to follow. The PD said not to give the sniffer dog treats, but Faulkner couldn't help it, Bison was too damn cute to not reward when he did a good job.

Lean bent over the tire tracks and gave them a good study. He pulled out his cellphone and snapped a quick photo with the flash on. He straightened back up and followed the grooves through the hardened mud toward the road. The tracks curved to the right where the lot joined the road. "Tracks go this way." He snapped and pointed his finger-gun down the road.

They had to backtrack through the woods to return to their cruiser. It gave them both time to think; plenty of time for Lean's optimism to dwindle. What started as a concrete trail had just widened right up to the bounds of comprehension. Bison wouldn't be any help tracking a moving vehicle, and that meant diligence and luck were just about all they had left to go on. Judging from the tread marks left by the vehicle, and how deep-set they were, Lean was confident the vehicle they were after was a truck, most probably a pickup, though no clues as to the make or model.

Lean thought about how much easier his job would be if Jonesborough were a big and rich enough community to have intersection cameras. He was jealous of city police who operated with bountiful access to security cameras. He would never leave Jonesborough, though. Not a chance. His father was born and raised in Jonesborough, and his father before him. Now both of them were buried over at Greenley's under the big oak tree. Lean wished to be buried there as well when his time came.

At present, his will stipulated that he and Trisha be buried alongside each other in her family plot, but now that their divorce was finalized, he could set about changing it back. He had been meaning to do it for a while now and kept forgetting or deliberately putting off the tedious paperwork.

When the officers were back in their cruiser and heading down the road with Bison in the back seat, they passed by the muddy lot and kept driving. Lean hoped to pick the trail back up as soon as possible.

Faulkner was ready to call it a night. His stomach growled loud enough for Lean to hear. "Whoop. There's my dinner bell."

Lean scrunched down and looked up at the sky through the passenger-side window. The sun was beginning its descent.

"Denny's or IHOP?" Faulkner asked, gripping the wheel lazily with one hand and fiddling with the radio with the other.

"Those the only two options?"

"If we're gettin' pancakes, they are. And, I don't know about you, but I am most definitely gettin' pancakes."

The cruiser continued down the road… and blew right past the narrow trail leading to Second Christ's holler. The officers were none the wiser.

Poison in His Pocket

Harry had hoped to see Andy once more before being locked up in Whitney's closet for the night, but Andy was no longer outside painting the home when Harry returned from foraging. Even a passing glance at his love would have done wonders for his psyche. He worried far more for Andy's safety than for his own.

The only silver lining that could be pulled from this dreadful situation was that it did nothing but confirm and magnify the love between the newlyweds. Harry would give anything to get Andy out of this awful place. He was ready to kill for Andy and he was ready to die for him too. He hadn't been sure of that when they said their vows, but now he was certain.

Cappie stood at Harry's side, waiting for Whitney to finish cleaning up the workshop from their day's labor to escort him home.

Harry looked longingly at the spot where he had last seen Andy. Much progress had been made on the east-facing side of the home. He hoped the familiar process of painting might have helped Andy to block out the full gravity of their situation even ever so briefly, though he knew it was a world apart.

He contemplated how he could make use of the poisonous berries filling up his pockets. He had been brainstorming on this topic since the very instant he spotted them clinging to the bush.

Poisoning the big, community pot of oatmeal the next morning seemed the most effective tactic of all he had considered thus far, but there were a number of variables and pitfalls to that course of action. He couldn't be seen tainting the pot in front of the others, which meant getting into the mess hall while it was vacant. He had yet to be left unguarded for more than a few seconds at a time, and he had no way of telling whether or not the mess hall was occupied before entering. Additionally, he would need a valid reason to avoid eating the oatmeal himself when it was served and he would need to somehow make sure Andy didn't eat it either. The two outsiders both abstaining from the same meal was sure to arouse suspicions, he figured.

Even if he could pull it off, he had no idea if the poisonous berries would be strong enough to adversely affect so many people after dilution. In truth, he didn't even know how strong the effect of the berries would be on an individual. He knew not whether it would result in sickness, debilitating pain, or outright death. He hoped for the worst fate possible to befall the eventual victim or victims.

"Thanks for hangin' around, Cappie," Whitney said as he stepped out of the workshop.

"No problem at all, Whit. He did well out there today, I gotta say."

"You don't gotta say that. Ain't no work deficit too mighty for his kind."

Cappie did not rightly know what that meant but, regardless, he said, "Oh, sure."

Whitney looked at Harry. "Dinner time. Get movin'."

Harry started toward the mess hall.

"Nope," Whitney barked. "I eat dinner at my own table, like a man. But I guess you wouldn't know anything about that, would you?"

Harry said nothing. His expression remained neutral. He altered trajectories and moved across the center of the village, between the outdoor pews and the stage, to Whitney's front door.

Whitney shoved Harry out of the way when he reached for the door handle. He opened it himself and was a little bit disappointed when Harry gave no pushback of any kind. It seemed to him that the newcomer's spirit was finally broken. *Almost a shame*, he thought. He enjoyed breaking a spirit more than having one broken, like a dog chasing a car but not knowing what to do with it if he ever caught one.

The empty dinner table was the first sight to greet Whitney, and it sent a hot, aggravated burst of air out of his mouth. He stepped inside, tugging Harry in by the arm, then slamming the door shut.

Harry inched away, seeing that Whitney was about to explode.

"Shiloh!" He screamed up the stairs. "Where the fuck's my dinner?!"

"It's cookin'," Shiloh's voice came from around the corner at the top of the stairs an instant before she did.

Harry looked into the little kitchen. He felt the hairs on his arms and the back of his neck stand up as he laid eyes on the bubbling pot of stew atop the stove. He needed to make a decision, fast.

"On the table when I get in, ain't that what I told ya?!" Whitney shouted up the stairs.

A strong dose for Whitney or a weak dose for a bunch of them? Decide Harry, goddamnit!

"It's *almos'* done," Shiloh said, coming halfway down the rickety steps. Whitney blocked her from coming the rest of the way down.

Harry didn't know if he could pull off the mess hall option. This one was right in front of him. He pulled the figurative trigger. Harry dashed the couple of feet into the kitchen. He gambled on being just barely out of Whitney's line of sight. A micromovement of Whitney's head would plunge Harry into his peripheral vision. As quick as he could, Harry turned out his pockets and emptied the berries into the stew.

"All the other wives get it right!" Whitney barked.

"I'm sor—" Shiloh cut herself off with a shriek as Whitney stomped up the stairs towards her.

He raised a clenched fist. "Why can't you?!"

"Wait!" Shiloh shouted, cowering against the rickety banister. "Ya cain't! Y'aint allowed yet!"

Whitney so badly wanted to lay into her with everything he had. His patience had long since run out. His fist trembled in the air above her head. With a loud groan, he lowered his arm. He couldn't bring himself to break one of Conrad's cardinal rules. He had more restraint than this, he told himself most every day. *It's only a matter of time*, had become something of a mantra to help Whitney contain his rage toward his wife.

Harry took up the wooden spoon resting beside the pot and used it to stir the berries into the chunky stew. He could tell the arc of the argument playing out a couple of feet to his right was drawing to a close. He continued stirring until the berries disappeared below the bubbling surface.

"Ya better straighten up, girl."

Harry retreated from the kitchen as Whitney turned around on the stairs and stomped his way back down to the ground floor. The blood felt cold in Harry's veins. He had to forcibly maintain a calm demeanor. His muscles were tight, and part of his brain was willing his body to sprint out of the home right then and there.

"Serve me, now."

Not out of the woods yet, Harry told himself, followed quickly by an explosive, internal, *fuck!* His pockets were still turned out, the white fabric dangling from the front of his jeans. *Don't draw attention to it,* he thought as he casually laid a flat hand over an exposed pocket. The other pocket, he covered with the wall as he leaned against it.

Whitney sat down at the table. Shiloh filled a bowl and brought it to Whitney with a wooden spoon and a cloth napkin.

Harry inched his fingertips up his hip. At length, he poked the pocket back into place, then got to work on the other one.

His eyes were locked with trepidation on Whitney as he took his first bite of stew.

Whitney glared up at him. "Y'aint gettin' any of my stew. Don't even fuckin' think about it."

Harry averted his eyes. He was thankful for Whitney's selfishness in that moment. He hadn't thought up a plan to avoid eating the poisoned dinner himself if it was offered.

Whitney took another bite and found himself thrown by the taste.

Any tension that had left Harry's body came back with a vengeance as Whitney raised his spoon to eye level and scrutinized the stew held within. Harry couldn't keep from fidgeting. He thought about ripping open the front door and bolting. He thought about lunging across the table and tackling Whitney before he realized the truth.

But he didn't have to.

"God damn it, Shiloh, your cookin' keeps gettin' worse and fuckin' worse. My gosh." He shook his head and took another bite.

"Ya juss love complainin'," Shiloh said as she stepped back into the kitchen.

Shit. Shiloh. Only then did Harry realize he may have been doing her harm as well. He watched her fill herself a bowl and take a seat diagonally across from Whitney.

She filled her spoon and lifted it from the bowl. She blew on the steaming stew.

Harry coughed loudly, drawing attention and buying himself an extra moment.

Shiloh stopped short of taking her first bite. She looked up at Harry, but so did Whitney. He couldn't risk trying to signal her.

Harry's mind went blank. "Um…" *Say something! Anything!* "I have to use the bathroom."

"Hold it," Whitney said bluntly, returning his spoon to his bowl. "I'll walk ya out to the edge of the woods after dinner."

"He can use our bathroom, c'aint he?" Shiloh asked, lowering her spoon.

"Not a chance in hell I'm lettin' his faggot ass touch my shitter." He stuffed another spoonful into his mouth. "Now shut up and eat your dinner."

Shiloh picked her spoon back up.

Do something! Harry shouted internally. "Hey, come on!" he exclaimed much louder than necessary with only half a plan in his head. He stepped forward.

Whitney rose to his feet.

"It's right there," Harry said, gesturing to the bathroom off to the right side of the narrow home.

"I said no."

"I'll just be in and out. Only take a second."

He made a weak attempt to circumvent Whitney and head for the bathroom.

"You ain't listenin'," Whitney said as he grabbed hold of Harry's lapels and shoved him backwards.

Yes, Harry thought. He threw himself off his feet and swept his arm across Shiloh's bowl, knocking it to the floor with him and making Whitney feel strong at the same time.

"Holy--" Shiloh said, popping to her feet. "Is you okay?"

Harry faked a groan on the floor, knocking the upturned

bowl off of his chest.

"Never mind if he's okay. He just wrecked your dinner, and I ain't sharin' with ya, so don't ask."

Harry picked himself up and wiped the stew off of his shirt. He would stink like stock and venison for hours.

"Aw, please, Whitney. Ah'm so hungry," Shiloh pleaded. "Ah'm as hungry as a horse."

Whitney slammed his hands down on the tabletop. "That ain't even the idiom, retard!"

Shiloh's lip trembled. She hated when Whitney or the others called her that word more than any other word in their entire vocabularies. It was a word classmates used to shout at her on the playground.

"Clean up this fuckin' mess."

At length, Shiloh made her way around the table, grabbed a rag, and wet it.

Harry thought he saw tears in her eyes as she knelt down over the mess. *I'm responsible for those tears*, he thought. "Sorry, Shiloh," he said softly.

Whitney glared at him.

"It ain't you," Shiloh said in an even softer voice.

"Less talkin', more scrubbin'," Whitney barked, lifting his bowl and eating from it while standing over his young wife.

Shiloh wanted to hug her sister more than anything. But her and Lindsay were always kept apart. She couldn't even remember the last words they had spoken to each other. Shiloh wanted to hug her momma and poppa too but it had been at least a year and a half since she had seen them. She wondered if they were still looking for her. She wondered if they thought she was dead. She wondered if they might prefer that to the truth. She couldn't remember the last words they had spoken to each other either.

A Lesson In Cruelty

Andy's cheek stung. "Please, stop," he said weakly. The red palm print didn't have time to fade from his skin before another painful imprint was stamped over it. His wrists were bound to the arms of a chair in the corner of the ground floor, his ankles bound to the chair legs. He had no means of defending himself. 'Helpless' had become his default state of being.

"No, no. Y'aint doin' it right," Hoyt said to his one-eyed wife Cilicia. "Close ya fist. And harder."

Cilicia wanted it to stop. She was taking no part in the joy that Hoyt was clearly getting from the beating. She felt bad for the pain she was inflicting. But still, what she wouldn't give to trade places with the outsider. He didn't know how easy he had it.

She made a fist like Hoyt wanted. This would only end when she had satisfied his cruelty. The quicker she reached Hoyt's threshold, the less cumulative pain she would be putting the stranger through in the long run, she rationalized. She took a swing. Her knuckles connected with his cheek.

Andy whimpered. He slumped against the side of the

chair, feeling his various injuries throb in synchronicity with the beat of his heart.

"You can do better'n that," Hoyt said. "Come on! Hit him like I hit you." He shook his fist in front of Cilicia's face. "I need'a remind ya how it's like?"

Cilicia shut her remaining eye and shook her head. She quickly raised her fist and threw a hard punch into Andy's ear.

"Harder! Hell, Cilicia, I'm doin' ya a favor here, and you're actin' like ya don't even wanna learn."

Andy couldn't take it in silence any longer. "I didn't do anything!" he shouted at the top of his lungs, bloody spittle spewing past his busted lips.

Hoyt went quiet. He showed Andy a look of utter disgust as he ground his teeth back and forth. "That don't sound like a repentant man to me." He popped a quick jab into Andy's eye, quicker than he could see it coming. "You ain't done nothin'? What ya sayin'? A whole lifetime'a sin don't count?! Sodomy! Immorality! Rejection of God's will! God gave you life, and you stabbed him in the back with your damnable ways!" He swung a right hook into the side of Andy's head that knocked his chair up onto its two side legs for a moment. He spun toward Cilicia and grabbed her by the shoulders hard enough to bruise. "Do it like that! That's how you hit a sinner!"

Andy couldn't take it. He just couldn't take it. He needed to escape in his mind if not in his body. He tried to block out the present and think back to the past.

He thought back to seeing Harry for the first time. He was studying a swirling cloud projection on the wall of the Seoul Museum of Art. He had his arm wrapped across his chest and a hand over his chin, rubbing at his stubble, while he studied the thirty-second loop of cloud bursting as if he expected it to be different on the eleventh or twelfth go around.

Even viewing him from behind and from across the room, Andy could tell he was American at a glance. It was in his stance; the way he stood so wide and so rock steady. He hadn't taken his sunglasses off when he came inside. Andy later learned that was to hide how hungover he was. He had tried baekse-ju for the first time the night before and had instantly become a big fan. He had considered calling off his planned trip to the museum and sleeping it off instead. They were both infinitely glad he decided to power through.

Andy shyly approached him and, in English, offered to give him a personal tour. Harry thought he was an employee of the museum, until Andy led him down the east wing, pointed to one of the paintings hanging on the wall, and said, "That's one of mine."

Harry spent three straight minutes studying the piece, then truthfully declared it to be his favorite work in the entire museum. They chatted and strolled the halls of the museum together for the next four hours, repeating loops and revisiting pieces, neither man wanting their chance encounter to end.

Eventually, Andy worked up the courage and offered to show Harry some of his works in progress back at his apartment. Harry gladly accepted. They walked the mile and a half from the museum to Andy's apartment building, chatting about the cultural identity of art sprinkled with bits and bobs of personal information about themselves. Once they were inside his apartment, it wasn't long before—

A tooth flew out of Andy's mouth, ricocheted off the wall, and clattered to the floor.

"Like that!" Hoyt shouted before shoving Cilicia forward.

Andy's escapism had been terminated. He tried to disappear back into his memories but it was no use. The alternating fists of Cilicia and Hoyt kept shocking him back into reality before the better times could get a foothold. His happy place was destroyed.

Andy's face was a bruised and bloodied mess by the time Clayton was satisfied. After forty-five minutes of pummeling, Clayton retired to bed.

Cilicia hung around a moment after Clayton had gone to offer her silent sympathies… but they were lost on the broken man.

Blotting Out the Moon

Officer Faulkner was bored and slowly running out of patience. After their dinner break, Lean had insisted on returning to work and repeatedly traveling down Old Cheney road, where their trail ended, looking for anything out of the ordinary. Doggedly retracing one's steps was a core tenet of investigation, and Faulkner hated it.

Old Cheney road connected to a four-way intersection about six miles from the muddy lot where Harrison and his husband were presumably loaded into a truck and driven God-knows-where. Nothing but forest and farmland in the intervening miles between the lot and the intersection. The officers had now spent the majority of their day driving slowly back and forth on Old Cheney road and each road that joined it at the intersection. The exercise seemed pointless to Faulkner but, as he had no ideas for where to look or what to pursue next, he entertained Lean's simplistic game plan.

As the night wore on, however, Faulkner became less and less of a willing participant in the pointless exercise. Now it was dark out, the official hours of their shift were in the rearview, and he found himself once again turning down Old

Cheney road, heading back toward the parking lot where they lost the trail.

"They could be anywhere by now," Faulkner said grumpily.

"I'm not ready to give up on this yet. We ain't got nothin' else, so… maybe we missed something." Lean continued to peer out the window as they drove. To him, the repetition was all part of the bargain. He wondered how a detective would approach the case. The Jonesborough police budget was not at a level capable of sustaining a fleet of detectives on payroll.

"Our trail is just about as fucked as could be, Lean," Faulkner declared. "Come on, let's pack it in for the night. We'll start checkin' the usual dumpsites in the mornin'." He was working on the assumption that the missing couple no longer belonged to the land of the living.

"I wanna check it on foot--"

"Are you kiddin' me?"

"No, I ain't kiddin' you. I actually like to do good police work on occasion if ya can believe it." Lean took a deep breath and lowered his voice. "Come on, park it. We know they were here."

They parked in the muddy lot. Lean readied his flashlight and climbed out of the passenger seat. Faulkner sat behind a moment, stuffing down his annoyance, before stepping out of the cruiser as well.

It was near pitch black in the lot now without the aid of the flashlights. The encircling trees blotted out much of the moonlight.

Despite it being harder to see, Lean had a theory that certain clues were easier to spot in the dark within the beam of a flashlight. His field of vision was narrowed to a singular spotlight under his control, his focus magnified on minute details illuminated with cold LED light. He scanned the earth for anything unnatural: a coin submerged in the mud, a cigarette butt left behind as litter, anything that could have fallen from one of their pockets…

Faulkner watched Lean, hunched low, pivot slowly with his flashlight aimed at the dried mud. Faulkner wasn't doing much investigating himself, mostly just waiting for Lean to tire himself out.

Lean stepped lightly. He was methodical in his flashlight scanning of the no-longer muddy ground. In his mind, he was dividing the parking lot into a grid and thoroughly searching each square in sequence before moving on to the next. It was a practice similar to one he had seen in a documentary employed for finding and defusing buried landmines in the aftermath of World War II.

The grooves left behind in the mud from the tire tracks caught brilliantly in his flashlight beams, the uneven surface casting a world of shadows along the ground. The tracks were even more visible in the flashlight beam than they had been to the naked eye in the broad daylight, which made him hopeful about the prospect of finding footprints.

He broke from his grid pattern and maneuvered from the tracks directly toward the trail into the forest. He crouched down low as he shuffled along, holding the flashlight only a couple of inches above ground level, hoping to catch the edges of any subtle depressions in the beam. At first: nothing. Then…

"Ah-ha! Got something!"

Faulkner, surprised out of his distracted imaginings, rushed over. "What is it?"

"Footprints." He moved the light over a wider area. They were too shallow to see in the daylight. "Whole lotta footprints."

"Oh, pshh," Faulkner scoffed. "That don't mean nothin'. Those could be anyone's footprints. They could be ours."

"Wasn't muddy no longer by the time we got here." Lean paused a moment to think, then remained strong in his conviction. "Only one set of tire tracks here before us. I think there only bein' one vehicle through here while it was muddy makes it a good bet that the only footprints through here while it was muddy ought to be from the same party."

"I don't know how safe a bet that is, Lean. What good does it do us anyway if they climbed into a vehicle and drove off right after?"

"It lets us know how many people we're dealing with. Look at these prints." He moved his beam slowly over the footprints. It was a jumble of overlapping tracks; hard to tell how many people had left them behind exactly. "Looks like maybe four or five peoples-worth of tracks."

"Hmm." Faulkner knelt down and looked the tracks over with less dismissive eyes. "Ya see this one set here?" He pointed with peace-sign fingers over one set of footprints in particular.

"I do. They stand out a little from the jumble somehow."

"That's because they're deeper. Which means…"

"Whoever left those particular tracks is a lot heavier than the others."

"One big'un and three or four little'uns."

"Neither of our missin' persons is on the big side."

Faulkner stood up straight and stretched his joints. "Well that's somethin'. Damned if I know how that helps us, but it *is* something." He turned and started back toward the cruiser. "All right, now let's get outta here."

"I wanna check the road on foot."

"What? Oh, no. No, no, no. We made a little progress, Lean, be satisfied with that. We're done for the night, time to pack it in and go on home."

"I ain't done yet. I don't wanna let this trail get any colder than it already is. Who knows if those footprints would'a still been visible if we came back in the morning? Could rain, or the mud could dry out the prints, or some other people could come hikin' through here. We gotta be thorough while we got the chance."

"God damn it," Faulkner said. He hated how convincing his partner was sometimes. The guy knew how to make his points; should have been a debate-team captain instead of a cop.

"Come on," Lean said. "You can bring Bison with us. We pick up a trail, we'll want him with us. Been cooped up in the back too long anyhow."

"Fine then."

Faulkner let Bison out of the car and wrapped the leash around his hand. The trio set off down the road by flashlight.

It Flashed on the Floor

Harry was back in the closet. His wrists and ankles were bound to the metal bars, but he no longer bothered to struggle. He could not escape his bonds on his own; he had accepted this. He hung forward with his head slumped uncomfortably against his shoulder, asleep. The majority of his body weight was suspended by his arms. His wrists and shoulders were being strained to near dislocation. He was so dreadfully tired and he knew he would need to keep his energy up if he had any hope of escaping the next day, and the next day it would have to be. One more day, Harry had decided. He didn't think he could play along for a greater duration than that, he couldn't stand to bide his time any longer and pretend to fall in line with these men while they continued to abuse Andy.

He was roused from his shallow slumber by the bumping of the bedroom door into the wall and by the loud creaking of the hallway floor under Whitney's bare feet. Harry creaked his tired eyes open and peered through the crucifix-obscured aperture at his captor, who was pale and sweating. He looked nauseous, like a sea-sick man aboard a boat on choppy waves. He staggered a couple of short steps down the hall from the bedroom.

By the time Harry was locked in the closet and Whitney went off to bed, the poisonous berries had displayed no effect whatsoever on Harry's captor. Now, they seemed to be taking him for a ride.

Whitney put a clammy hand on the wall to steady himself. He took another two steps, clutching at his stomach, before doubling over and vomiting on the floor. A ghastly moan came from his dripping mouth. He straightened up and used both hands to brush the profusely sweaty hair out of his eyes. "Shiloh! Come clean th—"

He gagged and clapped a hand over his mouth. Whitney turned and staggered down the stairs, supporting himself on the rickety railing the whole way. Sliding his hand along it left splinters in his fingers and palm, but he had bigger troubles at the moment.

As Whitney descended the steps, he left Harry's field of view from within the closet. As soon as Whitney was out of sight, Shiloh emerged from the bedroom. With frantic energy, she looked down at the puddle of chunky vomit dripping between the floorboards, then down the stairs, then directly at Harry past the holy mullion.

Fuck, does she know it was me? Harry considered pretending to be asleep, but it was too late, she had made direct eye contact with him.

Shiloh hurried toward the closet, put her hands against the metal door, and brought her face right up to one of the quadrant openings. "Ya gots'a help me, Mistah!" she whisper-shouted.

"Wha- What?" Harry was not prepared for her plea. He could hear Whitney heaving and puking in the bathroom downstairs.

"Ya gots'a help me hide it. Please."

"Hide what?"

Shiloh was in panic mode. "Ah got mah bleedin'! Whitney always check mah sheets right in the mornin'. Ah- Ah ain't ready!"

"Oh, uh, uh—" Harry stammered, unable to quickly process all that was happening.

"Please help me hide it. He been savin' up so many beatin's for me. Ah-" Tears began to roll down her cheeks. "Ah don't want mah silencin' yet! Please!" Her stifled cries became full-volume blubbering.

"Okay!" Harry whisper shouted. "Shh! I'll help. Shiloh, quiet, he's gonna hear you." Harry tried to keep an eye on the staircase but couldn't see it well with her face so close to the window.

"Ya will?" she asked, sniffling.

"Yes, I'll help." *Now or never*, Harry thought. He softened his true intentions for her. "Get me outta here, and I'll help you hide your sheets."

"Wha- Now?"

Harry felt a pang of hesitation. Maybe it would be better to let Whitney fall back asleep and then have Shiloh set him loose? *No. Fuck it.* "Yes, right now. Do it. Quickly."

Shiloh grabbed the closet latch and slid it open. The metallic screech was loud; loud enough that Whitney may have heard it over his heaving downstairs. She crossed the closet and grabbed onto Harry's knotted wrist. She fumbled with the rope, struggling to untie it.

"Cut it. Cut- get something sharp," Harry muttered frantically as he watched the unoccupied top of the staircase through the open closet door.

But there was no time. The stairs began creaking under Whitney's weight.

Shiloh shut her eyes for a moment to concentrate. She had watched Whitney tie and untie these knots dozens of times, sometimes on her own limbs. With her eyes closed, she felt the contours of the rope and performed the movements she had watched Whitney do so many times.

The knot came loose, and Harry's arm dropped from the bar. His shoulder was throbbing. He lifted his arm to work on the knot binding his other wrist. Shiloh knelt down and began untying his ankles.

The creaking of the stairs grew louder.

Shiloh was heaving short, panicked breaths as she worked on the knots.

Whitney came into view, ascending the stairs with no small amount of effort. He looked like he might puke again at any moment. His eyes settled on the two of them in the closet.

Harry's final limb came free. He gently pushed Shiloh aside to exit the closet. He balled up his fists and strode toward Whitney, as the captor reached the top of the stairs.

Whitney looked and felt even more ill than he did a moment ago. He swayed on wobbly legs, slow to understand what he was looking at as Harry headed his way. His vision was blurry but the sight was unmistakably alarming. "What in God's na—" He gagged and dry heaved. His hands clutched at his ribcage as he spewed bloody puke all over the front of his clothes.

Harry hoped it hurt; hoped it burned his insides on the way up. He stepped toward Whitney with his fist raised.

"Christ—" Whitney squeaked out before doubling over. Dark, chunky blood flashed on the floor and spilled over the edge, dripping down to the first floor below.

Shiloh gasped. "Holy Lord!"

Whitney's vision went hazy. The room appeared to be filled with fog.

Harry didn't need to throw his punch. His fist was left clenched in the air as Whitney tipped over backwards and tumbled down the staircase.

He rolled end over end, his legs busting through the rickety bannister as he twisted like a ragdoll. His momentum stopped on a dime when the back of his head cracked with a BANG against the floor at the base of the stairs.

Shiloh held a hand over her mouth. She was trembling as she inched over to the top step beside Harry and peered down.

A shaft of wood from the banister was embedded in Whitney's thigh, and one of his arms was broken with the bone piercing through his nightshirt sleeve. The break was in the same spot as Andy's injury.

A pool of blood grew slowly outward from Whitney's head. His eyes stared up at the ceiling, unblinking.

"Is he- What happened?" Shiloh was shocked, confused, and afraid.

Harry didn't answer. He took her hand in his and led her downstairs. They stepped over Whitney's motionless body.

Shiloh pulled away from Harry. She was filled with panicked energy and couldn't stay still. She paced the kitchen with her hands tugging at her long locks of hair. "What Ah- What'a we do? What'a Ah do?"

"We gotta get out of here," Harry said. He gambled on using her real name. "You can come with us, Trixie, me and Andy."

"Ah- Wha- Ya mean like leave for good?"

Harry knelt down over Whitney and checked his pulse. If he felt a single heartbeat, he was ready to squeeze the life out of the bastard… but there was no life left to squeeze.

"Is- Is he dead?" Trixie asked.

Harry ignored her question. The answer wouldn't help the situation. "We've gotta get outta here, Trixie. Right now."

"Ah- But Ah—" Trixie felt as though she was treading on quicksand. He mind ran in a million directions at once. A sinking feeling in the pit of her stomach just kept growing and growing.

"Where's he keep his gun?" Harry blurted out the moment the idea came to him. He couldn't believe it wasn't the first thing he thought of after Whitney took his tumble.

"Upstairs, but—"

Harry started back up the stairs. He made it halfway.

"Wait! Ah ain't know the combo, mistah."

"Combo? Fuck." *Of course.* He returned down the stairs and moved for the front door. He grabbed hold of the doorknob and looked back at Trixie who was standing still and thinking hard with her hands to her head. She was shaking badly. "Trixie, we *need* to leave. Right this second."

"Ah- ah- ah cain't leave wit'out Lindsay! Ah mean Eve! Nah, Ah mean Lindsay!" It had been many months since she had spoken her sister's real name aloud.

"Okay, okay, okay. We'll get to her," Harry said, unsure of how or if he could hold himself to that claim. "We'll find Andy and we'll find her and then we'll get outta here. Okay?"

Trixie took her hands away from her head. She nodded frantically.

Harry twisted the doorknob and yanked. He left the stench of blood and puke and bodily evacuations behind as he ran into the fresh air of a cool Jonesborough night, pulling Trixie along with him.

Under Second Christ's Watchful Eye

Harry shut the door behind them. He wouldn't chance a left-open door leading to an investigation and a raising of alarms. So far, he didn't think anyone else knew what had gone down; it hadn't been loud enough to carry to the next home over, he hoped. He was grateful for the generous spacing between each building.

He knelt down in the soft grass and had a cautious look around. Trixie crouched behind him, looking wherever he looked. Crickets surrounded the village, firing their nocturnal chirps into the cool air with reckless abandon.

Harry searched the darkened horizon for the narrow trail through the forest they had taken to get to the village. It seemed the best—and perhaps only—path toward freedom. The odds of getting helplessly lost in the pitch-black woods while attempting any other escape route seemed insurmountable.

At first, he was having trouble locating the mouth of the trail, then he spotted the cluster of vehicles and remembered where they were parked in relation to the trail. The silhouettes of two men with rifles stood beside the vehicles.

They seemed to be on guard, if not at attention, near the mouth of the horseshoe-shaped village.

Harry took Trixie by the hand and repositioned them both around the corner of the home. With their backs to the wall, Harry peaked out at the silhouettes. "Trixie, who has keys to those trucks?"

"Um… Ah dun- Ah dunno."

"All right, uh…" Harry didn't let himself dwell on the idea. "Do you know which house Andy is in?"

Trixie shook her head.

"Which house is, um…" *What's his name God damn it? Think, Harry, think!* "Uh, Hoyt! Which house is Hoyt's? Point it out to me."

Trixie's hand stuck out around the corner as she pointed to a home on the opposite side of the village.

Of course, it couldn't be next door, Harry thought to himself. They would have to cut through the center of the village, straight through the outdoor church, to reach Hoyt's house, or else spend the extra time skulking the long way around the perimeter of the village. Harry desperately didn't want to spend any more time out in the open than necessary and, having spotted two night-watchmen already, Harry was fearful of additional men patrolling the village. *Fuck it.*

Harry took off in a low crouch-run across the middle of the horseshoe-shaped village. Trixie sputtered, then followed behind in a matching stance.

The torches lining the outdoor church were not lit. The darkness provided good cover, Harry hoped, though given how well he could see, he figured anyone whose eyes were also adjusted to the dark would at least detect his movement if not be able to identify him outright. Moon and starlight shone down on the clearing that served as the base of the village.

Harry passed the grand decider and made his way between two rows of pews. *Halfway there!* Harry was out of breath, more from the exhilaration and the fear than the exertion. He slowed to glance over his shoulder at Trixie. She was keeping up well enough but she had to lift the hem of her nightdress to avoid tripping over it.

As he returned his focus forward, Harry caught sight of light and movement up ahead. Without taking the time to process the image, he dropped straight to the ground behind the pew. The grass was worn away beneath him from the shuffling feet of the congregants. Harry twisted in the dirt and clawed at Trixie, bringing her to the ground too.

He laid his cheek flat against the earth and peered under the bottom of the pew toward what had caught his eye.

It was Earl, emerging from his home with a candle in a holder in one hand and his guitar in the other. He lowered into the chair beside his front door, set the candle on the ground at his feet, and began plucking away.

His chair faced the outdoor church. If Harry and Trixie were to rise or exit either end of the pew, they would be directly in Earl's field of vision. Harry did not trust the darkness to hide them.

Harry tilted his head and looked at Trixie, who was quivering on the ground behind him. *"Don't move,"* he whispered. *"We need to wait here a while."* He was grateful when Trixie didn't ask any questions and replied only with a small nod of her head.

Initials

Officers Faulkner and Lean trudged along the side of the road, flashlights in hand. Lean's focus was locked onto his beam of light as he waved it over the ground ahead of them. Faulkner had lost hope of finding anything at all. Bison seemed to have given up too, Faulkner thought. He was trotting along beside them rather than sniffing the dirt, rocks, and grass that lined the side of Old Cheney Road.

"If I ain't there when Janey wakes up, she's liable to think I'm cheatin' again," Faulkner said, trying to avoid saying the words 'let's call it a night,' for the eleventh time.

"Oh, speakin'a which..." Lean cleared his throat. He had been waiting for the right time to bring this up all day. He hated going back on plans. "I have to bow outta the BBQ this weekend."

"What? Why? Janey already put together her slaw and macaroni salad." If Lean didn't come, Faulkner would be stranded alone with Janey's book club friends.

"Blame Trisha. She switched up her work schedule without consultin' me, and now I have Todd on the weekends."

"So, bring him along! The more the merrier—"

"Wait, shut up."

"Excuse me?"

Something shined brightly in Lean's flashlight beam. "Look-a-that." He jogged the couple of feet between him and the metallic object, knelt to pick it up, then held it above his head to show Faulkner.

"A belt buckle. So what? That could be anyone's."

"Anyone with our missin' person's initials." Lean stood upright and flipped the belt buckle over to Faulkner.

H.W. was engraved into the silver belt buckle. Faulkner ran his thumb over the letters. *Fuck*, he thought. He had put their chances of actually finding something here at a big, fat goose egg.

Lean felt a rush of energy; the long hours had been eclipsed by this discovery. He felt as though he had just taken his first glug of coffee at the start of the day. He moved with short steps, methodically scanning the immediate area with his flashlight.

Faulkner's hopes for the search had been reinvigorated. He swept his light beam along the center of the road, then along the brush at the edge of the forest. He spotted something in the tall grass and stepped over to it. Holding the grass aside and poking around revealed only discarded trash. An empty chip bag, some beer bottles and cans, and a used condom or two, all incidental.

For the first time since nightfall, Faulkner considered the possibility that their missing persons might still be alive.

As Lean shuffled down the side of the road, dragging his boots through dirt and stones, the forest edge caught his attention. There was a gap in the trees, and the ground running between them was worn with parallel grooves. He sprinted to the gap—alarming Faulkner—and confirmed his suspicion: tire tracks. The gap was just barely wide enough for a vehicle to pass through.

Lean stood at the mouth of the trail and shined his flashlight straight down the center of the tunnel of trees. It was pitch black, and his beam could reach no terminus. As he moved the light to the side, the intervening trees cast inky creatures along the trail.

He lowered the beam to the ground below his feet. Faulkner joined at his side, and they both knelt down. The grooves of the tire tracks caught the light. Lean took his cellphone from his pocket and pulled up the photo of the tire tracks left behind in the muddy lot.

"These look like the same tracks to you, Faulkner?"

"I'd say so, God damn it." Faulkner thumbed his radio. "This is car King-Adam-One-One, requesting backup. We're following tire tracks down an unmarked trail about five miles from the east end of Old Cheney Road."

Thelma's voice from the dispatch office crackled back through the radio. "Copy that K-A-One-One."

Lean stepped eagerly down the dark trail. Faulkner jogged a step to catch up. It was too dark and too far to see the first kink in the tight, twisty trail.

The woods were abuzz with life. Hooting, squirming, chirping, chittering.

The officers felt surrounded long before they actually were.

The Creak of Stairs Unclimbed

E arl belted a yawn and rose from his chair. He picked the candle up and gave the burning wick a gentle blow.

Finally, Harry thought, still lying in the dirt between the church pews. He looked back at Trixie and mouthed, *almost*. He watched through the gap underneath the pew as Earl returned inside and shut the door.

Harry counted to ten in his head, then got up onto his knees. He peeked over the top of the pews and had a look around. There was no one else in sight. He gestured to Trixie, and she rose to her feet.

Staying crouched, the two quickly covered the remaining distance to Hoyt's house. He checked the name plaque above the door to be certain. *Hoyt — Cilicia* the plaque confirmed.

Harry reached for the doorknob. He twisted just enough to tell the door was locked without rattling it. He knew sound would travel further within the home and he couldn't know for sure if Hoyt and his wife were asleep.

He moved on to the window. With just a light push, it began to slide open. Harry stopped. He took Trixie by the hand and led her around to the side of the house where he hoped she would be hidden. He held up a single finger and whispered a barely audible, *"one minute."*

Trixie shook her head and wanted to plead with him not to be left alone but she held her tongue when he turned his back on her and went out of sight around the corner. She counted in Mississippis.

The window got stuck only halfway open, and Harry was afraid of forcing it the rest of the way and making noise. He held onto the sill and the frame and hauled himself up, squeezing his shoulders through the narrow opening.

He stretched his leg out past the end table parked beneath the window and stepped down to the saw-dusty floor. His eyes found the staircase in the dark, and he moved toward it on bent knees. He feared the steps would creak underfoot, so he eased his weight onto the bottom step as gently as possible. The home remained dead-silent.

The next step was less forgiving. A low, wooden moan eased out from under Harry's shoe. He froze and looked up toward the second floor like a child awaiting disciplinary parents.

He listened intently and heard nothing but crickets. Harry advanced one more step.

"Harry?"

Harry twisted on the staircase and looked toward the darkest corner of the combined living/dining room space where the voice had emanated from. Andy's voice.

He was seated in a chair with his wrists bound to the wooden arms, his face obscured by shadows, but his whispering voice unmistakable.

Harry bounded over to him, momentarily throwing caution to the wind as far as noise was concerned.

Andy leaned forward as Harry approached, his face dipping into the faint moonlight streaming in through the window.

The sight refreshed Harry's rage. Andy's face was bruised and swollen like a boxer's after a losing bout. His lips were both split and bleeding, and his nose appeared to be broken.

Harry went straight for the knots. He worked at them as best he could while whispering, "Those motherfuckers."

"Is this it?" Andy asked. "Are we finally getting out of here?" Andy feared he was dreaming.

"Yes," Harry said confidently. He got one wrist untied. "This is all my fault. I'm so sorry I brought you down here."

"Harry, no. It's not your fault at all. Oh, I missed you more than anything."

"I won't let them hurt you anymore," Harry said, feeling ashamed of how far he had let this go.

When the final knot was thwarted, Harry helped Andy to his feet. They embraced and shared a passionate kiss. Harry cared not about the blood, and Andy cared not about the pain in his split lips. They moved together for the window.

"That girl, Shiloh, she's coming with us." It would take too long to explain her double-name situation. "I told her we'd get her sister too but… but if that seems too dangerous, then we'll go without her."

Harry supported Andy and was about to help him through the window when his blood ran cold.

Outside, in the center of the village, the Grand Decider blasted four deafening horns.

A Flood of Teeth

"Fuck!" Harry exclaimed, though he was drowned out by the blaring horns of the Grand Decider.

The bedroom door upstairs swung open and banged against the wall.

Harry abandoned the half-opened window. He unlocked the front door and threw it open, shoving Andy outside ahead of him.

Hoyt hurried downstairs just in time to spot Harry slipping out the front door. The sight threw him, it was not at all what he was expecting to see. "Hey! Get back here!"

Trixie was pacing over a short area in front of the home with her hands to her head when Harry stepped outside. "Oh no," she shrieked with growing urgency. "Oh no, oh no, oh no!"

Lanterns and torches lit up all across the village. Doors swung open, and the followers of Second Christ poured out of their homes. At first, they moved toward the pews to await further instruction from Conrad, then the men closest to the chaos took notice of the fleeing outsiders. They spread word to those further away with angry shouts as they began to close in.

"Go, go!" Harry shouted, taking Andy's hand and running for the forest. They didn't have a chance in hell of reaching the trail with everyone out of their homes. Better to dash for the nearest trees and try to shake them in the darkness of the woods.

Trixie ran after them toward the outskirts of the village but she wasn't as fast. She tripped over the hem of her nightdress and nearly wound up flat on her face. She recovered her balance and held the bottom of her dress high up off the ground but, by then, she was lagging behind.

Harry glanced back over his shoulder as he ran. Hoyt was hot on their heels, with others gaining right behind him. When Harry returned his eyes to where he was going, he found Bo and Duke running straight at him, a flaming torch in Duke's hand leaving a hot trail behind it.

Yanking Andy by his uninjured arm, Harry ran wide around Bo and Duke, but Hoyt was closing in behind them, and now Judd was sprinting at them from their side. More and more of the flock rushed in from all directions.

Andy swore between panicked breaths. "Shi-bal, shi-bal, shi-bal." The language center of his brain defaulted to Korean curse words.

Duke reached out for Andy.

Harry clenched his fist and swung as hard as he could. He sent Duke reeling with a broken nose.

Andy flailed wildly against Bo, who had wrapped his arms around him and was trying to wrestle him to the ground.

Hoyt caught up to Trixie. He dove and tackled her off her feet. She screamed and twisted as he knelt on her arms and pinned her to the grass.

Harry charged at Bo as he wrestled Andy. He raised his fist but found himself unable to throw the punch. Judd's meaty hand gripped his wrist.

Bo grabbed tight onto the bulge in Andy's hurt arm, making him cry out in pain. With a twist of his body, Bo pulled Andy against his hip and took him off his feet, flinging him to the ground with a heavy thud.

Judd got Harry's arm under control and spun the outsider around to face him. While Harry turned one way, Judd threw a punch in the opposite direction. The impact was like a jackhammer to the jaw; a massive right hook that knocked Harry out on his feet.

Harry staggered a couple of dizzy steps as his eyes bounced around like pinballs. Teeth slid out of his mouth in bloody drool.

Judd reached out and took hold of Harry's shirt, keeping him off the ground when his knees finally buckled.

Bo knelt on Andy's head, mashing his face into the ground. Earl and Clayton ran over and got ahold of Andy's legs to put an end to his thrashing.

Judd lifted Harry into the air and slung the limp body over his shoulder.

"Fuckin' God damn fuckin' faggot!" Duke shrieked, blood gushing from his nose. He stomped up behind Judd and dropped a hammer-fist onto Harry's unconscious face, dislodging another tooth already loosened by Judd's fist.

The tooth dripped from Harry's mouth and stuck in a phlegmy glob to the back of Judd's shirt.

"Bring him to the stage," Judd told Bo. He carried the unconscious man toward the outdoor church, where Conrad and Second Christ would level their final judgment.

Carnality Steeped in Suffering

Harry regained consciousness to find himself on his knees atop the stage. The congregants were amidst the pews, all on their feet and calling for blood. He looked to his left and saw Andy on his knees and with a gun barrel pressed against his temple. That's when Harry realized a gun was held to his own head as well. Judd and Joseph had their fingers on the triggers. The hunters stood tall above the outsiders, facing their whooping brethren in the pews.

The tall double doors of the church swung open, and Conrad strode outside with Second Christ bundled up in his arms. He thundered across the dark grass.

Clayton had Trixie wrapped up in a headlock. She continued to scream and thrash, but her efforts were in vain.

The male congregants shouted over each other, competing for their personal hatred to be heard.

"Fuckin' kill 'em!"

"Shoot 'em!"

"Death to the sodomites!"

"End the fuckers! Crucifixion!"

"Kill the faggots!"

"Crucify! Crucify!"

The shouts continued, spiteful words fusing together in the cacophony of condemnation.

Joseph glanced at Judd and spoke softly. "Do we know how they got out anyway?" He scanned the faces of the crazed crowd. "Wait, where the fuck's Whitney?" He hadn't spotted him in the chaos.

Judd squinted over the congregation. "I don't know. He wouldn't miss this."

"He was hosting yours, wasn't he?" Joseph gestured with his gun barrel toward Harry before setting it back against the side of Andy's head.

Harry shut his eyes and held his breath. He ran his tongue along the fleshy divots his teeth had previously occupied. He couldn't tell how many he had lost. His entire mouth tasted of copper.

Judd looked down at Trixie. He knew he couldn't count on Harrison for a straight answer, but Shiloh, on the other hand… "Where's Whitney, Shiloh?"

Clayton twisted her so she faced Judd. She hesitated.

"Answer him, Shiloh!" Joseph barked. "Did these faggots get the drop on him?!"

"What the fuck happened, Shiloh?!" Clayton shouted in her ear.

Trixie wet herself. "Ah- Ah- No!" She shrieked. "He were- He- No, he…." Blubbering overtook any discernable speech.

Joseph was getting worried now. "Somebody go check on— Oh…" He stopped himself and lowered his gaze to the planks of the stage beneath his feet in a show of respect for Conrad, as the Father began to ascend the steps.

A tense hush fell over the crowd of congregants in the pews. The only sounds came from Trixie as she continued to cry and struggle weakly against Clayton's grip.

Clayton slid his arm up Trixie's body until her throat was in the crook of his arm. He tightened his grip and choked off her voice.

Trixie's sister watched from the pews beside her eighty-five-year-old husband, Sardus. Eve bounced anxiously, sweating, fighting the urge to do something. But what could she do? She averted her eyes and toed the line.

Conrad was slow in crossing the stage. He took up a position between the two lost lambs and looked out at his congregation in silence.

Harry and Andy quivered at the ends of gun barrels. They each looked into the other's teary eyes and said, "*I love you.*"

Conrad cleared his throat. "Second Christ has made his judgement."

Hoyt blurted out, "Crucifixion!"

Duke joined in the outburst, "Death to the fags!"

Conrad shook his head slowly. "I hear your pain and I understand." He let a moment's silence cleanse the air. He knew his next remark would not be easily swallowed. "But these lambs are not beyond hope."

"*What?!*" Sardus exclaimed. "Bullshit!"

Hoyt overlapped him, "Are you fuckin' serious?!"

Conrad extended his hands in a gentle gesture. "Second Christ is offering them one final chance at redemption. A trial by which to--"

"Un-fuckin'-believable!" Sardus continued.

"They're devils in our midst! The Grand Decider said so!" Walt shouted.

Conrad had enough. He would not be disrespected this way. He lifted his leg and stomped his foot down with his full weight. The entire stage shook. Splinters and dust fell to the grass below.

"*You dare question Second Christ?!*"

His voice boomed, sending the congregation into pin-drop silence. Conrad's eyes drilled into Walt, forcing his gaze down to the grass.

Walt wished he could rewind time just a few seconds and hold his tongue. His veins coursed with hot shame. With his eyes shut and his hands clasped, Walt spoke. "I'm sorry, Father Conrad. Second Christ, forgive me, please."

Conrad took his eyes off of Walt and looked over the other silent faces, moving from man to man at a deliberate rhythm. "Straight from Second Christ's lips, I bring you gospel. We preach faith before violence. We preach growth over destruction. We preach sanctification over condemnation." He let his words hang in the air and gave his followers a moment to reflect. "We shall give these corrupted sinners one final chance for true repentance."

"Amen!" Cappie shouted. A couple of dirty looks came his way, but he did not care. Nods of approval came from others; mostly from the women, who knew Conrad's words of mercy did not apply to their gender.

"The method of transfiguration has been clear from the outset," Conrad declared, "but a quandary exists." He swept his arms over the congregation. "There exists no woman amongst our flock who stands unbetrothed. After much deliberation, and with time an ever-pressin' factor, Second Christ deemed an exception from carnal law permissible."

Murmurs rippled through the crowd as understanding set in.

Conrad spoke softly. Each congregant hung on his every word. "An act of selfless charity need be made for the greater good." He did not know how his followers would respond to his request. "I shall need two volunteers." He looked expectantly to the crowd as a whole, settling his gaze upon no individual.

Walt bolted upright, seeing an opportunity to redeem himself for his earlier gaffe. "Marabella volunteers!" He bowed his head. "Please accept this sacrifice as my penitence, oh great Second Christ."

Marabella, whose bleeding had arrived only the year prior, felt a flash of worry. Her face was already swollen with fresh bruises and welts, she wasn't ready for another trip to the round building.

Sardus, following Walt's lead, rose to his feet and bowed his head. "Eve volunteers as well, Father Conrad. Please forgive my outburst."

Eve failed to hide her surprise and discomfort. She tried to hold out hope. Surely Father Conrad or Mother Mabel would intervene. They wouldn't let her be the one sent to the round building twice in a row. It would break tradition.

But not so.

"Thank you, Walt. Thank you, Sardus. Your generosity shall not be forgotten."

Eve felt her husband's wrinkly hands on her shoulders, shoving her along the pew. One row back, Marabella was receiving the same treatment from Walt.

"Who shall go first, Second Christ?" Conrad reached his hand into the bundle held by Mabel.

Harry couldn't help but glance over at the sound of a baby's cry coming from within the bundle. It was the first sound he had heard come from the being. There had been no crying during the shouting, nor Conrad's stomping and shaking of the stage… but now there was. It was a short cry; over as soon as it began. Harry had doubted any creature lived within that bundle until that very moment.

Conrad gestured down at the chosen wife. "Marabella, escort this lamb to his trial."

Harry felt Conrad's big hand grab hold of the back of his collar. Conrad brought him to his feet and shoved him toward the stage steps. Harry felt lost. He had a guess as to what was expected of him but he hoped he was wrong.

Marabella stepped rigidly toward Harry. She hesitated and found Walt's fist shaking in front of her face.

"Don't you dare shame yourself in front of the whole

flock!"

She cowered and nodded repeatedly. Marabella hurried over to Harry and took him by the hand. She led him over to the round building where they were met by Conrad, with the key in his hand.

Conrad unlocked the door and ushered them inside, Marabella first. "Last chance, lamb. Don't waste it." He slapped a meaty hand down on Harry's shoulder, pausing him in the doorway. "Second Christ's genesis lays the patterning for all coition. The carnality must be steeped in suffering."

Harry had no clue what Conrad was saying to him. He was unbearably anxious and sweating profusely. He began to stammer out a response.

Conrad smiled. He spoke plainly, "She ain't allowed to enjoy it, so make sure it hurts." And with that, Conrad shoved him the rest of the way into the round building and locked the door behind him.

In the Round Building

Marabella moved deeper into the round building. She hoped to get this over with as quickly as possible. She approached the low, soft platform that occupied the precise center of the building's one large room. She climbed atop it. The cushioned material squelched beneath her knees as she sunk into the plush material. It was still wet with the sordid and assorted fluids from Sardus and Eve's recent visit.

Harry struggled to process the images his eyes transmitted to his brain. He looked around in utter bafflement. Every last inch of the rounded perimeter was lined with whips, paddles, blades, ropes, needles, harnesses, and other pain-bringing toys and tools of the BDSM trade. Some of the implements were familiar to Harry and would be to Andy as well. Despite their familiarity, they seemed alien and barbaric now that any pretense of consent had been stripped away. Harry repeated Conrad's elusive words in his head, *Second Christ's patterning lays the genesis for all coition...*

Dried blood of varying ages and shades transformed the

wooden floor into a mandala worthy of monastic appreciation and impermanence. Clumps of hair of all colors littered the floor. If a blacklight were swept over the room, it would explode out of sheer excitement.

"What the fuck?" Harry muttered aloud as he stepped deeper into the round room toward Marabella.

Marabella filled her hands with the hem of her dress and lifted it up and off over her head. Her entire body was bound with black, hemp rope tied in intricate knots into a tight harness.

The rigid movements of the village's women finally made sense to Harry. The ropes were bound the tightest around Marabella's joints, strangling any bend or large movement. Circulation was cut off to various parts of her body. Her breasts, her forearms, bulges of flesh: all distended and discolored red and purple.

Harry staggered toward her, absently, feeling sick to his stomach. *She's just a teenager*, he thought as he studied her distorted body in horror. Beneath the hempen harness, there was not an inch of skin free from bruising or scarring. Her skin was bumpy and textured like rice paper. Marabella's body was a manifesto of pain written in braille.

"I- What? I- I-" Harry stuttered, lost for words as well as coherent thoughts. His senses were wholly overwhelmed. The heavy, stale air within the round room burned his nasal passages.

Marabella gestured urgently to the wall of implements. She needed Harrison to do what was demanded of them both, or else her punishment would be quantifiably worse.

He looked where she gestured but stood immobile. When he looked from the hanging toys and tools back to her, she nodded desperately. Harry shut his eyes. He could hear the muffled voices of Conrad and the congregants praying outside. He had come too far to draw the line anywhere short of freedom. Feeling disgusted with himself, Harry approached the wall on autopilot. He reached up and pulled a tool off the rounded wall at random: a leather tawse.

Marabella was grateful for the impending pain. She knew it couldn't be easy for him, and she had learned to bear worse. She sat on her heels, awaiting punishment, bracing herself.

Harry stood at the base of the platform. He knew what was being asked of him now and he knew that for his sake and Andy's, he would have to deliver. He lifted the thick tool above his head but couldn't bring himself to swing. The tawse trembled in his grip. He had a promise to keep. A promise to Andy.

"I… I need to. I have to do it. I'm sorry." He turned his head away as he swung the tawse. Marabella shrieked, and Harry felt like he was going to vomit. If his stomach were less empty, he might have. He looked back. The split leather thong had left two parallel lines of red across her shoulder, but her eyes were urging him for more.

Marabella knew the wounds would have to be severe for Conrad and the others to be satisfied. They would check her over thoroughly to make sure the act wasn't faked, inside and out.

"I'm so sorry," Harry said. He tried to imagine it was Conrad or Hoyt or Clayton he was striking, but Marabella's innocence was inescapable.

The tawse came down a second time, then a third. The third strike broke skin. Marabella shrieked, projecting her voice to ensure those outside the round building could hear. She bled onto the soft pedestal as she reached out for Harry's waist to pull him closer. She unbuttoned his pants and grabbed hold of the zipper.

Harry struck her again with the tawse, his eyes full of tears. He tried to apologize again, but no words came, only sad, breathy noises halfway between speech and sobs.

Marabella reeled from the smack with a yell, nearly

falling off the pedestal. Regaining her balance, she returned forward and finished unzipping his pants. She knew this could not end until she had gathered his seed. Conrad would accept nothing less.

She slid her hand through the flap of his boxer-briefs.

It's for Andy. It's for Andy, Harry kept telling himself as he did what Conrad wanted.

For the first time in the round building, both parties were miserable during the act of coition.

All-Consuming Darkness

Lean and Faulkner both held their flashlight beams steady to the ground directly in front of them as they moved. It had proven easier to follow the tire tracks than the trail itself. With how narrow and twisty the path was, it would be easy to wander off it and into the thick of the woods in the impenetrable darkness.

Bison seemed on edge to Faulkner, but he was aware he might have been projecting his own frayed nerves. The dog dutifully sniffed along the tire treads but had picked up no trackable scent thus far.

"Where ya think this goes?" Faulkner asked.

"With any luck, directly to our missin' persons."

"Yeah but… whatta ya think's at the end'a this trail? Place-wise I'm talkin'."

"How should I know?"

"I don't know." Faulkner trudged in silence for a moment. "Just ain't ever worked a case quite like this before," he muttered softly.

"You sound nervous, Faulkner," Lean said with a hint of judgment behind his words, or maybe he was teasing in a manner intended as playful.

"So, what if I am? Stumblin' around in the dark, headed God-knows-where into God-knows-what."

"We can't afford to be nervous. Leave that to the two we're tryin'a save and the people we're tryin'a save 'em from."

"Oh, can it with the Goody Two-Shoes act, Lean, will ya?"

Lean did not reply. The officers walked side-by-side in silence for a moment.

After several breaths, Faulkner sighed. "Sorry."

"Blame it on the nerves," Lean quickly added.

The ends of their flashlight beams shone upon rusted chain-link fencing. The sight gave Lean a tiny explosion of eager energy while it clamped down further on Faulkner's nerves.

Lean raised his beam along the fencing until the light landed on a metal placard bolted in place. The letters *H, A,* and *Z* were printed in faded paint. A patch of rust had overtaken the intervening letters between the *Z* and the *ICALS* on the other side.

Bison whined and pawed at the dirt at the base of the fence.

Lean lowered his beam back down to the ground. The tire tracks clearly continued straight through the fence. He grabbed hold of the chain-link and pulled. The fence rattled without giving way. He moved further down the fence, found the loose spot where the fence was cut, and began tugging it aside. "Li'l help?"

Faulkner grabbed hold of the fence and helped his partner clear the path. The continuing trail past the fence seemed impossibly dark to Faulkner, if it were even scientifically possible to be darker than what they had already traversed. He thought about asking Lean to wait here for backup to arrive but knew the proposition would be shot down with moral grandstanding about precious moments being wasted. He carried out the whole argument in his head and knew Lean, the Goddamn boy scout, would be the victor in the end. With the sensation of lead weights filling up his lower intestines, Faulkner stepped into the all-consuming darkness.

Transfiguration

ndy was shocked. For the first time, he was shocked not by the zealots holding him captive, but by his own husband. If what he heard while knelt atop the stage was to be believed—if the screams of pain from within the round building were truly caused by Harry—then he was not the man Andy believed him to be. He didn't want to believe. He didn't want to think his husband capable of inflicting such pain on an innocent.

Conrad held his wide stance in the doorway of the round building, cradling Second Christ with one arm, murmuring a prayer of salvation and transfiguration. Shouts of pain continued to fly from the building at irregular intervals. The rest of the congregation recited their standard prayer of fertility, all except for Walt who couldn't bring himself to pray for the outsider's seed to impregnate his wife before his own. He formed his mouth into the shapes of prayer words without producing any sound.

Eventually, the screaming stopped, and so did the prayers.

Andy felt horrified and heartbroken as Conrad stepped aside, and the door swung open to reveal his husband. Harry staggered out of the round building, buttoning up his pants, looking pale and nauseous. He was drenched in sweat and shame in equal measure.

Oh, Harry, no, Andy thought with crushing disappointment and heartache.

Conrad peered in through the doorway at Marabella laying atop the pedestal; bleeding, nude, used. He smiled. "Walt," he said. "Check on your woman."

Walt couldn't bring himself to look at Harry. He felt a different kind of hatred for the man now, one tinged with a peculiar type of envy. He entered the round building and quickly crossed the floor to Marabella, who had adopted the traditional post-procreative position on her back with her knees pulled against her chest.

Conrad wrapped an arm around Harry's shoulders, dwarfing him like a bear would its cub. "Do you feel the salvation? Can you feel Second Christ's love surging through your veins?"

Harry feebly nodded. He realized he needed to really sell it or all this torment would be for naught. He pulled himself together and nodded again, this time with conviction. Harry did feel different, deep in the core of his being. Oh, what had they turned him into? He had crossed a line he could never uncross.

Conrad smiled and let out a short, giddy laugh. "Ah, I can see it in you. Do not worry. The fatigue you're feeling is only natural. A transfiguration as bold as yours is sure to *take it out of one,* so to speak." He rested his forehead against Harry's. "I am proud of you, young Harrison." He turned to the congregation and proclaimed, "We have a success!" He clapped his meaty hands, setting off a ripple of compulsory applause through the congregation.

All followers of Second Christ joined in the applause, save for Walt, who pretended to be busy checking over Marabella, and Joseph, who still had his gun to Andy's head.

Conrad put an end to his clapping and waited for the others to follow suit. "Send forth the other lamb. And pray for a two-fold recovery from sinful continuance."

Andy was ushered down the stage steps.

Sardus shoved Eve toward the outsider. She stumbled and fell but quickly righted herself. She took Andy's hand as he passed from the final wooden step onto the earth. His hand was limp in hers.

Andy watched Marabella exit the round building, limping, bloodied. He looked at Harry in disbelief, his mouth hung agape. "Harry… how could you?"

Harry's heart stung. He wanted to explain—to explain that he did what he did for love. He did it for Andy. He wanted desperately to explain that it was the only way to live through this… but he couldn't let his façade falter in front of the others now that they believed him to be converted or transfigured or whatever the hell they believed him to be. He didn't know if explaining it would have made Andy feel any differently anyway. "You have to do what they want, Andy. It's the only way." He eyed Conrad, who was watching over them closely. "It's the only path to salvation."

"I'm not— I—" Andy's shock overpowered speech.

"Just do it! For God's sake, Andy, please!" Harry pleaded as Andy was brought to the round building. "For Second Christ's sake," he added.

Andy did not reply. The wounded expression remained on his face as he was pulled away, searing itself into Harry's battered mind.

Judd stepped up to Harry, getting between him and Andy. "I had faith in your conversion all along," he said jovially. "Welcome to the righteous path." He reached out for a handshake.

Harry had to fight to hide his disgust. He looked Judd square in the eye and shook his hand with confidence whilst wishing he could rip the hand off and force it down his throat.

Conrad returned to his stance in the round building's doorway after shepherding Eve and Andy inside.

***

The numb sensation drained from Andy as he laid eyes on the rounded wall of implements. "What the hell is all this?" he muttered to himself in Korean.

Eve hurried over to the central pedestal, climbed atop it, and yanked her dress off as quick as she could. With both arms, she beckoned him forward.

He moved towards her, absently. "I, uh— What is—"

Eve reached out for his zipper.

"Uh, no, wait—" He pushed her hands away. "Wait, stop."

She looked up at him in dismay, her eyes full of terror. Eve nodded feverishly and reached for his zipper again.

Andy pushed her away and backed up. "This— This is insane."

Eve got off the cushioned platform. She ran to the wall and pulled a slender blade off of it.

Andy yelped and stumbled backwards into the wall as she ran at him with the knife. A flogger and a buckled arm splint fell to the floor with a clatter.

Eve forced the knife into his grip. With both hands on his wrist, she guided his hand to her stomach and pressed the tip of the blade down into her navel hard enough to let a trickle of blood escape.

"No," Andy said firmly. He released the knife, letting it fall to the floor. "I can't— I— I can't do this. I won't do it."

Eve grabbed onto Andy's collar and pulled him in close. She needed him to do this. She needed him to know what would happen to her if he didn't. She opened her mouth and tried to explain. The sounds that came from her mouth sounded more like the panicked grunts of a rabid animal than a human being's attempt at speech.

There was no tongue in her mouth.

"Reeaaoouuu!"

Andy shrieked, "What are you do—"

"Eeaaee!"

"Fuck! Get— Stop!" He tried to push her away, but she clung to him.

"Rouuu aaavv ooooh!"

She smacked herself across the face, hard, then she motioned for Andy to do the same. When he didn't, she balled up her fist and punched herself in the eye as hard as she could.

"Fucking hell!" He moved for the door, but Eve grabbed back onto him and made him face her.

"*Ooouu eeeeiiih!*"

He shoved her again, with more force this time. She stumbled back, losing her balance as she tripped over the buckled arm splint on the floor. Andy ran for the door and ripped it open.

Conrad was there waiting for him. His meaty hands grabbed hold of Andy's hair and dragged him off his feet. He was done giving extra chances.

Crucifixion

"Andy, no!" Harry screamed. He tried to run to Andy, but Judd effortlessly threw him to the ground, flat on his back.

Judd knelt on Harry's chest at the base of the stage and stuck a finger in his face. "Don't throw away your salvation."

Conrad dragged Andy by his hair toward the wooden steps. Mabel stood atop the stage, rocking Second Christ back and forth in her arms.

Andy kicked and screamed and squirmed as Conrad dragged him onto the stage, banging against each step on the way up.

"Kill him!" Earl shouted. "Kill the degenerate!"

At the same time, Hoyt yelled, "Crucify! Crucifixion!"

"Kill them both!" Bo screamed, competing to be heard.

"Death to the devils!" Duke added to the vocal fray.

Conrad slammed Andy down in the center of the stage. He pressed his foot against the outsider's chest.

Joseph hurried over and pressed his rifle barrel to Andy's cheek.

Mabel brought Second Christ over to Conrad.

"Level your judgment, Son!" Conrad knelt down and cupped Andy's entire head in his hand. With his other hand, he reached into the bundle in Mabel's arms.

A loud, layered cry came from within the gilded shroud.

Conrad listened and nodded with understanding. He returned to his feet and faced his followers.

The congregation leaned forward in silent anticipation.

After a moment's pause, Conrad declared, "Crucifixion!"

The congregation erupted into raucous applause.

Harry twisted furiously under Judd's weight. "No! No, stop! You fuckers! You evil mother fuckers!"

Conrad gestured delicately to Joseph, then to Andy with a flutter of his pillowy hand. Joseph slung his rifle over his shoulder, lifted Andy, and flipped him over onto his stomach.

Andy's head overhung the edge of the stage. He looked down at Harry directly below him in the grass. Tears began to stream down his face. "Harry!" He wailed hopelessly. He knew his time was coming to an end. Andy wished the appropriate final words to his husband would spring to mind, but his senses were overwhelmed and his lungs struggled to draw in the breath needed for speech. His sobs were deep and debilitating.

"Judd, fetch the cross, boy," Conrad ordered. "Bo, bring me nails. The big'uns."

Duke and Hoyt took Judd's place over Harry as he left for the workshop. Harry tried to slip free in the exchange but it was no use. In an instant, they were knelt atop his limbs with their full bodyweights, pinning him to the grass. If only he were stronger. If only he hadn't brought Andy into the woods. If only. If only.

As Judd and Bo entered the workshop, Second Christ

began to wail in his bundle in Mabel's arms.

Conrad brought his ear in close. "What's that now?... Garlic?" He listened a while longer until the crying stopped. "Ah, I see." He nodded with understanding, then withdrew a hooked gutting blade from his robes.

Andy's tears fell like raindrops upon Harry's face below him. "You're gonna be okay, Andy!" Harry shouted. "I'll save you! You'll be okay!" he announced, dropping the transfigured façade. He couldn't keep it up any longer. It was obvious to everyone. All bets were off.

"I love you, Harry!" Andy declared. He could feel it in his bones, that he didn't have much longer to live. He could practically count the seconds ticking down. He couldn't expire with a rift between him and his love, however slight and sudden.

"I'll fix it! I swear to God, I'll make it right!" Harry fought with all his might but couldn't get his limbs free from under the knees of Duke and Hoyt. Maybe if he weren't so drained from the debauchery in the round building, maybe if he weren't so sleep deprived, or so undernourished, maybe if he had exercised more often before ever coming on this trip; his brain sparked with *what-ifs* and *could-have-beens*. Andy's face above contorted as a scream was forced out of him. "Andy!" Harry wailed without purpose.

Conrad was on both knees behind Andy, dragging long, vertical slits down the backs of both of Andy's calves with his hooked knife. Conrad paused, blade in flesh, and looked back toward the bundle as Second Christ continued to wail. He nodded with conviction. "Yes, Second Christ. Thy will be done."

He grunted as he got back on his feet. Conrad stepped over Andy and reached down into one of the stage-top cornucopias. He pulled from it a clove of garlic and ripped it to pieces.

Conrad knelt back down behind Andy. He peeled apart

the flesh of Andy's calves and shoved the pieces of garlic inside.

From down on the ground, Harry didn't know what was happening but he could see just how much pain was being inflicted on the love of his life. Andy screamed and cried at the top of his lungs, matched only in energy by the joyous cheers of the male members of the congregation.

Judd ascended the stage with the ten-foot cross balanced over his shoulder. He laid it down beside Andy, then he and Joseph forced him onto it. They stretched his arms out wide as he wriggled weakly. Judd ripped the splint off of Andy's arm so that it would lay flat against the wood.

Bo hurried up the steps and brought Conrad a wooden mallet and a basket of thick, iron nails. Conrad listened to Second Christ's cries and brought a hand to his wife's cheek. "Mabel, our son is tired. Bring him to rest."

Mabel gave a downward tilt of her head, the broad smile still plastered on her face. She descended from the stage and made her way toward the church, rocking Second Christ back and forth the whole way.

On his back atop the cross, looking up into the dark sky, Andy could no longer see Harry, but he could feel his husband's presence beneath him and could still hear Harry's furious exertions as he continuously struggled to break free. Andy stared up at the stars and tried to drown out the shouting voices all around him, tried to block out the searing pain in his legs and in his arm. He again attempted to compose a goodbye to Harry in his final moments of life. He began, "Har—" but got no further as the sounds of his own screaming overpowered all else.

Conrad struck the nail for a second time, then a third, driving the iron nail through Andy's wrist joint into the wooden cross.

"Andy!" Harry screamed from the grass.

Conrad pulled a second nail from the basket, then handed

the rest back to Bo, who bowed his head and set about returning them to the workshop. Conrad rested the tip of the nail between the two tendons of Andy's arm, stretched tight. He brought the mallet down hard on the head of the nail.

Tears and spit and snot leaked out of Andy. "Please, please, please…" he could manage just the single word. His faculties were no longer his.

From the ground, Harry watched the cross rise into the air.

Judd hauled the cross upright and slotted it into the square opening in the center of the stage.

Fresh blood fell upon old blood. Andy's bodyweight hung entirely by his wrists. His legs thrashed, and his feet searched for purchase where there was none, two-and-a-half feet above the surface of the stage. Skin tore, and his body sagged lower until the nail nestled against the bones making up his joints and hung sturdy.

Harry roared, "You fuckers! You Goddamn mother fuckers!"

A new voice came from behind them all. "Freeze! Hands in the air!"

Rescue

Conrad stopped, bloody knife in hand. He turned atop the stage and came to face Officers Lean and Faulkner, standing beyond the pews.

Both officers had their pistols drawn. Faulkner had Bison's leash wound twice around one hand while wielding his handgun in the grip of his other. The gun rattled in his hand. Bison growled viciously and tugged taut against his leash.

Slowly, the congregants all turned to face the officers, who drew closer to the outdoor church at a creeping pace.

Faulkner stared in horror up at the cross mounted on the stage and the weeping man nailed to it. "What in the fuck is goin' on here?!" He asked the universe rather than any individual.

"Don't move!" Lean shouted at two congregants who had begun circumventing the pews. "I said freeze!" he shouted at two others. But they kept moving, slowly, more of them now, too many to aim at all at once.

The officers swept their guns back and forth over the flock, doing all they could to hold them back and slow their approach. Backup was already on the way. They had radioed from the mouth of the trail, so they should arrive any moment, or at least, that's what the officers hoped. A voice came from down on the ground.

"Help! Help us! Oh, thank God!"

Only then did Officer Lean notice the bloodied man under the knees of Duke and Hoyt. *Harrison Winters*, Lean thought. He was in rough shape, but Lean felt certain it must be one of the men they were after.

Andy could not manage any words; the pain was too great.

Harry was elated. The first good thing to happen in days was finally arriving. He laid his head back in the grass and watched the approaching officers upside down. "Yes, yes, yes, thank you! We're saved!" He craned his neck to look up at Andy past the edge of the stage. "Andy, it's over! We're saved!" he joyously proclaimed.

He laid his head back in the grass and watched, upside down, as a third figure approached the officers from behind the pews. It was Bo, returning from the workshop with his shotgun at the ready.

He strode up behind the officers, moving silently across the grass.

"Hey, wait, wait, look out!"

Before Faulkner could turn to look, Bo blew his head off with a shotgun blast.

"*NOOOOO!*" Harry screamed in utter devastation.

Bone and brain slapped and stuck to the side of Lean's face.

Bison barked and leaped at Bo, but his leash went taut—still wrapped around Faulkner's hand—and jerked him back down to the ground. The dog snapped at the air.

Joseph aimed his rifle from atop the stage and drilled a hole through the sniffer dog's chest. Bison flopped onto his back, legs kicking, whimpering weakly.

Lean pivoted on his heels and swung his aim toward Bo—

But Bo fired first, shredding Lean's uniform with hot buckshot.

Lean's body spasmed, and his pistol fired into the sky as he felt the ground rush up and slam against his back.

"*God damn it!*" Harry wailed. "*No, no, no!*"

Bo racked his shotgun and strode over to the officer.

Lean brought a trembling, bloody hand to the radio mounted on his shoulder and thumbed the talk button. His voice came out ragged. "Officer down. Off—"

Bo squeezed his shotgun's trigger, blowing both the radio and Officer Lean's head to bits. Shards of plastic and wires intermingled in the grass with chunks of skin and teeth.

The decay of the gunshot was slow above the holler. Bison's whimpering was getting on Bo's nerves, so he walked over to the dog and brought the heel of his boot down on the animal's skull.

Some of the followers of Second Christ fell silent, others began pacing, and others still entered into full-blown panic.

"This is not fucking good!" Walt declared.

"We can't kill police," Sardus said, as if it were a line they had all agreed never to cross.

Cappie and Earl shouted at the same time: "This is too far!" and "We're so fucked!"

"Enough!" Conrad said loudly but not angrily. He waved a hand over the congregation, and they fell into attention. They were in need of leadership. Conrad took a moment to think and to collect himself. He spoke in a calm, confident tone. "Now is not the time for panic. Now is the time for preparation." He had a slow look around, gauging the faces of each of his followers. He shut his eyes and nodded, knowing that what was about to come would result in more hardship and bloodshed than his followers had ever experienced as a community nor as individuals. "With Second Christ's protection, we will get through this, but it will be a trying time. A test of our faith and of our resolve." The followers of Second Christ needed to prepare for battle. Conrad had witnessed firsthand how police respond to the slaying of their own.

When he was a young man attending his first year of college, he had watched from his fourth-floor window in the UT dormitory as the entirety of the Knoxville police force flooded the low-income housing block four streets over. He repurposed his star-gazing telescope to watch the streets as police went door to door, dragging random people out of their homes, beating them, handcuffing and zip-tying them, throwing them into paddy wagons or gunning them down and leaving them to bleed out in the gutters. It was a week later when he learned that a vice detective had been stabbed by a black man in a drug bust, and the rest of the police force accused every black person in the city of harboring the fugitive. Turned out, he had crossed state lines the night of the stabbing. Thirteen people were murdered by the police in the aftermath, and another forty-five were injured to the point of hospitalization.

"Earl, Cappie, get those bodies gone," Conrad ordered calmly. "Duke, get Harrison tucked away until our land is secured."

"We should crucify him too!" Duke shouted up at Conrad. "You heard the way he—"

"Do not question me!" Conrad's voice boomed, compelling Duke into reflective silence. "Time is of the essence. He will be dealt with at the appropriate moment. Must I bestow your duty upon another?"

"No!" Duke blurted. "No, Father Conrad. You can count on me." Duke pulled the knife from the sheath on his belt and brought it to Harry's throat. With Hoyt's help, he hauled Harry to his feet, got behind him, and hooked an arm under his armpit to grip the back of his neck and hold him in a docile position. He held the knife against Harry's throat and pulled him backwards towards his home.

"The rest of you," Conrad said, "take up your arms. We're sure to have more foes inbound. Prepare to defend our homeland. These will not be police officers storming into our holler. They will be enemies of Second Christ. Devils in disguise. Do not hesitate in proving your devotion."

The outsider wrenched around in Duke's grip as the twosome staggered away from the others in tandem. The knife cut into Harry's neck as he struggled. The wound was shallow. Blood trickled down the blade and along Duke's hand.

Harry stopped struggling and let Duke drag him as he watched Conrad turn his attention to Andy. *No, no, no*, he thought over and over again, *it can't happen. It can't happen. Not after all this. It can't happen. It can't.*

He watched from the distance as Conrad brought his hooked knife to Andy's jugular…

And dragged the blade across his throat.

Part III

The Stench of Festering Death

Harry went limp in Duke's grip. His legs dropped out from underneath him. His wide eyes shimmered with tears, and his mouth hung agape.

A waterfall of red gushed from Andy's throat. The newlywed choked and gargled, trying desperately to draw breath through a windpipe split in two. The life drained from his eyes as his torso was saturated in blood. His final thought was of the look of disgust he had shown Harry for doing what he believed had to be done. The colors of the world before his eyes muted like a bleach-bypass photograph. In an instant, there was no color at all. Seung-jeong Oh saw nothing but darkness, heard nothing but silence, and felt nothing but pain for a half-dozen heartbeats. Then, the pain finally stopped, and so did the beating.

Conrad needed him out of the picture in the gunfight that he knew was on the horizon. No distractions. No risks. He wiped most of the blood from his blade onto Andy's leg, then turned and dispassionately descended the stage steps.

He made for the church. All around him, his followers

prepared. They armed themselves with guns and ammunition. Husbands tucked their wives away in their homes. Doors were locked and windows were blocked with bookcases.

Conrad opened one of the church's two tall doors and stepped only a foot beyond the threshold. He called to Mabel at the far end of the holy building, "Mabel, stay with our son and do not leave the church, no matter what happens."

Mabel bowed and did not look up from the floor until Conrad had left the building and pulled the door shut behind him.

It was clear that something bad had happened to Whitney for the outsiders to escape, and Judd intended to find out precisely what before the holler was flooded with adversaries. The best he could hope for was to find his fellow congregant unconscious or tied up. Judd marched across the center of the village toward Whitney's home with his rifle in tow.

He pulled open the front door and caught a glimpse of Whitney, dead on the floor, and of the flies circling his body. Judd averted his eyes with a sickened groan. He stepped inside the home and pulled his shirt collar up over his nose to combat the awful stench of festering death.

Judd's wishful thinking had been dashed. He hadn't thought Harrison had it in him to kill. Judd stared down at the blood puddle, at Whitney's broken arm, at his dead eyes staring up at the ceiling.

He felt a pang of regret, followed by one of guilt. He never got the chance to clear the air with Whitney, especially after their scuffle in the truck but also for all the other times before. It was obvious to everyone in the village that there was animosity between them, and it had been growing for a while. Judd would have to live with that bad blood going unanswered on his conscience but so too would he have to live with the responsibility of playing a hand in his death. If Whitney had it his way, the outsiders would have been shot dead right where they were found in that clearing. The outsiders never would have stepped foot in their holler.

Oh God, Judd thought. "Second Christ, forgive me," he said aloud, realizing that everything that had happened and was about to happen was his fault. Those police never would have come to the holler if not for his attempt to save the souls of the men he had come upon in the clearing. The war that was about to be waged could have been avoided entirely if not for his actions. All of the blood that was about to be spilled was on his hands, and he hated himself for it.

"No," he told himself. It was not his burden to carry. At least, not his alone. *I was doing my Christian duty*, he reminded himself. He could almost hear Conrad whispering the words in his ear, talking him down from this self-destructive ledge as he had done so many times before. *This is on Harrison*, he rationalized. *It's his fault. All of this is on him.* "Evil faggot," he growled as he turned away from Whitney's corpse, stormed out of the home, and slammed the door behind him.

Through the Sockets

With her hair wrapped around his fist, Sardus dragged Eve across the room. "Made a God damn fool outta me!" She yelped as he yanked her by the hair onto the dining table. "Sit still," he said, releasing her hair and turning his back on her.

Eve did as instructed. She laid flat on the wooden table, her legs dangling off the end. She had learned long ago that struggling only made it worse. Sardus maneuvered his old bones up the stairs, muttering to himself the whole way, "bitch" this and "cunt" that. Eve remained motionless.

When Sardus returned, he had a bible in his hand along with a length of rope. He usually used the rope to tie her up, but, this time, he used it to bind the bible to his hand. "I can't be havin' ya do this to me," he murmured, pulling a knot tight. "Ya gots'a learn discipline." With his empty hand, he grabbed onto the front of her dress. His bible-bound hand rose high above his head, then came down with a hard, flat thud against the side of Eve's head.

***

Clayton was pissed. Somehow, he had gotten stuck with Shiloh as everyone else ran off and geared up for battle. Conrad had neglected to offer guidance in the matter of dealing with her. He looked around for Whitney but could not locate him. He hoped he would be found in his home and was not taking a defensive position in one of the communal buildings.

Shiloh was not making it easy to transport her. She had continued to wriggle and wrench since he first laid hands on her. He had one of her arms pinned behind her back and one of his arms wrapped around her throat. They slowly shuffled backwards toward Whitney's house. It was an arduous process to cross the village with her in tow.

As they drew near, Clayton heard the door open. He glanced back over his shoulder to find Judd exiting. "Hey! Whitney's in there, yeah?"

Judd shook his head. "He's dead."

"What?" At first, he thought Judd was kidding, but the expression on Judd's face convinced him of the truth. "What?" he repeated. "Did this—" He tightened his grip around Shiloh's throat and leaned back, picking her up off the ground. "Did this fuckin' bitch do—"

"No," Judd said quickly. "It wasn't her. It was the queer."

"Fuck. Fuck that fuckin'—"

Judd started to walk away.

"Wait!" Clayton called after him. When Judd turned back around, Clayton asked, "What do I do with her?"

Judd gave it a moment's thought. "Conrad and Second Christ need to determine her fate, but you best not bother him at a time like this. Tuck her away in your place until the dust is settled."

That meant hauling Shiloh all the way back across the village to get to his house. Clayton groaned with frustration. Judd took off, leaving Clayton alone in his task.

***

Duke dragged Harrison like dead weight through the doorway of his home. He kicked the door shut and carried the limp man over to the foot of the stairs. He deposited Harrison onto the bottom step, out of breath.

"You killed him," Harry muttered, staring into the distance. "He's dead…"

Duke retrieved a length of black rope and wrapped it around Harry's wrists. But, before a knot could be tied, Harry's hands shot up.

Harry roared as he rose from the staircase and buried his thumbs into Duke's eye sockets. He didn't care who heard. He didn't care who saw. Blood gushed as they staggered in tandem across the living room. Duke screamed bloody murder.

Duke banged up against the front door. Harry growled through gritted teeth as he jerked Duke forward, then slammed his head against the wooden door over and over again, his thumbs sinking deeper with every impact.

The screaming stopped, and the legs of the corpse that had been Duke a moment ago went limp, taking the body to the floor with Harry's thumbs still lodged in the skull. Twin spurts of blood followed the squishing as Harry withdrew his thumbs. It felt good. It was exhilarating for the agony to finally go in the other direction.

Harry had not a moment to think before gunfire erupted outside. He took up Duke's fallen knife and dashed to the window. He knelt at the corner of the sill and peered outside.

A half dozen or more police officers were advancing from cover to cover through the village, exchanging gunfire with the residents of Second Christ's holler. Most were wielding pistols but a couple had pulled shotguns from their cop cars which they now took cover behind.

Fuck it, Harry thought, *fuck it, fuck it, fuck it*. The words kept echoing in his head. It was hard to think of anything else. What did he have left? Why shouldn't he? "Fuck it!" he yelled as he ripped open the front door and sprinted outside into the affray.

Trixie & Lindsay

Clayton was fumbling with the doorknob, trying to get it open without losing his grip on Shiloh, when the first gunshots rang. "Shit!" he said and twisted to see the staggered line of police officers advancing on the village.

Trixie wriggled out of his grip while he was distracted. She gulped air and backed away from him.

He pointed at her. "Don't you even think about—"

She wheeled and broke into a sprint.

"Stop!" Clayton gave chase. Shiloh rounded the corner of his home. By the time Clayton rounded the same corner, she was already disappearing around the next one. He gave it his all and sprinted to the back of his house, losing his footing and falling to the ground in the process.

When he looked up, Shiloh was nowhere to be seen.

Clayton picked himself up. "Aw, screw it," he said to himself. *Let her be someone else's problem.*

Trixie counted to one hundred before emerging from behind the storage crates around the back of the mess hall. She peaked out with just one eye to make sure the coast was clear before stepping out from her hiding spot. Her blood was pumping at maximum pressure. She could feel her heartbeat in her fingertips.

Even though there was no one in sight, Trixie realized she wasn't ready to move yet. She tucked herself back behind the crates as gunfire echoed through the holler on the other side of the mess hall. *What to do, what to do?* Should she find Harrison, she wondered. *No,* she decided. *Gots'a get Eve.* She winced and cursed herself. *Lindsay! Her name's Lindsay!*

Trixie crept away from the back wall of the mess hall. Sardus and Eve's house was at the right terminus of the horseshoe-shaped village. Two buildings separated her from her destination. She made her way to the edge of the mess hall's back wall and peeked out toward the village center.

She saw Cappie making a break for it. He burst out through the front doors of the mess hall and sprinted through the gunfire toward his home on the opposite side of the village. He made it about halfway before he caught a cop's bullet in the side of his head.

Trixie gasped and covered her mouth. She watched brains spill from Cappie's ear, then watched his lifeless body topple one of the pews on its way to the ground. She felt sick. Cappie was the nicest man in Conrad's congregation by a country mile. *Oh, but how could the police know? They just tryn'a save the women.* She hoped Harrison wouldn't get shot by mistake. It would be easy to mistake him for one of the residents with everyone running around like chickens with their heads cut off.

Sticking to the outside perimeter, Trixie dashed as fast as she could across the open space to the next home. She flattened her back against the wall and tried to calm her breathing. Next was the workshop, and then Sardus and Eve's house.

Trixie slid along the back wall of the home and laid eyes on the workshop. She quickly pulled back around the corner when she laid eyes on Judd, taking cover behind the workshop's one wall.

Judd popped out from behind the workshop and took aim with his rifle at an advancing police officer. Before Judd could pull the trigger, a different police officer got a bead on him and fired first. Judd grunted as a bullet passed through his massive bicep. He pulled back behind the wall, tore a strip off of his flannel shirt, folded it over, and wrapped it around the wound to stop the bleeding. He twisted a simple knot and pulled it tight with his teeth.

Trixie turned ninety degrees and ran straight for the tree line. She slid on fallen pine needles and grabbed onto a tree as she hid behind it. When she was confident she hadn't been seen, she progressed along the edge of the forest behind the back of the workshop.

From his cover in the shade below the stage, Joseph could see Judd's predicament. There were two officers focused on him, alternating fire. Joseph signaled to Earl, and the two of them laid down suppressing fire, driving the cops down into cover.

With them cowering, Judd had line-of-sight on one of them. He leaned halfway out from the workshop wall, brought his rifle to his shoulder, shut one eye, and squeezed the trigger. His bullet slammed into the cop's chest. The officer fell to the ground beside his cover. His bulletproof vest saved his life but left him with a cracked rib. He gasped for air. Joseph and Earl took aim at the exposed cop and finished him off posthaste. Judd pulled back into cover as the other officer turned and unloaded an entire pistol magazine at him, weakening the structural integrity of Judd's cover.

Trixie yelped as a stray bullet struck a tree right beside her and blew bark through the air. She dropped straight to the ground and laid flat. She hoped no one heard her exclamation over all the gunfire. Staying low, Trixie crawled over the bugs and pine needles, inching closer to her destination as the violence continued a few yards to her right.

Finally, she reached a point parallel to the house Lindsay was in. There were two-dozen yards to cover between the edge of the forest and the back of the home. Trixie waited for Judd's focus to be drawn to his gun sights, then she lifted the hem of her dress and sprinted as fast as she could for the home.

She slammed right into the siding, unable to stop her momentum in time. She felt elated, she had made it. Trixie maneuvered around to the side of the home that was blocked from Judd's view. She crouch-walked over to the side window, peered inside, and saw the old man.

Sardus was ashamed of the fear he felt. He knew he should have been out there fighting for his home but all he wanted to do was go up to his bedroom and hide under the covers until it was over just like he had done as a little boy whenever there was a thunderstorm. Instead, he preoccupied himself with Eve's punishment. As long as he was disciplining her, he could tell himself that he had a halfway-valid reason for not jumping into the battle.

Trixie watched through the window as Sardus raised his bible-bound hand high above his head. She fidgeted uncertainly as he brought the bible down hard on her sister's bloody-and-bruised head. *What to do, what to do?* She had no idea.

The cover of the bible was beginning to pull free from its binding. Sardus didn't care. It was an outdated tome. He would never treat the new bible so roughly, once Conrad and Second Christ had finally finished it.

His arm was getting tired. Sardus hauled the bible above his head once again. Eve braced herself as best she could in her weakened state.

Earl shouldered open the front door and dove to the floor, barely avoiding the bullets intended to end his life.

Trixie ducked out of sight below the windowsill.

Sardus spun to face Earl, who picked himself up off the floor. Earl seemed surprised to see him.

"Sardus, what're ya doin'?! Where's ya gun?! We need all hands on deck!" Earl fished a handful of shotgun shells out of his breast pocket and began reloading from inside the safety of the home.

"I was just—" Sardus began but stopped himself. He realized how transparent his excuse was and couldn't risk letting his fear show through. He wouldn't be able to stand the judgement. "Uh, right." He slid the rope and bible off of his hand and went to fetch his rifle.

Earl looked at Eve in silence as he finished reloading his shotgun and waited for Sardus to return.

"Okay, ready," Sardus said, taking the safety off of his rifle. He cleared his throat and stretched his fingers. They were sore from the bible beating.

"S'about time, old-timer," Earl said, patting the older man on the shoulder. They left the home together and soon went in different directions.

Trixie counted to ten, then climbed inside through the window. She rushed over to her sister, who was stunned to see her. Trixie wrapped her arms around her and squeezed her tight. It had been two months since they had last been within touching distance. "Oh Lindsay!"

Hearing the name made Lindsay do a mental double-take. It felt like she was being shaken awake from a bottomless daze. It seemed like a lifetime ago that she had been called by her true name.

Trixie stepped back from the hug but kept her hands on her sister's shoulders. "We gotta go now, Lindsay. It's time. And Ah mean get gone real far away fast."

Lindsay nodded, slowly at first, then more eagerly as her consciousness continued to pry its way out of the fugue. Memories were flooding her mind that she had thought were lost forever. She stood up off the table and took one rigid step before stopping. She turned and hurried into the kitchen, taking up the steak knife she was never allowed to touch and lifting up the hem of her dress. She brought the blade to the rope harness binding her joints and sawed through the fibers at different points until the whole thing snapped apart.

She cut herself in the process but she did not care. She was free from her hempen bondage. She lifted the tattered, knotted harness above her head and slammed it against the floor as hard as she could. Lindsay took her first uninhibited steps in a good, long while, and the sensation felt entirely new. She returned to Trixie and hugged her again, this time, able to reach all the way across her back and clasp her hands together and hold her tight.

"I love you, Lindsay. I've missed ya somethin' awful." Trixie rested her head against Lindsay's chest for a moment, then the gunfire outside returned the sense of urgency. "The police'll help us," Trixie said. "We just need'a get to them without any'a Conrad's people stoppin' us." She suddenly remembered, "Oh! We need'a get to Harrison first—"

Lindsay shook her head and made a noise that sounded close enough to "no" for Trixie to get the message.

"But, no- but he helped me. He got me away from Whitney. I wooden'a got to you without him."

Lindsay grabbed onto her sister's shoulders and shook her head fervently.

"Oh," Trixie said, saddened. "Okay." She felt bad abandoning Harry but she wasn't about to argue with Lindsay in the middle of all this. With so much gunfire, Harry might have been dead already for all she knew.

Lindsay hugged Trixie again, then they moved for the front door that Sardus had left open behind him.

The stepped cautiously outside, intending to sneak toward the officers positioned behind their squad cars, but when a bullet struck the wall of the home right beside them, they each jumped and broke into a sprint. Lindsay's joints were unaccustomed to such movement, and she lagged behind. Trixie held onto her hand and tried to pull her along quicker.

They ran toward the cruiser parked sideways at the edge of the village, and the two police officers crouched down behind it. Trixie waved her hand through the air and shouted, "Help! Help us! Me and mah sistah need help!"

The two police officers behind the cruiser heard her cries in between pops of gunfire. They turned, aimed over the hood of the cruiser, and opened fire on the sisters.

Blue Blood

The cops riddled Trixie with holes.

Lindsay belted an animalistic scream as her sister fell to the ground. She never let go of her hand. Before her scream had reached its apex, the cops filled her with lead too.

Blue-blood had been spilled. As far as the police were concerned, any living soul in the village without a JPD uniform was the enemy, and they would be executed with extreme prejudice.

Sardus moved hastily around the corner of one of the homes and put his back to it. He was unsure whose home he was taking cover behind. His old heart was beating so fast he was afraid it would give out. He took a couple of deep breaths, then leaned out around the corner and raised his rifle. He squeezed the trigger without a chance in hell of hitting what he was aiming at.

A bullet whizzed right over his shoulder and flew into the woods with the sound of a speeding hornet. Sardus felt a bit of urine leak out and soil his underpants. He pulled back behind the corner and thanked Second Christ for swerving the cop's bullet. His hand was shaky as it worked the bolt of his rifle, chambering the next cartridge.

Sardus was more afraid than he had ever been in his entire eighty-five years of life. He wished to live long enough to die a peaceful death in sleep. He had never faced his mortality so directly. He had gone as far as to dodge the draft to maintain his safety. This was now the closest to war he had ever come.

There was a break in the gunfire, and Sardus considered leaning out to take another shot. He waited too long, and the gunfire started up again at irregular intervals. The sound of running footsteps became audible between the pops of pistols.

Sardus turned to his side where the sound came from and spotted Harrison, covered in blood, sprinting towards him around the back of the home. "What the fuck are y—" Sardus began to say but never finished.

Harry ran right into him and buried his knife in the old man's heart. He seethed with rage as he tore the blade out and plunged it back in the same spot twice more.

Sardus's legs went soft. His rifle fell to the ground. He reached a trembling hand up toward Harrison's face as he collapsed onto the bloody grass. His heart was no longer beating too fast; it was beating too slow. And then, it wasn't beating at all.

Harry moved on, seeing red. He didn't care whether he lived or died. He just wanted to drag as many of the mother fuckers down to hell with him as he could.

The gun battle raged across the village.

A cop made a rush through the center of the village, trying to close distance on the cultists. He took a bullet in the stomach and dropped to the ground. He rolled onto his side and checked the damage. The bullet was lodged in his guts; it had snuck in below his vest. He'd live, he thought. He crawled forward, flat on his chest, and got behind the stone well near the middle of the village. He groaned in pain as he propped himself up and laid his back against the uneven stones. Bullets impacted the opposite side of the well, shooting stone dust up into the air and blasting apart the wooden bucket suspended above the mouth of the well.

Bo made a break for his home with Li'l Rhoda in his arms, screaming. He didn't make it halfway before his back and legs were hammered with bullets. He was dead before he hit the ground.

Li'l Rhoda had the wind knocked out of her as she slammed into the ground. Bo's perforated corpse landed on top of the five-year-old and formed a cage around her. Her screams were muffled by his body as his blood stained her skin red.

***

Conrad stood alone inside his home, watching the chaos through the two windows on either side of his thick front door. He could see dead bodies dotting the landscape and was sure there were more corpses outside his field of view and that more would be made out of men before the day was through.

He pondered how many of his followers he could stand to lose before his congregation saw a total collapse. This could not spell the end of all he had built, he would not stand for it, and Second Christ shouldn't either. He wished his son would intervene and put an end to the bloodshed. *I should be in there with my wife and child*, he thought, staring at the doors of the church. But he remained immobile, fearful of opening his doors to the outside destruction.

He could stand to lose a few of his men. The weaker ones. *The weak shall perish so the strong may prosper*, he thought, beginning to compose his first sermon for after the dust had settled. He hoped to keep the deaths of the women to a minimum. Finding more men to join the village would be a simple enough task, but bringing in fresh women without raising too much alarm or leaving too much of a trail was the real challenge.

Pray Until Death

The mess hall was filled with fearful energy. Bethany and Cilicia cowered near the center of the building, hugging onto each other as if sharing in their fear could offer some form of protection.

They had shoved the tables and benches up against the double doors as a barricade. Gunfire boomed like thunder outside. Bright flashes of light shined through the gaps between the boards of the mess hall's wooden walls.

At length, Bethany let go of Cilicia and lowered onto her knees. She clasped her hands together, shut her eyes, and faced the ceiling. She silently prayed for the police to come out of this battle victorious and put an end to her bondage. She was unsure whether to pray to Second Christ or another. She wasn't sure what she believed anymore.

Cilicia followed Bethany's lead and knelt beside her. Unlike Bethany, Cilicia prayed out loud, despite her lack of a tongue. The words came out malformed but she knew God wouldn't care. Her intent was clear and would be understood. She prayed for the death of Conrad and every last one of his true believers.

The women prayed side-by-side. Bullets began punching through the wall in front of them. Spirals of smoke shone in the narrow beams of light. The women cowered but did not cease in their prayers.

More and more gunfire struck the mess hall. Cilicia took a bullet in the arm before she took one in the face. Bethany felt three sharp thuds strike her chest before her world went black. Her final thought was spent wondering which side killed her.

***

Judd needed to relocate to get an angle on the cop behind the well. He slid along the back of the workshop wall until he reached the other end. He knelt down, stepped one foot out from the wall, and found the cop's head at the end of his rifle sights. He steadied his breathing, then pulled the trigger, drilling a hole through one end of the cop's skull and out the other.

He returned upright and pulled back behind the wall. That's when he heard the growl approaching from behind him. Judd spun around and registered Harrison charging at him with a blood-covered knife raised high.

Judd covered up his face just in time for Harry's knife to sink into his muscular forearm. A spasm of pain shot through Judd's entire arm up to his shoulder. The rifle fell crookedly from his grip and landed on the grass with a dull thud.

It took force for Harry to free the blade from Judd's flesh; it had gone in all the way up to the handle. Harry attempted a second stab, but Judd caught onto his wrist and held him at bay.

Judd grabbed onto Harrison's other arm as well and twisted with him. He slammed the outsider's back against the workshop wall and pinned him in place. "Fuckin' faggot!" he roared. "We gave you—"

There was a crazed look in Harry's eyes as he lunged forward and tore a chunk out of the large man's jugular with his teeth.

"What the fuck—" Judd muttered in disbelief.

Harry spat a mouthful of Judd's flesh onto the ground, then sunk his teeth back in for a second bite.

"Holy fffff—"

With his jaw clenched tight, Harry jerked his head back and tore a huge piece of Judd's neck-meat out. Severed arteries sprayed wildly into the air, coating Harry in a fresher shade of red.

Judd released his grip on Harrison and staggered backwards. He couldn't believe it. *The faggot killed me....* He attempted to bring a hand to his wound but found himself unable to move his arms. They felt heavy, like the blood in his veins had turned to stone.

Harry watched the color drain from Judd's face. The giant man's expression spelled terror as he hit the ground gasping. Harry never even considered picking the rifle up off the ground. He was already moving on to the next son of a bitch he could find and put his knife to. *Fuck it, fuck it, fuck it,* continued to ring in his head like a madman's echo in a cavernous cathedral.

He stomped right on Judd's head as he broke into a sprint, mashing the bigot's face into the dirt.

Fuck It

The firefight between the cops and congregation raged on. Moves were made, distance was closed, guns were reloaded, bullets were fired, and blood was spilled. And through it all, Harry ran.

He sprinted through the village looking like a wild animal. He had no end game and no destination in mind. That is, until he laid eyes on Conrad's home and saw the Father's face peering back at him from beyond a window. Harry yelled as he altered course and charged for the grand home beside the church.

Suddenly, he was on the ground. How did he get there? He was lying on his stomach in front of the church. He looked around, disoriented. Then, he felt the pain. He rolled onto his back with a groan and felt the bullet hole in his side.

Bullets whizzed overhead, not necessarily fired at him. Harry attempted to gauge his wound. It was difficult to tell how bad it was with how saturated in blood he already was. He propped himself up on his elbow and bent his arm to feel for a hole in his back. He couldn't find one, which he took to mean the bullet was probably still inside of him. *Fuck it,* he thought. What did it matter? He was dead anyway. Andy was dead anyway.

He breathed deeply in and out. There was a lull in the gunfire as some of the combatants broke to reload. The sound of a baby crying became audible in the silence. The sound of Second Christ crying.

With a grunt of pain, Harry forced himself back onto his feet. With his head ducked low, he staggered the couple of feet up to the church doors and slipped inside as bullets splintered the wood right beside him. He pushed the door shut behind himself and got a look at the interior of the church for the first time.

The floor was made of carefully arranged stones packed in the earth. Poorly rendered tapestries in Conrad's likeness hung from the walls; four in total. In fabric, he was a bit more slender and stood atop a hill, surrounded by doves and angelic rays of light. A halo hung above his head, and Second Christ napped in his arms.

With a hand clutching his wound, Harry made his way down the center aisle between the tall pews. At the head of the church, in place of a pulpit, was a gilded bassinet. Second Christ cried loudly within it, and Mabel stood at his side. A door to the outside world hung halfway open at the back of the church; Mabel and Second Christ's escape route should the police breach the church.

When the door had creaked open with only one set of footsteps to follow, Mabel had expected Conrad, finally come to join her. She was furious at the sight of the outsider bleeding upon their hallowed church floor. She strode toward him with a look of disgust upon her face as clear as day. It was the first time Harry had seen her without a smile. She silently thrust a pointer finger toward the door as she and Harrison drew closer together.

With a wild swing, Harry lifted the blade from beside his hip and slashed her throat in a single motion. He lost his balance as he woozily staggered over her. He caught himself on a pew and continued forward. Harry could hear Mabel gurgling on the stone floor behind him but he cared not enough to glance back at her.

Harry pressed on, feeling lightheaded. He clamped down hard on his gunshot wound with his empty hand. He stumbled right into the edge of the bassinet. With a scowl on his face, Harry peered down at Second Christ.

The baby's face was a twisted swirl of knotted flesh. Harry was taken aback. Second Christ's mouth was nothing but a wet flap. It opened and closed flatly like a fish gasping on dry land as he cried. His eyes were wet, black beads that shimmered in sunken sockets.

Harry didn't know whether to feel hatred or pity for the tiny creature. He looked up from the bassinet to the back door and considered making a break for it. *Fuck it. I'm dead. Andy's dead. Fuck it.* He looked back down at Second Christ and growled.

"Fuck you to hell!"

Harry lifted the knife high above his head with both hands, letting his gunshot wound leak onto his shoes unplugged. With a roar, he plunged the knife down into the bassinet.

When his knife struck Second Christ's skin…

The blade shattered.

Second Christ

"Oh, Christ!"

The baby's cries rose sharply in intensity. His screams echoed throughout the church.

Harry released the handle of the broken knife, letting it fall into the bassinet beside the shards of broken metal and the crying infant. He stumbled away from the bassinet in wide-eyed terror as Second Christ began to rise up into the air.

The baby's cries continued to grow louder and louder until they seemed to come not from his wet flap of a mouth but from high up in the sky above the roof of the church. Second Christ rose from the bassinet, lifting higher and higher in the air.

"Fuck me!" Harry yelled. He turned and ran for the doors.

Second Christ let out a deafening wail and sent a blast of air rushing out in all directions like a shock wave. The tall pews were knocked over like dominoes, and Harry was thrown clean off his feet.

He crashed through the church doors and landed flat on his chest on the ground outside. Harry moaned in pain and tried to stand but wound up collapsing back down to the ground. He made one last exertion and found himself passing out.

***

The police could hear the resounding cries from high up above now. Officers looked around for the source of the sound.

Thunder boomed, and a white substance began to rain from the sky: breast milk.

The gunfight slowed to a stop as each participant was doused in the strange precipitation.

The Grand Decider pumped its bellows. Five horn blasts rang through the air, one more than the followers of Second Christ had ever heard in succession. More horn blasts followed, on and on without pause.

The cops were confused. The congregants were terrified. They knew such an outcry from the Grand Decider was possible, but it was not a sound they ever expected to hear within their lifetimes.

The ground began to shake as the horns continued to blare.

An officer lost his balance in the rumble and fell to his knees on the grass. He braced himself on the trembling ground with both hands. *An earthquake?* But how could he rationalize the white rain?

A bolt of lightning struck the ground in the center of the village.

Clayton threw down his gun. "Fuck, fuck!" He tried to understand Second Christ's message but Conrad was not available to interpret.

Gusts of wind whipped through the village; strong enough to knock an unbraced man over. A second bolt of lightning was cast from the sky and set Earl's home ablaze.

"What the fuck is happening?!" one of the officers yelled but was muted by the rumbling earth, whipping wind, and deafening cries from above.

Earl dropped to his knees in front of his burning home and clasped his hands in prayer. "Second Christ Protect us! Offer us protection in our time of need—"

The earth split open, carving a jagged mouth through the center of the holler. Grass and dirt and rock gave way to a dark pit with no bottom in sight.

An officer stared dumbfounded at the sight. "Holy mother of—"

The chasm widened. The chunk of earth the officer stood upon gave way and sent him screaming into the void.

Boards and nails gave way as the roof was torn off the church in a gust of wind. The shelter swirled in a dark cyclone. Second Christ rose up out of the church. His gilded cloth, still wrapped around his tiny body, flapped wildly in the torrent of wind. He continued to rise higher and higher into the sky as his cries boomed like thunder.

Clayton laid eyes on Second Christ and threw his hands in the air. He dropped to his knees and attempted to translate God's tongue. "Yes, great Second Christ! I understand!" he shouted over the raging tempest. He stuck his tongue out and opened his mouth to the white rain.

Joseph watched Clayton drink from the sky and wondered if he should do the same. He let his rifle fall to the ground.

Clayton laughed joyously, feeling safe for the first time since the gunfight broke out. He turned toward Joseph and smiled. "It's milk!" he proclaimed. "Drink of Second Christ's milk! It will protect us from harm in—"

"Fuck this," the fallen officer said as he returned to his feet and took aim at Clayton, kneeling out in the open.

A bullet entered the back of Clayton's skull and blew his brain out through his forehead.

Before Joseph could react to Clayton's death, he felt a

tugging sensation on his ankle. He looked down and saw nothing, then he found his leg yanked out from underneath him by an invisible force. He was lifted, upside down, into the air.

"What in God's name?!" the officer exclaimed, watching Joseph rise up above the cover he had been hiding behind.

Joseph twisted and thrashed. *Why me?!* he thought in a panic. *Why me, Second Christ?! Why?!* He let his arms hang limp and he looked straight down. He was fifteen feet off the ground and still rising higher.

A bolt of lightning split the sky and struck Joseph, setting him ablaze.

Joseph screamed in agony and flailed in every direction as Second Christ lifted him higher.

Conrad watched through his window with a hand clasped over his mouth as his first-ever follower roasted alive in mid-air.

Joseph continued rising up, moving faster and faster until he shot into the sky like a shooting star.

Conrad's meaty fist slammed down on the windowsill. "No, no, no!" he shouted. "Wrong! False!" He could sit idly by no longer. He stormed outside into the white rain.

Ribbons of Flesh

Conrad's robes were instantly soaked in the rain of milk. He ran toward the church.

Li'l Rhoda, having finally squirmed out from beneath Boyd's corpse, ran toward the Father. Her husband's blood ran down her little body anew as it was saturated by the rain. "What do we do?!" she cried. She grabbed onto the bottom of Conrad's wet robes. "I'm scared, Father Conrad! What's happening?!"

Conrad placed his palm on the child's forehead and shoved her to the ground. He pressed on to the church.

The remaining police officers no longer had interest in this fight. They turned tail and ran for their cruisers parked at the mouth of the horseshoe-shaped village as bolts of lightning struck the land all over.

The earth began to shake again as the pit grew wider, swallowing up the stage. The cross upon which Andy was crucified lowered into the sea of black like the mast of a sinking ship. Earl, still on his knees praying, was cast tumbling into the pit. He tried to accept it in his heart as his rightful end under Second Christ's loving eye even as he screamed into the abyss.

Conrad looked down at blood-soaked Harrison as he neared the church. He took him for dead and stepped over the motionless body into the church. He ran down the center aisle past the toppled pews toward the cyclone that swirled beneath his son.

He felt a tremor seize his heart as he registered Mable lying on the floor: dead. He stopped for a moment and reached a trembling hand down toward her as his eyes grew wet. He stopped himself. *Now is not the time*. He forced his panicked eyes back to Second Christ, high up in the sky above. *Sorry, my love.*

Conrad side-stepped his wife's lifeless body and continued forward until he was as close to the cyclone as he would dare get. He thrust his arms into the air and shouted over the rushing wind, "My son! Stop! You are reckless! You are killing our own people!"

Lightning struck the ground right beside Conrad, blackening the corners of four stones packed in the earth.

Conrad reeled and fell over onto one of the upturned pews. He quickly righted himself and reapproached Second Christ. "Son, please!" he shouted as loud as he could, near muted by the cyclone. "End this destruction before all is lost!"

A powerful gust of divine wind took Conrad off his feet and broke six of his ribs in the process. He was sent careening backwards, all the way down the aisle, and crashed through the church doors. One of them splintered and was taken clean off its hinges as it was struck by the full brunt of the mountainous man's body.

Conrad landed on his back outside the church and slid a few feet through the wet grass before coming to a stop. He blinked the milk out of his eyes and watched his son continue to throw a fit in the sky. Conrad brought his hands to his chest and gasped for air. His chest was crushed, and he struggled to draw breath.

Then, a third hand landed on his chest as Harrison crawled his way over and flashed a demented smile. He stuck his hand into Conrad's robes and fished out the hooked gutting blade that had ended his husband's life.

Harry went to town on the Father. He knelt atop Conrad's thick torso and carved him up; slashing, and ripping, and tearing away ribbons of flesh until there was hardly anything left of the Father that appeared human. White rain pooled in the crevices of the mangled flesh.

Panting and white as a sheet, Harry flopped over onto his back and looked up at Second Christ and his temper tantrum. The infant was barely visible beyond the swirling cyclone of wind and lightning.

A ghoulish chuckle escaped Harry's bloody lips. He didn't know why but he suddenly found the whole thing funny. In fact, it was downright hilarious. He stared with dead eyes into the raining milk. Harry cackled with mad delight, laughing harder with each passing second.

The Mad Delight of a Broken Man

The Grand Decider's bellows continued to pump and its horns continued to signal the end. Earl's flaming home crumbled inward, crushing and searing Bethany as she sheltered within. The crust of the earth cracked loudly as the pit grew wider, taking in fleeing cops and wives with no distinction between them.

"Oh shit, oh shit, oh shit!" one of the officers repeated to himself while he ran as fast as he could toward the cruisers. He threw himself against the driver-side door of his cruiser and fumbled for the door handle. He looked around for his partner and couldn't find him. He couldn't find any of the colleagues he had arrived with. He was alone.

The officer got into the driver's seat and locked the door behind himself. It didn't make him feel any safer. He started up the engine and slammed on the gas. The cruiser traveled no more than a few feet before the split in the earth progressed into its path. He slammed on the brakes with both feet.

The bumper and front tires overhung the chasm. The officer threw it in reverse and prayed to his version of God as he gunned it backwards. The tires spun ineffectually against the wet ground as it rumbled beneath the vehicle.

Harry was on his feet. He didn't remember standing up but there he was. Tears streamed down his face and got lost in the white rain. He wandered up to the corpse of a cop with a bullet through his head. Harry stooped and picked up the officer's fallen handgun. The safety was already off. Harry held the gun above his head and aimed at Second Christ.

He pulled the trigger five times and watched as the bullets flared against the outside of the rain-wrapped vortex of wind and lightning that swirled around the puerile God. It felt to Harry like the satisfying punchline to a long-winded joke. Staccato laughter tumbled from his mouth. A wail of despair followed, then he was back to laughing without knowing precisely why.

The sound of a roaring engine approached. Harry turned and laid eyes on a cop car swerving towards him in reverse. The officer inside was screaming in a panic. Harry braced himself and leaped as the side of the metal body swung and crashed into him at a crooked angle.

Harry was carried against the bulk of the vehicle until it slammed into a tree at the edge of the village and sent him flying away from it with great force. He felt a pop in his shoulder as he hit the ground and flopped over onto his stomach. His moan of pain dissolved into hysterical laughter. It all just kept getting funnier.

The officer in the driver's seat wiped blood out of his eyes. He had a gash in his forehead from where it had just slammed against the radio console in the sudden stop. He put the vehicle in drive and hit the gas but nothing happened. The trunk of the tree had crushed a significant portion of the back half of the car. One of the tires was bent to an unworkable angle and the others spun ineffectually against the wet grass. He jerked the wheel from side to side in a full-blown panic.

The pit opened wider and began to swallow whole buildings. The workshop and two of the homes were gone in an instant. The Grand Decider teetered for a moment on the edge of the drop-off before taking the plunge. The horns continued to sound as they fell deeper and deeper into the earth, changing pitch and adopting an echo.

The cop tried to open his door but found the twisted metal frame pinned in place. He frantically shuffled over to the passenger seat and popped open the door to find the widening pit rushing towards him. The earth shook, and the cruiser was rocked onto its side, sending the officer tumbling out of his seat.

He grabbed onto the inside door handle and dangled above the endless chasm. The terrified officer screamed his prayers into the sky. He begged for God to spare him. But Second Christ wasn't interested. Chunks of earth broke free and plunged into the abyss. The cruiser lost purchase on any solid ground and carried the officer down into the depths.

Second Christ continued screaming and crying until the pit had grown large enough to devour the entire village. The stagnant water of the pond drained into the void. The surrounding trees of the village's perimeter fell, roots and all, into the black nothingness. The village was erased. The slate was wiped clean.

Second Christ's screams and cries slowed to a stop, as did the swirling wind, rain, and lightning. At length, the gaping pit began to seal back up. Second Christ slowly lowered to the ground as it reformed beneath him. An earthen crust was formed of thin air, and lush, healthy grass populated its surface.

The divine infant settled down on the ground, wrapped snuggly in his divine cloth. The little guy was exhausted. Within seconds, he drifted off to sleep.

Skin and Glass

Ma and Pa were asleep in bed, tucked warmly under their blankets. It had taken Ma a good long while to drift off, wracked with worry as she was. Pa's time in the military had left him with the ability to sleep anywhere at any time regardless of the conditions. He snored like a lawnmower failing to start.

Ma stirred. She thought she heard something downstairs but couldn't be sure it wasn't a part of her dream. She wasn't left wondering long. A series of loud bangs against the front door shocked Pa from his slumber and woke Ma the rest of the way up.

"What was that?!" Ma asked, knowing her husband couldn't possibly have any more information than she did.

Pa rubbed his eyes, put on his glasses, and climbed out of bed. The banging repeated downstairs. Pa slid on a pair of slippers. He made his way out of the bedroom and down the hallway. Ma stuck close and hid behind him. As they inched down the stairs, the front door came into view.

A figure, shrouded in shadows, jerked around on the other side of the beveled glass set in the door. The dark figure thrashed violently against the entrance.

"Who's there?!" Pa projected from the middle of the staircase.

The figure slammed the door again, louder, harder. The doorknob rattled.

Ma hung onto the back of Pa's shirt and clenched it tightly in her fists. They reached the bottom of the stairs together. "I said, who is it?!" Pa shouted at the door.

The figure disappeared from the door, not backing away but moving to the side. The living room window shattered.

Ma shrieked, and Pa jumped. They held onto each other. Pa put himself between his wife and the dark figure that flopped inside through the broken window, landing face-first on the glass-covered floor.

Ma shut her eyes and screamed. She buried her eyes into Pa's back.

"Wait!" Pa declared. "Wait, it's Harrison!"

Bewildered, Ma reached out to the wall and flipped the light switch.

Harry was illuminated, wide-eyed, and caked in dirt and blood both old and new. He cringed at the light and moved toward his parents in the hallway.

"My God!" Pa uttered.

"Oh, Harrison!" Ma rushed over to him. Avoiding the glass that clung to him, Ma hugged her son, caring not about the mess.

Harry did not hug her back but he immediately burst into tears.

"What happened to you?"

Through the tears, Harry spoke, "Andy's dead. He- I- he- it's my fault."

"Tell us what happened, son," Pa said.

"I killed him. It's my f- I brought him- and I- he—" A spurt of mad laughter interrupted his cries. He thought about how if he hadn't taken Andy out into the woods, if he hadn't brought him on this trip, if he hadn't brought him to the U.S., if they had never even met, then Andy would still belong to the land of the living… and Harry couldn't contain his laughter. It was just too damn funny.

Ma released him from her hug and backed away at the sobering sound of laughter. She and Pa noticed the hole in his torso and the pistol in his hand for the first time. The gun was loose in his grip and the barrel knocked against the side of his knee as he cackled.

His laughter became strangled. The sobs and the laughs intermingled, shifting between one and the other; sometimes forming a singular sound, other times remaining dissonant. "I need to kill- I- I need to- the- Christ, Christ, Christ!"

Ma and Pa shared a fearful look. Pa moved slowly for the kitchen where their landline hung on the wall in its cradle.

Harry doubled over in laughter, then dropped to his knees, weeping, pushing shards of glass deeper into his knees. Oh, how funny it was that the pain just kept coming. Harry giggled as he returned to his feet and flicked the side of one of the glass shards sticking out of his kneecap. The opposed emotions flickered back and forth, no longer waiting their turns in his broken mind.

"Honey, can you- can you put that down?" Ma asked softly, gesturing to the gun. "Let us help you. Let us take care of you."

Pa picked up the receiver and quietly dialed 9-1-1.

"I need to- to- to- to- to- to kill. I need to kill the baby." Harry couldn't remember what he had gone there for. To say goodbye? *Why would that matter?* he wondered. How funny.

Pa whispered into the phone.

"Can you talk to me, honey? Let's go sit down on the couch and you can tell me what happened." With slow, non-threatening movements, Ma reached her hand up toward Harry's shoulder and touched him gently. She shepherded him into the living room, and he followed, shuffling his feet and sobbing. "It's okay, Harrison, it's okay. Sit with me."

They reached the couch. Ma tried to get Harry to sit, but, instead, he turned away from her and moved for the window.

"Harrison?"

He laughed. "The baby. God. Christ. The baby. The Chri- the Ch- Ch- Ch—" Harry climbed back out through the window.

"Harrison?! Come back! Stop!"

But he was gone, disappeared into the black of night.

Blood-Soaked on Main Street

The sun was beginning to rise, and that meant it was time for Carlotta's Breakfast Nook to open up shop for the day. Carlotta got dressed and descended the narrow flight of steps from her apartment above the Breakfast Nook.

She twisted open the long Venetian blinds that covered her storefront windows and was about to flip over her 'OPEN' sign when she laid eyes on a bloody man staggering down main street with a gun in his hand. She gasped and went straight for her cellphone.

The cloudless sky was awash with orange and a hint of pink. Harry moved with slow, shuffling steps, right down the middle of the road. He was lost in a town he knew like the back of his hand. He had been down this street 10,000 times yet it looked alien to him. Everything was unfamiliar, and he couldn't think straight. He tried to rub his forehead and accidentally poked himself in the eye with the barrel of the pistol. He laughed at himself for how foolish he was. He laughed at the world for how foolish it was. He cried at the world for how cruel it was, then he couldn't help but laugh again at that very same cruelty.

A cop car rose up over the orange horizon and headed in his direction.

I know how this one goes, Harry thought. He was ready this time.

He lifted the pistol from his side and aimed directly at the sun reflecting in the cop car's windshield. He pulled the trigger. An unsatisfying click was all that followed. He pulled the trigger twice more to the same effect.

The gun was empty this whole time?! It was the funniest thing Harry had ever heard of. He growled angrily, lifted the gun above his head, and whipped it at the pavement as hard as he could. The polymer handle chipped, and the gun bounced into the air before settling in the muck of the gutter.

The police cruiser pulled to a stop several yards from Harry. The town's two remaining police officers, Crystal—the desk officer and Bobby—the newest recruit, stepped out of the cruiser with their guns drawn.

"Put your hands behind your head!" Crystal yelled.

"Get down on the ground!" Bobby shouted over her.

Harry did neither. Instead, he laughed and cried in their faces in equal measure.

Crystal fought her impulse to gun him down and get it over with. She needed information out of him.

The continued shouts of the officers fell on deaf ears as they closed in on the crying, laughing, bleeding man in the middle of the street. He was tackled to the ground, and his arms were pinned behind his back. Crystal accidentally popped Harry's shoulder back into its socket, and that was even funnier than the gun being empty. Harry howled with laughter, his eyes filling with tears. He had never laughed even half as hard in his entire life.

Harry hardly registered their touch. He was too enraptured by the emotive battle in his mind to worry over such slight debasement of his corporeal being.

Blind Man's Memories

Harry was seated in a flimsy chair with his hands cuffed through a metal ring welded to the table. The small room surrounding him was built of painted cinderblocks. A metal door was to his back. A security camera recorded him from the corner up near the ceiling.

He was sure he had been seated in this chair for at least five minutes but couldn't remember entering the room or sitting down. His short-term memory was hazy; a watercolor rendition of a blind man's memories. His brain was an answering machine on loop, recording over old messages with random bursts of information breaking through.

Jonesborough PD's only living faculty, Crystal and Bobby, stood across from the unhinged man, though they were unsure if he was aware of their presence or not. Crystal smacked the metal table to get his attention.

"We are missing officers who went looking for you!" This was her third time repeating the information. It seemed to finally get through to the man this time. "You had a firearm belonging to one of our officers. What happened out there? Where are our men? Whose blood is all over you?! We need answers, God damn it!"

"Dead. Dea- dead, dead. Andy's dead. He's dead. Andy!" he shouted past the officers, "I'll save you, Andy! Andy!" A ghoulish chuckle escaped Harry's lips, followed by a pained wheeze, and then a flood of tears.

"Did you kill your husband?" Bobby asked.

"Forget the husband," Crystal said. "What happened to our men? Where are they? We've searched the woods and we can't find a damn—"

"My fault," Harry said through the tears. "It's my fault. Because of me. I did- I brought- I- I killed him- I- because of me. I did. I—"

"This guy's wiring's fucked up," Bobby said quietly to his colleague.

Crystal slammed the table again. "Tell us what happened out there! What happened to our officers?!"

"God," Harry said, laughing. "G- God- Go- God- G- G- God killed them." *God wiped out the entire police force.* Harry couldn't even get the words out. The thought made him so deliriously happy and crushingly depressed. "Second Christ. The Second Christ. Christ. The Second Christ—"

"Stop saying, *Second Christ*!" Crystal screamed. She looked to the new recruit. "What the fuck is wrong with this guy?"

"He needs help. From doctors, not us."

Harry sputtered, "I- wha- the- I- I need to—" Harry stood up out of his chair. The handcuffs stopped him from going very far but they didn't stop him from trying. "The baby. I need to- The baby needs to- I- I need to- I need to kill the baby. The baby needs to die."

"What the fuck are you talking about?" Crystal questioned. "What baby?"

"I- I- The baby. Christ. Second Christ. I need to kill the Second Christ. The baby needs to die. It needs to die. I need to kill it."

"This guy belongs in a fucking asylum, not here."

Harry yanked repeatedly at his handcuffs. He dragged the chain back and forth in a sawing motion against the metal ring, then he was back to brute-force pulling. He laughed and cried harder with every tug.

Babe In the Manger

octor Elswit and his wife Marjorie had recently celebrated their fifteenth wedding anniversary. He worked as an optometrist in the city and she taught history at the nearby community college. They had sent the kids to their grandparents and had a night of expensive Italian food, passionate lovemaking, and whispered promises of new plans to keep the spark alive.

It was a bright Sunday morning and the forest was warm but breezy. Birds sang in the trees above. The husband and wife made their way down a sunny trail, side-by-side. Oliver and Marjorie Elswit had recently taken to morning hikes for their exercise and alone time. Alone time typically doubled as quiet time; a welcome respite from the deluge of noise pollution that crowded their daily lives. Their entire Sunday was mapped out. Hike, shower, pick up the kids, church, brunch, Junior's soccer game, Mindy's playdate with the Walker girls, supper, bedtime for the kids, alone time for the parents, Reverend Kenneth Johnson's evening sermon on the TV, bedtime for the parents.

Then, back to work on Monday. Doctor Elswit was

looking forward to retirement. He was looking forward to old age in general. Hanging around the house with the people he loved and not worrying about a damn thing sounded picture perfect to him.

Marjorie, on the other hand, wanted life to slow down. She had hoped to be a tenured professor at a respected university by the time she was thirty-five. Now, here she was, almost forty years old and still puttering around a two-year institution. At least she was getting close to finishing her master's online.

They rounded a bend in the trail and slowed at the sound of a baby crying off in the distance.

"Do you hear that?" Dr. Elswit asked. He could tell from his wife's expression that she did.

"I think it's coming from over here." She led the way off of the trail and through the brush.

The Elswits pushed their way through some shrubbery and emerged into a clearing. In its center was a baby swaddled in a gilded cloth.

"Honey, look! Someone left a baby." Marjorie rushed over.

Oliver scanned the area. "Hello?! Anyone here?!" His eyes searched the perimeter of the bright clearing.

Marjorie knelt down beside Second Christ. "Hey there, little fella. Don't worry, you're not alone." She delicately picked him up, then she got a look at his knotted face. "Oh, God," she said instinctively. "Honey, I think something's wrong. This baby- something's wrong with him."

Oliver hurried over. He glanced at the child and reeled. "Holy—! What did they do to you?" With a scowl Oliver scanned the horizon. "What kind of Godless monsters could abandon such an innocent, helpless soul?"

"Should we bring him to the police? Or to Child Protective Services?"

Dr. Elswit considered it.

"No," a low voice said from everywhere and nowhere.

Dr. Elswit knew not the origin of the word but he did not feel confused or surprised by its utterance. He felt comforted by it. The sound was warm honey on his ear drums.

"I am yours," the low, calming voice said, wrapping the doctor in a blanket of isolating sound. "You must care for me."

Oliver's insides felt warm. He looked at the deformed baby, swelling with paternal love.

"Should we, honey?" Marjorie asked.

"No," the Doctor said. "Our home is large enough to welcome him in."

"But shouldn't we do what's—"

"Who knows where he'll end up in the state's care. You know how often those programs ruin lives. We'll make sure he's raised right, in a good, Christian household."

Marjorie didn't need any more persuading. She was happy to have him. She smiled down into the bundle. "Ya hear that, little fella? We're gonna take care of you. You're safe now."

Second Christ put an end to his crying. He settled down into the warmth of Marjorie's arms.

She stood, and the Elswits carried their new child from the clearing.

A tiny, satisfied yawn came from the baby's flap of a mouth before Second Christ drifted off to sleep in the arms of his Second Mother.

About the Author

Sam Kench is an author, screenwriter, and filmmaker based in Los Angeles.

A lover of all forms of art and storytelling, it was the world of cinema that first drew Kench to writing. He writes in all genres with a particular affinity for the dark and twisted and a penchant for stories that change throughout and keep readers guessing.

Outside of storytelling, Kench is an avid poker player and has worked as a professional film critic since he was 15. In 2014, Kench was named one of the most important defenders of free speech by the National Coalition Against Censorship.

In 2022, Kench was included in the top four screenwriters under the age of 25 as chosen by the Black List and the Writer's Guild for the Michael Collyer Fellowship.

His debut novel, *The Fall of Polite*, was self-published in 2020. *South of the Mason-Dixon* is his second novel.

Other HellBound Books Titles
Available at:
www.hellboundbookspublishing.com

The Horror Zine's Book of Ghost Stories

"This collection of ghost stories is fresh, varied, and entertaining. Perfect company for a long winter's night."
– Owen King, co-author with Stephen King of the New York Times #1 Bestseller Sleeping Beauties

Twenty-six brand-new tales of ghosts, spirits, and the afterlife to chill even the most hardened reader to their very marrow. Grand masters and newcomers alike serve well to petrify with stories to keep you laying awake in the dead of night - long after the last of the light has died - listening for that telltale scratching at the door, a soft whisper of disembodied voices, and the icy caress of long-dead fingers upon your ankle…

The Horror Zine's Book of Ghost Stories is delighted to present to you original, never before seen, spine-tingling tales from Bentley Little, Joe R. Lansdale, Elizabeth Massie, Graham Masterton with Dawn G. Harris, Tim Waggoner, and the very best up and coming writers in the genre. Includes a foreword by Lisa Morton.

"An incredibly creepy collection of stories of the recently and not so recently dead, written by some of the finest writers in horror. I suggest that when reading, do so in the daylight, because reading these at night will only make you more aware of your own, unempty house."
– Susie Moloney, author of The Dwelling and The Thirteen

Invasive Species

A monster has come to Maldus, Arkansas, and the residents of the small mountain town are too busy to notice. With the monster comes something even more terrifying and threatening than gnashing teeth or razor-sharp claws.

The monster has brought change.

The residents of the small mountain town are too busy to notice at first. Busy with things such as addiction, racism, work, or land deals.

Unnoticed, the change the monster brings in its insidious wake spreads like wildfire.

Unnoticed, the town of Maldus falls prey to an Invasive Species.

Secret Harbor

Tony Carpenter loves Karina. It doesn't matter that they're only fourteen, because when they're together they forget about their abusive homes.
They run away, leaving a trail of murder in their wake, until Tony is caught and sent to Secret Harbor School - a boy's home on a remote island in Washington State's San Juan's.
Run by corrupt staff with no accountability to anybody who cares about the abuse administered daily to its residents, Secret Harbor School is among the state's best kept secrets.
Tony has no intention of staying. The first chance he gets, he plans to escape and do whatever it takes to get back to Karina.
Even if it means more people have to die.
Secret Harbor is a dark, fast-paced, psychological thriller that will make you laugh, cry, and scoot ever so slowly toward the edge of your seat...

Sam Kench

The Horror Writer
"The most definitive guide into the trials and tribulations of being a horror writer since Stephen King's 'On Writing.'"

We have assembled some of the very best in the business from whom you can learn so much about the craft of horror writing: Bram Stoker Award© winners, bestselling authors, a President of the Horror Writers' Association, and myriad contemporary horror authors of distinction.

The Horror Writer covers how to connect with your market and carve out a sustainable niche in the independent horror genre, how to tackle the writer's ever-lurking nemesis of productivity, writing good horror stories with powerful, effective scenes, realistic, flowing dialogue and relatable characters without resorting to clichéd jump scares and well-worn gimmicks. Also covered is the delicate subject of handling rejection with good grace, and how to use those inevitable "not quite the right fit for us at this time" letters as an opportunity to hone your craft.

Plus... perceptive interviews to provide an intimate peek into the psyche of the horror author and the challenges they work through to bring their nefarious ideas to the page.

And, as if that – and so much more – was not enough, we have for your delectation Ramsey Campbell's beautifully insightful analysis of the tales of HP Lovecraft.

Featuring:
Ramsey Campbell, John Palisano, Chad Lutzke, Lisa Morton, Kenneth W. Cain, Kevin J. Kennedy, Monique Snyman, Scott Nicholson, Lucy A. Snyder, Richard Thomas, Gene O'Neill, Jess Landry, Luke Walker, Stephanie M. Wytovich, Marie O'Regan, Armand Rosamilia, Kevin Lucia, Ben Eads, Kelli Owen, Jasper Bark, and Bret McCormick.

And interviews with:
Steve Rasnic Tem, Stephen Graham Jones, David Owain Hughes, Tim Waggoner, and Mort Castle.

**A HellBound Books LLC
Publication**

www.hellboundbookspublishing.com